Emergency Drill

Danny Verity, PI #1

Chris Blackwater

CITY STONE
PUBLISHING

City Stone Publishing

ISBN (paperback): 978-1-915399-23-6
ISBN (ePUB): 978-1-915399-24-3

A CIP catalogue record for this book is available from the British Library.

Chris Blackwater | www.chrisblackwater.co.uk

City Stone Publishing | www.citystonepublishing.com

First printed:
Second edition: February 2022
Third edition (City Stone Publishing): September 2023

To my wife, the one and only Chris, with all my love

Glossary

A&E – Accident and Emergency

Accommodation – Pressurised module containing main sleeping, eating, and recreation facilities

ALQ – Auxiliary Living Quarters

Back-to-Back – Colleagues who swap places offshore/onshore, usually on a two-week rotation

Cellar Deck – Lowest deck on an oil platform

CID - Criminal Investigation Department

Chloral Hydrate – A short-acting sedative

CPR - Cardiopulmonary resuscitation, a lifesaving first aid technique

ECG – Electrocardiogram, records the electrical signal from the heart

EXB – Extra-broad. Wide-shouldered passengers are allocated specific seats in the helicopter

GA – General Alarm

GBH – Grievous Bodily Harm

GP – General Practitioner, a family doctor

H2S - Hydrogen Sulphide, a highly poisonous gas

HR – Human Resources

HSE – Health and Safety Executive

Irn-Bru – Carbonated soft drink made in Scotland

KPI – Key Performance Indicator

MBA – Master's in Business Administration

Medevac – Medical evacuation of a casualty

North Utsire – Shipping forecast area close to the Norwegian coast

OIM – Offshore Installation Manager. The senior manager on an oil platform

Oppo – Opposit number; the other half of a pair of workers

PA – Public Address system

PAPA – Prepare to Abandon Platform

PI – Private Investigator

POB – Persons on Board

RMP – Royal Military Police

Sat Level – Measure of blood oxygen saturation

Special Branch – Police counter-terrorism unit

Temazepam – Drug used as a pre-med and to treat sleeping problems

TLQ – Temporary Living Quarters

Vantage Card – Identity card issued to North Sea oil workers

Void – Empty space between modules, sometimes used for equipment access

Wee Free – The Free Church of Scotland (epithet)

Chapter One

THE CRAMPED, OVERHEATED PLANE rocked and rolled its way past the line of thunderclouds menacing the Scottish coastline. When it reached Aberdeen, a fierce crosswind forced the pilot to fly crabwise across the airfield. At the last minute, the plane banked right and nose-dived towards the tarmac. It hit the ground hard and bounced to a halt, perilously close to the end of the runway.

Danny Verity puffed out his cheeks and relaxed his death grip on the armrest. After a few minutes, the plane turned and taxied to the stand, a short, wet walk away from the terminal.

As soon as his battered dry bag arrived on the carousel, Danny grabbed it and headed outside. The rain was easing, but it was bitterly cold. Rather than pay for a taxi, he lugged the bag half a mile along the service road until the smell of kerosene and cigarette smoke signalled his destination.

A huddle of oil workers blocked the entrance to the heliport. Danny took a lungful of dank Aberdeen air and elbowed his way through the crowd.

'What's your hurry, pal?' said a wiry old boy in a grimy hi-vis jacket, squaring up to him and barring his way.

'I'm late for check-in.'

'Relax. There's a storm coming. You're going nowhere.'

Danny hoped he was right, though he could ill afford a night in an overpriced airport hotel. At least if he checked in for his offshore flight, he'd get a day's pay and a hot meal. It wasn't much, but better than nothing.

The old boy spat out the remains of his roll-up and ground it into the tarmac with the sole of his boot. He seemed to have lost interest in Danny, who took the opportunity to squeeze through to the entrance. A blast of warm, fetid air, heavy with the aroma of frying bacon and stale sweat, enveloped him once the glass double doors slid open. A babble of voices with accents from every shipyard and port in Britain filled the room.

To Danny, the heliport looked more like a cross between a refugee camp and a hospital waiting room than an airport terminal. There were bodies everywhere, sitting shoulder to shoulder on long rows of seats, perched on flimsy tables, or squatting on their kitbags. They were talking in disconsolate huddles, hunched over smartphones and books, or staring blankly at the early morning news on the TV screens overhead.

At the front of the departure hall, another screen displayed a rolling ticker-tape of numbers and abbreviations that meant absolutely nothing to Danny. He scanned the room for anything that might guide him to the right check-in desk, then gave up and asked a bushy-browed, moon-faced man at the back of the nearest queue.

'Cuillin Alpha?'

'Nah. See the baldy fella over there? Him with a face like a skelped arse?'

It was easy to see who he meant. Danny kicked his bag across the aisle and took his place alongside a short, stocky woman in her early thirties, wearing a company issued polo shirt several sizes too big. She had a gorgon's mop of mousy hair and a permanent scowl that could have curdled UHT milk.

'Hi,' he said. 'You flying to Cuillin Alpha?'

'I was fancying Malaga myself, but I hear it's shite this time of year. Full of English bawbags. Worse than Edinburgh and that's saying something.'

Danny assumed this was a quaint Scottish insult and opted to change the subject.

'I didn't think there'd be any flights today, what with Storm Erin on the way.'

'Don't you kid yourself, pal. My back-to-back's a shifty bastard. He's not gonna stay on the Alpha a second longer than he has to. If you ever want to get off a platform in a hurry, make sure you're on the same flight as the heli admin. We always get where we're going, believe me.'

'Is that right?'

'Aye. And what's it to you?'

'I'm Danny Verity. The new medic.'

He held out his hand, but she gave him a look like he'd offered her a dead rat.

'Temporary medic. That figures. I check everyone who's coming aboard my platform. Too many dodgy characters on board already. You look worse in real life than you do on Facebook, by the way.'

'Give him a break, Gemma,' the man in front of her said in a rapid-fire Belfast accent. His unkempt red hair, bandy legs, and long arms gave him the look of an undernourished orang-utan. 'I hear the last medic quit before he even got back to Aberdeen. Said you intimidated him.'

'I'll do more than intimidate that lazy bastard if I ever see him again. That boy was sicker than most of his patients. I swear he never left his cabin. Even more of a slacker than you, Callum Jarvie.'

She presented herself to the agent at the desk who checked her passport and, in a dull monotone, told her to put her bags on the scales. Carefully avoiding eye contact, he motioned for her to step on the platform herself. She leaned over to check her weight and sighed.

'Too much drink and not enough sex, that's ma problem.'

'Says that every fecking time,' Callum said once she was out of earshot. 'Does my head in.'

Danny was still expecting the agent to bump him off the flight. Instead, he waved him through with barely a word.

'Can't manage without a medic,' Callum continued. 'I swear the entire platform's held together with sticking plaster.'

Danny didn't find that particularly comforting. He glanced around the lounge, vainly searching for a seat. Eventually, he joined his new colleagues, squatting on the floor by the toilets where Gemma was examining the crude bandage on Callum's wrist.

'What happened to you?' she asked. 'Out on the lash, were you? Is that the story?'

'As if, Gem. It's against the rules. You know I'm a stickler for the rules. I just tripped while I was phoning the wife. Distracted walking, they call it.'

'Sure you weren't sending explicit texts to your new girlfriend?'

'What girlfriend? I'm as faithful as the day is long, as you well know.'

'Aye. A wet winter's day in the Shetlands, maybe.'

Danny offered to look at the injury, but Callum waved him away and returned to trading insults with Gemma.

The departure screen still claimed that all flights were on hold. The more optimistic passengers were watching the display over by the canteen. It was showing a live feed of the weather radar. A colourful array of storm clouds was approaching from the north and the wind speed was steadily rising. If there was no improvement, they might as well go home. With a hundred or more disgruntled oil workers camped out in departures, no one seemed ready to make that call just yet.

Danny was about to fetch a bacon bap and a mug of coffee from the canteen. Before he made it to the door, an announcement came over the PA.

ATTENTION ALL PERSONNEL. FLIGHTS TO THE CUILLIN, CAIRNGORM, AND GRAMPIAN FIELDS WILL RESUME SHORTLY. WILL ALL PASSENGERS FOR THE CUILLIN ALPHA REPORT TO DEPARTURES WITH YOUR VANTAGE CARD AT THE READY.

Gemma was convinced they'd jumped the queue because of the machinations of her colleague offshore, but Danny thought it must have been a break in the clouds in North Utsire. Reluctantly, he followed the other nineteen passengers as they shuffled through the scanner and sat in an airless, claustrophobic room watching a safety brief on different ways to die if your helicopter crashed in the North Sea.

A cheery young guy with a blond ponytail handed him a survival suit. Danny pulled it on and immediately started sweating like a pig in a blanket. He picked up his lifejacket from the rack on the wall and wrestled with the belt and the uncooperative crotch strap. As he sat back down next to his new buddy Callum, the oxygen bottle jabbed him in the ribs, and he squinted at the pressure gauge to check he had a full thirty seconds of air.

'I just hope this isn't a long flight.'

'An hour or so on a fine day. In this weather, who knows? Last month we got there and the fecking platform was fogbound. Had to fly all the way back. I was dying for a piss.'

The ground crew bustled around, keen to get them underway before the weather closed in. The blond guy frogmarched the passengers across the tarmac and herded them into the waiting Sikorsky S-92. After a few incomprehensible words from the Norwegian captain, they lifted off and bobbed around a few metres off the ground as she adjusted the trim.

Danny was already losing the feeling in his left arm. The regulars had grabbed the best seats and had left him perched by the aisle next to a bearded giant wearing a chequered "extra-broad" armband. He could either cosy up to the guy or sit with one buttock hanging over the edge. Eventually, he found an uncomfortable compromise by sliding down the seat until his shoulder fitted under the big guy's armpit.

As they rose into a leaden Aberdeen sky, the noise became deafening. He adjusted his earplugs and pulled on the ear defenders. He felt strangely detached from the outside world, but at least the noise had reduced at a bearable level.

After a while, the pulse of the rotor became quite soothing. Danny noticed his fellow passengers dozing. It was as if they'd been hypnotised. He was convinced the noise and turmoil of the journey would keep him awake, but soon he was nodding off with the rest of them.

He awoke with a jolt as the chopper hit a patch of turbulence and realised he'd been fast asleep. There was a stack of black clouds directly ahead and the pilot banked steeply to avoid them.

He glanced around for his nearest available exit. It was on the other side of his extra-broad companion. Not that he fancied his chances of surviving a crash landing.

The chopper continued to rattle its way through wispy fringes of low cloud. Danny was hypersensitive to every change in the engine's tone. This rollercoaster ride was making him decidedly queasy. There were a few more dramatic dives, but no immediate sign of them falling out of the sky.

Eventually, they lost altitude. He watched the descent through the observation window by the co-pilot's foot. He could just make out flames belching from a tall steel structure, barely visible against the grey-green sea. As they descended towards the helideck, the chopper began bucking like a bronco and the rattling rose to a deafening clatter.

'Jesus Christ!' the extra-broad man said, nearly elbowing Danny in the face. 'This job will be the death of me.'

They were now at eye-level with the swirling inferno of the flare, surrounded by rigs, stacks and towering cranes. The slightest impact could shatter the rotor and send them spiralling to a watery grave. With one hand, Danny fumbled for his oxygen mask and, with the other, pushed himself back into the seat and braced for impact.

Chapter Two

FOR A FEW STOMACH-CHURNING seconds, the pilot wrestled for control, then bowed to the inevitable. With each gust, they edged closer to the flames. Gradually, Danny realised they were moving up and away from the platform, not lurching further into danger. Once clear of the superstructure, the passengers breathed again and there was an outburst of swearing. Danny hoped the pilot hadn't heard the extra-broad guy's scathing opinion of female pilots and Norwegians. If she had, she kept it to herself.

'Sorry guys. We are having some turbulence here when there is a strong westerly. If things improve, we try again. If not, we go back.'

They hovered about a hundred metres off the stack for a few minutes. Conditions seemed worse than before. Abruptly, the shaking abated, and the pilot made a dive for the helideck. Again, they hit turbulence as they approached, and it looked like they were in for a repeat performance.

Even with his eyes closed, Danny knew when they were passing the flare. He could almost feel the searing heat on his face. They seemed to descend faster than before, or were they free-falling? The nose of the chopper reared up and, with a last shudder, they powered through to calmer air. Before Danny could think of some fitting last words, they slammed down onto the deck, pitching back and forth on the landing gear until the downdraft clasped them securely in place.

For a while, no one spoke. They just sat there listening to the pulsing rotor. Even the pilot seemed lost for words. Then Gemma piped up from the back seat, 'Well, that was fun, eh, lads? Who wants to do it again?'

A face appeared at the window and a man in a fireproof suit opened the main access door and folded the steps down onto the deck. He gave the ashen-faced crew a thumbs up and beckoned them to disembark.

Danny gingerly followed his new colleagues down the steps. As he stepped out of the chopper, an icy gust knocked him sideways. One of the deck crew reached out a hand to keep him from losing his feet entirely until he could grab hold of his bag for ballast.

It was impossible to hear what the man was shouting. He gestured towards a barrier which led, via four flights of open stairs, down to the main deck. Danny dumped his bag and followed his fellow passengers through a set of double air-locked doors, down another flight of stairs and into the brightly lit briefing room with its rows of grimy vinyl-covered chairs.

Through some magic, Gemma was already in place in the adjacent heli admin office, isolated from the rest by a reinforced glass screen. She appeared unfazed by their crash landing, or the queue of impatient oil workers waiting for their cabin allocation, and was calmly flicking through a clipboard full of thumbed notes.

The room smelled of aviation fuel and sweat and the chairs had lost the last of their stuffing years ago, but at least it was warm and dry. He thought Callum might hang around to show him the ropes, but he'd already grabbed his gear and gone, so Danny ripped off his survival suit and slumped down on the nearest seat. He was just regaining some composure when a tall figure with a cadaverous face loomed over him.

'Daniel Verity? I'm John Haldane, B shift medic. Here are the stats for the last trip: a couple of cuts and bruises, but nothing major. Incident list is at the back. Snakey will fill you in about the near miss in the mud locker. Anyhow, you'd better see him for your induction soon. That's one of his KPIs. Gotta go, the rotor's running. Enjoy!'

Haldane disappeared through the door and away up the stairs.

So that's all the handover I'm getting?

It did not surprise Danny that Haldane wanted to get on that chopper and fly out of here at fast as humanly possible.

He did not know what a mud locker was, or where to find Snakey, whoever he might be. Right now, all he needed was someone to point him to the mess and then the sickbay. According to the forecast, it would be several days before the storm passed, so no one could kick him off the platform even if they wanted to. Surely by then, he would have worked out what the hell he was supposed to be doing.

He waited until the rest of the new arrivals had been dealt with before he strolled over to the heli admin desk. Gemma glanced up and rummaged around in the desk drawer.

'Here you go, Doctor Dolittle. These are the sickbay keys. Dinna drop them over the side like that moonhead medic we had last trip. "Can you no get another set cut?" he says. I'm surprised he never asked me to get his shoes mended while I was at it. What a prick.'

Danny clipped the keyring to his belt, promising to guard it with his life.

'John Haldane said I had to see some guy called Snakey.'

'That'd be Jack Blake, OIM. Offshore Installation Manager. Don't you ever call him Snakey unless you want to swim back to shore. Snakey is God Almighty out here. Or so he thinks. If you want something doing properly, see me. Maybe I'll tell you to piss off, but it never hurts to ask. Not unless I'm on my break, anyway.'

Danny attempted to follow her bewildering directions to the mess. He could use a stiff drink, but since that was out of the question, he would have to settle for a strong coffee. He was regretting even taking this job, but he needed the money if his soon to be ex-wife had anything to do with it.

As he stepped through the airlock and into the accommodation module, Danny heard a muffled explosion. The fans fell silent. One by one, the lights went out.

Chapter Three

THE EMERGENCY LIGHTING FLICKERED back on, followed by the deafening tones of a general alarm. A steady stream of crew brushed past Danny as he stood on the stairs, examining his safety card for directions. No one seemed to be in a great rush, so he assumed blackouts must be a common occurrence on the Cuillin Alpha.

Most of the crew seemed to head down to the mess, so he followed them, figuring that at least he could get a coffee and maybe ask for directions. As he shuffled past the serving counter, he spotted Callum heading in the opposite direction and asked him what was going on.

'Did you hear that bang?' Callum replied. 'Must have blown a big old breaker somewhere. Don't worry. We'll get the generator back online soon enough. We're not pumping any oil, so Snakey will be on the warpath. He'll never get his bonus at this rate. I'd keep your head down if I were you.'

Danny promised to keep his receding hairline firmly below the parapet and went in search of his muster point. It was next to the stainless steel serving counter, hidden behind the ice cream chiller. There was only one other name on the muster list, that of Archie Grier, a taciturn lifeboat cox, who bore a passing resemblance to the ancient mariner. Everyone else sat chatting and moaning around the rows of folding tables in the main dining area.

Danny's muster point didn't even have a chair. It looked like being a long and tedious drill. Since there were twenty oil workers between him and the coffee machine, he wandered over for a scoop of ice cream, until Archie called him back.

'No eating or drinking during the muster. It's against the rules.'

Seemingly exhausted by such a long speech, Archie leaned against the wall and lapsed into a sullen silence. Eventually, the main lighting flickered back to life, lifting the gloom in the mess. As the announcement came over the PA for the crew to return to work, Callum reappeared with an older, round-bellied technician in tow.

'This is Stevie Dunn. Best sparky in the field. Couldn't have done it without him.'

His new colleagues didn't seem in any hurry to get back to work, so Danny joined Stevie in the queue for the coffee machine. He could cope with the lights going out, but surely some critical systems relied on mains power. He hoped the techs were taking the situation serious.

'So what caused this power outage? It sounded like a gun going off.'

'Don't worry, mate. Just a short circuit somewhere,' Stevie said. 'Still don't know where exactly. Could happen again anytime. I'd keep a torch with you if you're heading out onto the plant.'

That was hardly reassuring, but there wasn't much he could do about it. Suitably reinvigorated by a double espresso, Danny lugged his bags up the stairs to his cabin, adjoining the sickbay. There were some advantages to being a medic. Most of the cabins were two-bunk cabin affairs. Only the medic and the senior managers got a room to themselves.

He dumped his gear and wandered through the internal door to the small, but well-equipped sickbay. Out here, you couldn't just phone for an ambulance. The medic had to deal with a lot more than your average GP onshore. It was a mini A&E department; he was nurse, doctor and surgeon, all bundled into one.

He sat down at the consultation desk and swivelled the chair around aimlessly. From here, he felt like a proper doctor fresh from some smart school of medicine, ready to diagnose and prescribe. He searched all the drawers, looking for a stethoscope or those rubber hammers that he assumed all GPs carried around, but all he found was a stack of bandages, a first aid kit and a set of inflatable splints.

To his left was the resuscitation couch. It came complete with an oxygen cylinder, suction unit, ventilator, and a pulse oximeter. Hanging from the wall was a portable ECG with its tendrils of multi-coloured wire. There was an examination chair and another sickbed to the right designed for a short-stay patient. Danny could have used a nice long nap, and the sickbed looked very inviting; eventually, he decided he really ought to check in with his new boss first.

The safety handbook included a diagram of the platform layout. When he got to the supposed location of the OIM's office, the door was shut, and the nameplate had been covered with insulating tape. Danny knocked.

A gruff voice summoned him inside.

Jack Blake was a balding, overweight Aberdonian in his fifties. He did not look happy to see Danny, but then again, he looked like the guy who only ever smiled at funerals. With an audible sigh, he told Danny to close the door and take a pew.

'Welcome to Cuillin Alpha, Mr Verity. Is this your first time offshore?'

Danny nodded.

'You'd better hope it's not your last. I suppose you think you're here to heal the sick, comfort the afflicted and all that shite.'

'Among other things.'

'Aye well, you concentrate on those other things. You're here for the same reason as the rest of us, to earn some cash and piss off home in one piece. I've worked offshore nigh on forty years. Guess how many sick days I've had.'

Danny shrugged. He figured Snakey was going to tell him anyway.

'None, zero, zilch. If some snivelling bastard comes to you saying he's got a poorly wee tummy or a nasty cold, give him an aspirin and tell him to fuck off back to work. You're not here as a nursemaid. Downtime costs money. It might even cost me my bonus, and you do not want that, believe you me.'

So much for joining a caring profession. In an attempt to impress Snakey, he recalled something he'd read in the *Emergency Medicine Journal*.

'I'd like to focus on preventative medicine. Stop people getting sick.'

'Good man. I'm all for that. But remember, you're not just the medic. Foremost, you're the safety officer. Incidents and accidents, that's what you should think about. The target for lost time incidents is zero. It's a KPI. My number one Key Performance Indicator. Completely unachievable, of course, but that's the oil industry for you. Run by MBA pricks who've never been offshore in their lives. You know the biggest cause of accidents offshore?'

Fortunately, Danny had a risk assessment form in his hand, so he just trotted out the first item on the list.

'Slips, trips and falls?'

'Aye well, maybe that's what they teach you at medic school, but what's the root cause of all that malarkey? I'll tell you for nothing. Stupidity. That's it in a nutshell. Stupid people doing stupid things with no thought for the consequences. You won't ever find that on a risk assessment, but it ought to be right there at the top. Your job is to keep these cack-handed dimwits out of the sickbay. That's the bottom line.'

'I'm not sure how you prevent stupidity.'

'Not even the Good Lord can manage that, and he must have invented it. But when some moron trips over his own feet, it had better be his own stupid fault, not ours. You scour this platform for anything those Health and Safety bastards could nail us for. You risk assess every rivet and rusty nail if you have to. And that's another KPI, mind. If we haven't generated enough reports to crash the server by the end of the year, that's another chunk of my bonus gone.'

And to think I'd been worried about being bored out here. Not that he was looking forward to churning out reams of paperwork, but it was better than watching daytime TV.

'Sounds like fun.'

'You're not here to have fun, Mr Verity. If you see anything dodgy going on, you tell them to stop it right there and then.' Snakey showed by holding out his hand like he was stopping traffic. 'There's a wee form for that as well. I'll give you a stack. You'll need them.'

'And what if it's something that's going to affect production?'

'Well, that's the safety dilemma, right there. If there's an accident you could have prevented, I'll be down on you like a ton of bricks. But if you stop the oil flowing for no good reason, then you'll be on the next chopper home.'

'That's doesn't sound fair,' protested Danny. The odds of him surviving a full two weeks on the Cuillin Alpha were decreasing all the time.

'Nay, it's not, but then the offshore life's not a game of cricket. See, we've not had a decent medic on this shift for nigh on a year now. Johnny Haldane and Malc Macallan were here for twenty years or more. Then Malc the Knife jacks it in and retires to the Seychelles with some foreign lassie half his age. So instead we get agency quacks. Useless bastards mostly, believe me. They've set a pretty low bar for you to crawl over. So you just get out there, keep your wits about you and try not to bugger it up.'

Chapter Four

Suitably motivated, Danny trudged back to the sickbay with an armful of processes and procedures to digest. As he sat down in his consulting chair, he realised he'd completely forgotten to ask the OIM about the mysterious mud locker incident. Snakey promised to send his Operations Manager, Blair Scorgie, round to give him a tour of the platform. Maybe he could show him the scene of the crime.

He sat at the desk for nearly an hour, flicking through Haldane's cryptic handover notes and trying to decipher the password for the medic's PC. He was just about to give up and go for another shot of caffeine when there was a sharp knock at his door. Without waiting for an invitation, in walked a tall, effusive Scot, sporting a Hawick rugby shirt and an outlandish Hollywood smile. After introductions and a knuckle-crushing handshake, Blair ushered him down to the non-smoker's locker room to get suited up.

They strolled round the escape routes: first the lifeboats, then up to the helideck and down the steps to the cellar deck, where Blair proudly showed him the rickety-looking escape to the sea ladder. They spent little time admiring the view. The swell was already swamping the ladder, and each time a wave struck the platform leg, spray burst through the open grates of the deck floor, soaking everything in its path.

Blair backed up and took Danny on a tour of the equipment of last resort: the life rafts, the abseil descenders, and a dubious-looking knotted rope. Danny offered a silent prayer to Poseidon in the fervent hope that he would never need to use any of them, especially the damned rope.

There were at least ten flights of steps from the cellar deck up to heli admin, and Danny was panting hard by the time they finished. Though Blair's rugby playing days were probably long gone, he obviously kept himself fit. Much fitter than Danny.

'I assume you've met Gemma Gauld, our heli admin clerk?'

'Oh, yes. She's hard to miss.'

'Gemma can certainly be a little abrasive, but she's an invaluable resource. Flights, accommodation, communication, she's your first port of call. Let's pop inside and get a weather report. Vital part of your safety evaluations, especially with conditions as they are.'

Gemma didn't look pleased to see them.

'About time. I've been trying to get hold of one of your idle techie bastards all morning. You know we lost satellite reception? And then the fibre optics went down during the power outage. All my comms are on the blink. How am I supposed to organise the flight schedule? Tell me that, eh?'

'Don't worry your pretty little head, Gemma,' Blair said, seemingly oblivious to her look of disgust. 'It looks like the wind blew the satellite receiver out of alignment. We have our best man on it.'

'Is that right? I didn't know you had one.'

'I sent Scott Viklund. He's staying on board for another week. Ken Mundie didn't show up at the heliport. Scott volunteered. That shows how keen he is. You're in safe hands.'

'Well, that's a comfort, I'm sure. But he'd better hurry. It's Aberdeen v Celtic on tonight. There'll be hell to pay if there's no reception on the TV.'

'So what's the forecast for the next few days?' Danny asked, hoping to avoid a debate about Scottish football. He knew nothing about either team and cared even less. 'Is this wind going to die down soon?'

'No. It's gonna get worse.'

'How much worse?'

'Did you not see the news? The BBC is saying it's naught but a wee gale, just like that dunderhead Michael Fish said right before the last hurricane.

But the shipping forecast says force ten and strengthening. It's going to be bad, boys, so I'd batten down the hatches and prepare for the worst.'

'Now, now, Gemma,' Blair said. 'No need to be an alarmist. We've seen plenty of storms out here and we've always been just fine. I might have to cancel some over the side work, but I'm sure we'll cope. I'll get your comms fixed. Don't you worry.'

'Don't come crying to me when the wind blows you to Kansas, or wherever.'

'You mean Oz. Dorothy's house was in Kansas and it got blown to the Land of Oz with her in it. I love that film.'

Gemma gave Blair a look that the Wicked Witch would have been proud of and slammed down the shutters on the heli admin booth. As they left the departure shack, her gravelly alto belted out a song about someone who had straw for brains.

Blair hummed along, seemingly oblivious.

Danny decided he'd better check out the satellite system; he followed Scarecrow Scorgie's directions across an exposed walkway towards the main drill derrick.

———

Squalls and salt spray were battering the upper decks. When Danny reached the pipe level, the drill team was busy battening down the hatches and retreating inside. Mud-splattered figures swarmed across the deck, gathering up tools and equipment with an increasing sense of urgency.

On the communications gantry above, Danny could make out Scott Viklund, crouching by the giant satellite array. It didn't look like a safe place in these conditions. He decided that if Scott hadn't finished the job soon, he was going to call a halt until the wind subsided. He would not be very popular with the crew, but he was prepared to risk an outbreak of football violence rather than see someone seriously injured.

A gust of wind swirled around the pipe deck, sending Danny staggering back into the safety barrier. He heard a stifled cry from above, and shouts of alarm. As Danny craned his neck to see what the commotion was about, Scott's hard hat came skittering down the gantry, bounced twice and disappeared over the guardrail into the grey murk of the North Sea.

Danny watched as Scott hurriedly packed away his tools and made for the access ladder. His foot was barely on the top rung when the full force of the gale struck. As Danny clung to the barrier to steady himself, he heard an ominous metallic squeal from above. A sound like ricocheting bullets echoed across the steel deck. One by one, the support bolts sheared. The giant parabolic reflector peeled away from its mounts and swung, with unstoppable force, towards Scott's exposed perch.

Danny's warning cry was plucked away by the wind. He could only watch as Scott, with a hundredweight of metalwork heading towards him and nowhere to go, threw himself backwards off the ladder. He fell, with his hands outstretched, like he was diving into the arms of the angels.

Scott hit the pipe deck hard and lay there unmoving, his body contorted inside his bright orange overalls, like a broken crash test dummy. Danny barely noticed. The reflector dish, about the size of a town hall clock, slammed against the module wall, snapping the last of its bolts. As gravity overcame momentum, it spun and tumbled towards him as he stood, transfixed, in its path.

The dish landed less than ten metres away, on a rack of artillery-sized pipes, bouncing the top dozen into the air before coming to rest with the outer rim looming over his head. The impact made Danny's ears hiss and the ensuing shockwave slammed against his chest, sending him toppling backwards onto the deck. He watched helplessly as the first pipe came loose from the stack and rolled inexorably towards his prone body. It struck a crossbeam and rolled over his foot, pinning him to the deck.

Chapter Five

As Danny lay trapped, another pipe bounced towards him. One end struck a shipping container. It fell awkwardly, with one gun barrel end pointing straight at Danny's head and the other wedged under the container. The remaining pipes fell in a confused heap, like jackstraws, a tangled barricade shielding him from another avalanche of falling debris.

Danny tried desperately to drag his boot free, but every time he moved, spikes of pain shot up his leg. Biting back the urge to scream, he tried to wiggle his toes. They felt like they were on fire, but there was enough movement to give him hope that the damage was not permanent.

Saved by a safety boot, he thought. Despite reading all those endless Health and Safety reports, Danny never expected a bit of steel and leather to spare his leg, or maybe even his life.

'You okay?'

A bearded driller with a mud-smeared face leaned over him. Danny nodded, not wanting to speak. He wasn't sure if he was going to laugh hysterically or howl like a baby.

'I'm Olly, the tool pusher. The lads are fetching the lifting gear. We'll get you free in a jiffy.'

Soon, there were half a dozen drillers gathered round him. Two were dragging a portable hoist, while the others wielded scaffolding poles, like Neanderthals hunting a mammoth. Olly began directing operations, using a rolled up work permit as a makeshift megaphone.

'After three. One, two, heave...'

The pressure came off his boot, and two lads grabbed him under the armpits, dragging him free. As the blood surged back into his foot, the pain knifed up his leg and Danny stifled a scream. He thought he was going to pass out, but after a few seconds, the searing agony subsided, his breathing slowed, and his vision cleared.

'You're one lucky boy, so you are,' Olly said. 'It's amazing nobody was killed.'

Danny stared at him in disbelief. Wrapped up in his misery, he hadn't stopped to wonder why he was the centre of attention. Surely, Olly realised he wasn't the only casualty?

'Scott. He was up on the gantry. He fell. Must be under the debris somewhere.'

'Jesus Christ!' Olly said and scrambled towards the pipe stack.

Danny forced himself up onto one leg and hopped after him, frantically looking for the body he saw fall from the sky only a few minutes ago. Searching among the mess of metalwork, he feared the worst, but then a shout came from across the deck and he felt a brief surge of hope.

Scott was lying close to the module wall, partly obscured by the up-turned shipping crate. With Olly's help, Danny limped around the detritus and dropped next to the casualty. Scott was barely conscious. A gasp of pain accompanied every shallow breath. Danny didn't need paramedic training to know that the man was in a bad way.

'Look at the state of his leg,' Olly said.

The right ankle was sticking out and there were deep cuts all down his flank. It was a mess, but that wasn't what was concerning Danny. Something had carved a deep gash into his left temple. There was a lot of blood and the blow might easily have fractured the skull. He could stop the bleeding, but God knows what an impact like that would have done to the brain.

'Head hurts,' Scott groaned.

Danny eased him down and tried to make him comfortable.

'Can you move your feet?'

'Not sure. They're all numb. But my head hurts. Got any aspirin?'

'Just hold on, Scotty. I've got some stuff that's way better than aspirin. Then we'll get you up to sickbay, okay?'

Danny leaned over and lifted Olly's ear defenders, hoping he could talk to the tool pusher without Scott hearing.

'He has to get to hospital right now. Tell the control room we need a chopper. Tell them to get the stretcher team up here. I'll prep him for evacuation.'

'I think he's going to be out of luck. There's no way a helicopter can get here in these conditions, not even for a winch rescue. We could lower him onto a boat, but that's going to take way too long, right?'

Olly trotted away to make the call, while Danny chewed away at his lip and tried to staunch the bleeding with the least oily rag he could find. Within minutes, a couple of first responders arrived carrying a stretcher and a medical bag. He rummaged through the contents until he found a clean bandage and some painkillers.

A driller handed Scott a half-drunk can of Irn-Bru, which he used to wash down the pills. While Danny bandaged the scalp wound, the responders set to work on the fractured legs as best they could, strapping them into makeshift splints. Scott whimpered intermittently, but the pain relief seemed to do its job.

Danny supported Scott's neck with a head restraint as they lifted him slowly onto the stretcher. As they got ready to transport the casualty off the pipe deck, Olly returned, shaking his head.

'All flights are grounded until further notice. That includes safety and rescue, sorry to say. Our support vessel can't even get close. The wind's too strong and there's way too much swell out there. You're on your own, mate.'

Danny lurched to his feet and grabbed one corner of the stretcher, but he could barely stand, let alone carry a casualty down several flights of stairs. He'd be needing a stretcher himself, he thought, as he perched back down on a nearby crate, with his injured leg outstretched, and helped himself to a couple of painkillers. There was no Irn-Bru left, so he took a swig of saline solution from the eye wash station and gulped the tablets down.

Olly and his oppo, Jed Santo, took the back of the stretcher; together, the four bearers carefully lowered it down the steep stairwell across the main deck and back up the outside of the accommodation module. Danny hobbled painfully behind, leaning heavily on the railing. By the time they had lugged the stretcher through the first airtight sliding door, word had got around.

Helping hands cleared the way to sickbay. The procession made its way through the gym, solemn faces lining the corridor. They looked uncomfortable like mourners paying their respects to a funeral cortege.

Gemma detached herself from the group and followed Danny into the sickbay. She stood to one side as he supervised Scott's transfer onto the treatment table. Once his patient was secure, Danny sat down at the PC and logged onto the medic's secure network.

'Please tell me that satellite dish wasn't the only way of communicating with the mainland.'

'Don't be daft, pal. There's our dodgy fibre optic link and, if all else fails, I can radio the support vessel. I'll keep the lines open. That's my job. Who do you want to call?'

'There's an emergency response unit at the Edinburgh Royal Infirmary. Whoever's on duty should be able to set up a video conference. I need to talk to a neuro consultant, someone who knows how to deal with brain trauma.'

'You should be able to get through on the medic's phone and the internet is still working, just about. Go see if you can get through. I'll keep an eye on Scott.'

'So you're a first aider as well, Gemma?'

'Aye, and I trained as a nurse back in the day. God help us.'

'No end to your talents, then?'

'Save your breath. I was a crap nurse. The bedside manner of an undertaker. I don't like healthy folk much, let alone sick ones. Hopefully, some of the training stuck.'

Apart from screeching at him for not holding the handrail, Gemma had barely spoken to him since they arrived. Danny knew that on a small platform like the Cuillin Alpha, most people had more than one job, but she seemed to have a finger in every pie. As well as a radio operator, she was the platform's heli admin clerk, and now it seemed she was part of the emergency response team.

Danny limped through the door to the sickbay and plonked himself down on the threadbare swivel chair. The adrenaline was wearing off and his leg was killing him. He peeled a laminated notice off the wall and punched the number into the sickbay handset. His hands were shaking, and it took him a couple of attempts.

Eventually, he heard a distant ringing tone and a recorded announcement which assured him that his call would be answered as a matter of priority. The machine then played "Greensleeves".

As he waited, Danny kept a weather eye on Gemma over by the resuscitation couch where she was busy patching up Scott's leg. The bleeding was under control, but a fair amount of oil and mud had worked its way into the wound. It took some time before Gemma was happy enough to bandage him back up. She noticed Danny leaning round the door and scowled. He wondered if she had a specific problem with medics or just the whole world.

The tinny music stopped and a A&E nurse picked up the phone. She took some details and soon, the irregularly oiled machinery of the emergency response system creaked into action. She got him to boot up his laptop and directed him to the video conference address. Within a few minutes, three doctors were peering at Danny through the screen as he walked around the bed waving a remote webcam at his semi-conscious patient.

There was a lot of shaking of heads and a flurry of impractical sugges-
tions, involving scans and tests which Danny barely understood and had
no access to. In the end, he lost his temper.

'You're not listening! I'm not a bloody brain surgeon and I haven't got
a sodding CT scanner. I'm just a paramedic on a forty-year-old oil rig in
the middle of the North Sea. This is my first proper serious incident. My
patient has a serious head injury and he might be about to seize. Just tell
me what the hell I'm supposed to do.'

There was a brief silence. Dr Weber, the senior consultant, leaned over
and glared into the camera. She was a middle-aged woman with steel-grey
hair who spoke calmly to Danny, in a soft lilting accent.

'You make him comfortable, Mr Verity. If he has pain, give him
painkillers. You talk to him. Maybe he hears, maybe not. You hold his hand
and say everything is okay. Maybe it's a lie, but say it anyway. I have seen
patients survive worse than this. Not so many, but we can hope. Then you
wait for a change in his condition, or maybe a change in the weather. And
so, nature will take its course for better or for worse.'

Once Danny calmed down, Dr Weber took him through a few basic
checks. He felt like a fool. How long had he spent training to be a medic?
He should know this stuff. Panicking would not help Scott. He needed to
get a grip and do his job.

Danny powered up the mobile patient monitor. Scott was still drifting
in and out of consciousness. Either the painkillers were making his patient
drowsy, or the pressure on the brain was causing him to black out intermittently.

He stuck electro-cardiograph pads to Scott's chest, clipped the oximetry
sensor to his finger, and wrapped the inflatable cuff around the upper arm.
The ECG showed a reassuringly regular waveform, but the heart rate was
way too high, and blood pressure too low. Danny fitted his patient with an
oxygen mask and watched the readings normalise, little by little.

Dr Weber got him to check Scott's eyes. The left pupil was slightly
dilated.

'This is the trauma side, yes? There could be swelling of the brain. If it is small, maybe he will be okay. If not, maybe some brain damage.'

She had Danny stick a pin in various bits of Scott to check his responses. Danny thought he saw the man twitch once or twice. The stimulus checks seemed to confirm that Scott had cerebral oedema, localised somewhere near the head wound.

'It is too risky to do anything now,' Dr Weber said, before she signed off. 'You must wait for improvement or good weather. If not, then maybe you must try a little brain surgery. Tell me, are you a good man with a drill?'

Chapter Six

NOBODY CONSIDERED DANNY TO be any good at DIY. Not with a drill, or any kind of power tool. When he and Kelly first moved in together, he'd made a pitiful attempt at decorating. This included some bodged wiring repairs that nearly burned down the house. She insisted on calling in professionals. When she left him, three years into an increasingly miserable marriage, she took off with a guy who ran a property maintenance company. He probably should have seen that one coming.

As for his abilities as a surgeon, Danny had attended a few lectures on emergency field surgery and a couple of live operations. Most of the time, he'd focused on not throwing up.

Of course, he'd been taught how to patch up serious injuries during his training as an army medic. But he'd trained for triage, not brain surgery. The thought of performing surgery on Scott's skull made his guts churn.

Danny left Gemma in charge of the patient, closed the office door, and slumped down in the chair. His hands were steadier now, but his pulse was racing and his mouth was desert dry. He gripped the arms of the chair and tried to calm himself down, but no amount of deep breathing exercises was going to do the trick. A large Scotch might have helped; another thing you couldn't get on an oil platform, not even for medicinal purposes.

His foot was throbbing, and it was a couple of hours before he could self-medicate again. He was still wearing his work boots and part of him didn't want to take them off to assess the damage. He unzipped one and gently peeled it off his injured foot. It didn't hurt as much as he'd expected until it was fully out of the boot and the blood started pumping around his toes.

The steel toe cap had done its job well enough, but the nails were turning black and the bridge of his foot was turning into one impressively livid bruise. Nothing seemed to be broken, though since everything hurt, it was hard to be sure without an X-ray.

There was not much he could do, apart from strapping it up with a compression bandage. Maybe a steward would bring him some ice if he asked nicely. He was about to reach for the phone when there was a soft tap at the door.

'Come!' he shouted.

The door opened and in loped Callum, looking rather sheepish. He grimaced at the sight of Danny's foot. 'That looks pretty bad, man. Sorry to disturb you. I came to see about Scotty. He only just joined the tech team. I'm supposed to be his mentor, God help him. How's he doing?'

'It's touch and go. We're trying to get him medevacked, but the forecast is looking dire.'

'You heard he was due to go off yesterday?' Callum said. 'Talk about bad luck. His back-to-back doesn't show up and then this happens. I guess Blair badgered him into staying on. Most folk would have told him to go hang, but Scott's too soft by half.'

'We'll try to get him off the platform as soon as we can.'

'I don't suppose this is what you expected, either. You must wish our flight never took off.'

'Too right. I feel like jumping on the medevac with Scott and never coming back.'

'So why don't you?'

'I can't leave until there's a replacement medic onboard. God knows when that will be. Right now, I'm more worried about how long it will take to get a chopper for Scott. I just hope his injuries aren't as bad as they look.'

'Well, if you need someone to watch over him, just let me know. I don't know much about medical stuff, but I can check the monitors or whatever. I'm good with monitors.'

'Thanks, Callum. Gemma is with him now. You could ask her.'

'Ask her what?' Gemma was poking her head around the door.

'Alright, girl?' Callum asked. 'Anything I can do for ya?'

'You could fetch me a comfy chair, Cal. Or how about a wee neck massage?'

'I'd love to, but I'm short-handed,' Callum replied, holding up his right arm, where a livid bruise now covered his wrist.

'You'd better let our medic look at that. It's your wanking hand, after all. Wouldn't want you to lose it.'

Reluctantly, Callum held out his arm. Danny gently manipulated the wrist that seemed to have the full range of motion despite Callum doing a lot of wincing and sucking of breath.

'Looks like a simple sprain right enough. How bad does it hurt?'

'Bad enough to keep me awake last night. Not bad enough to keep me off work, I guess. Not without Scotty for cover.'

Danny put a support bandage on the injury and gave him a pack of anti-inflammatory tablets for the swelling.

'Take it easy, okay?'

'Cheers. I always do. You get no thanks for overdoing it out here. Scotty could tell you that.'

'Oh yeah?'

'Our high and mighty bosses reckon we don't need two tiffies on the day shift. I don't know what they think we do all day. Sit on our fannies and drink tea, I suppose. So that's one of us for the chop from each rotation. Scott's the new boy, so I'd say he was favourite to go.'

'Looks like I got into this business at the wrong time,' Danny said.

'Oh, you'll be okay. They can't cut the medic's job, can they? And you're not such a prick as most of them.'

'I'm not so sure about that,' Gemma said. 'Don't forget. I see the HR records. Tell him what you did before you landed up on this dung heap, Danny-boy.'

'I was a medic in the army.'

'Aye, and before that?'

'Royal Military Police.'

'You signed up to be a copper and a soldier all rolled into one? For what? I canna think of anything worse.'

'My dad was in the RMP. He died when I was twelve. One of his old buddies suggested I follow in his footsteps. Maybe he pulled a few strings. I don't know. They accepted me anyway. It seemed like a good thing to do, but I'm not sure I was ever ideal military police material. Liked the detective work though.'

'So what happened? You tire of beating up squaddies?'

'I had a run-in with a superior officer. He got a promotion, and I got "reassigned". They paid for me to retrain. If I couldn't be a detective, I would have liked to become a doctor but wasn't smart enough. Being a medic seemed the next best thing.'

'So you got the job you wanted all along, eh? Why d'ya quit? I suppose it canna be much fun with IEDs and guys with missing legs.'

'True enough. I coped with it well enough until I got married. Kelly hated the travelling and the worrying about if I was going to come home in one piece. It got to me. I decided it was time to settle down and get a civvy job. I guess working offshore was not quite what she had in mind, but we had a mortgage to pay. This was the best paying job. So here I am.'

'Aye. Here we all are,' Gemma echoed. 'And some of us have work to do. Don't you have some of them instruments to fix, Cal?'

'Sure. I'll get out of your hair. Just let me know if you need anything that doesn't need heavy lifting or inappropriate touching, hen. And thanks for taking care of Scott, the both of you.'

Callum walked out with his injured hand raised, like a boxer keeping up his guard.

Gemma waited until he was well out of earshot before saying her piece. 'If he thinks I'm his hen, you know what that makes him, right? What was that story he came out with? Distracted walking, my arse. He's alright, but if I were his wife, I'd keep a tracker clamped to his ankle. He's keeping two fancy women that I know of and I don't suppose that's even the half of it.'

'So what do you think happened?'

'Maybe he was having it away with some lass and her fella caught him at it. It wouldn't be the first time he's had to hop out of the window and make a run for it. He never learns, that boy.'

Danny limped over to check on his patient. There was no change and no sign that Scott was aware of people talking about him as he lay there unconscious.

Despite Gemma's colourful character assignation, Danny decided he liked Callum and felt he should stick up for him somehow.

'Callum's not all bad, eh?' he suggested. 'He seemed pretty upset about Scott.'

'Aye, so he did. Like I said, he's alright if you're not married to him. But maybe he's feeling a wee bit guilty right now.'

'What do you mean? It's not his fault Scott was injured.'

'Oh, aye, I guess not. But don't pay any heed to what he says about the lay-offs. If they have to let one of the tiffies go, then the management out here would get rid of Callum and keep Scott.'

'Nothing to do with his infidelities, then?'

'More to do with the fact that he's a lazy wee bastard. He's meant to look after communications. Always happy to come round for a look at the radio if it's warm and dry outside. And he's keen as mustard if there's a chance of a chat and a cuppa. But climb up the comms tower with a storm coming? I don't think so. I'd say he was hiding away in the tea shack when that job got handed to Scotty.'

Whichever way Danny looked at it, he was desperately short of friends or allies on the Cuillin Alpha. Maybe Callum wasn't the most dedicated worker, but he was going to need all the help he could get over the next few days. Not that Danny cared to pick a fight with Gemma. There was sure to be only one winner.

Gemma settled herself back into the tattered examination chair and made herself as comfortable as she could. Danny took himself off to his cabin next door, making her promise to wake him if there was any change in Scott's condition.

Danny got undressed and crawled into bed, but there were too many worries buzzing around in his head for him to sleep. He sat up and began checking emails on his tablet.

He took a sly look at his wife Kelly's Facebook status. She seemed to enjoy herself far too much for his liking. There were a few drunken pictures from a night out in York. She was surrounded by a bunch of women he'd never seen before. Maybe they were new workmates. She was wearing a new dress, at least one size too small, and she'd daubed herself with that terrible fake orange tan. No sign of Andy the handyman, but he doubted if she would be daft enough to unveil her new boyfriend. Not until the divorce was settled and she'd got her cut.

***

Kelly couldn't understand why he'd taken a job where he had to commute to work by helicopter.

'Going offshore won't solve anything,' she'd said. 'It might be pretty isolated on an oil rig, but there are still people out there. You'll have patients to deal with.'

'I don't have a problem with patients.'

'No, I suppose not, so long as they're barely conscious. I mean, why join a caring profession when you don't give a shit about anyone?'

'That's harsh,' Danny said.

He did care about some things. Kelly, for one. Not that he would ever tell her. Their divorce was still pending, and he was getting menacing letters from her solicitor every other day.

It amused him she would still phone him up to start a row. Under different circumstances, he might have been flattered, but the taxi had been due and he hadn't even finished packing.

He held the phone with one hand and bundled his overalls and boots into the battered black dry-bag with the other.

A horn sounded outside.

'What are you running away from, Danny?'

He didn't bother to reply. It was getting to be quite a long list. On the coffee table, next to the solicitor's letters, was a stack of unpaid bills. The unopened letter from his GP was presumably about the alcohol counselling session he had no intention of attending.

His career in the army hadn't been a great success. Suppose this job went the same way? Or suppose he couldn't last two weeks without a drink? What then? There was only one way to find out. He slammed the door on his troubles and bounded down the stairs to the waiting taxi.

Chapter Seven

DANNY COULDN'T KEEP HIS eyes open any longer. He was emotionally and physically drained, and despite the thoughts and fears churning around in his head, he dozed off.

A rap on the door woke him. Danny's first thought was that it must be morning and time to take over the watch from Gemma. With no windows or natural light inside the accommodation, it was hard to tell.

It didn't feel like he'd had a solid night's sleep and he fumbled for his alarm clock. It was 3 a.m.; he'd barely slept a couple of hours. He opened the door a crack. It was Gemma. She looked serious.

'The wee man's going downhill fast. His heart's racing. And you should see his eyes. They look like pissholes in the snow.'

Danny struggled into his work clothes, not caring that Gemma was watching his semi-naked contortions. He followed her back to the sickbay and took a quick look at the ECG. Scott's heart rate was pounding away at over 120 bpm. He gently eased open each eyelid. Even the right pupil was dilated now; the left was just a blank black disc. He flashed his torch into both of Scott's eyes. There was no reaction.

'He's tachycardic and unresponsive. Cerebral oedema maybe. That's life threatening. I'm going to call the infirmary and I've got a nasty feeling of what they're going to say. Can you get hold of Callum? Looks like I'll need his help. Tell him to bring his drill jig. And tell him to wash his bloody hands before he gets anywhere near my sickbay.'

'What's the plan, pal? No, don't answer that. If it involves a tool monkey and a power drill, I don't want to know.'

Danny picked up the phone and called the emergency number at the infirmary. There was no answer, just a continuous tone interspersed with static. He tried the main hospital switchboard with the same result.

'Shit! The phones are dead. That's all I need.' Gemma poked her head around the door, scratching away at her unruly mousy locks like a dog with fleas.

'Cal's on his way. God help us. Maybe he'd be more use trying to trace that phone fault.'

'I don't think there's enough time for him to go running around the platform searching for a loose wire. We need him in sickbay.'

He asked Gemma to wake Jack Blake. Danny knew what he had to do, but he wasn't about to go ahead without some kind of authorisation. A few minutes later, Callum rolled up with Stevie, the rotund, ever cheerful electrical technician. They were carrying a lashed-up clamp assembly that resembled a medieval apparatus of torture and some industrial power tools. Danny shook his head.

'You realise this is a surgical procedure? What the hell did you think I was going to do with an angle-grinder?'

'Cal's seen too many horror movies,' Stevie explained, holding up the hand drill and a Heath Robinson jig. 'Will this do the job? It's pretty accurate. We use it for slotting bolt holes in sheet metal.'

By the time Gemma had woken a bleary-eyed Jack Blake and persuaded him to come to sickbay, the two technicians had fixed the drill to the jig and set it in place next to the bed. Danny put a brand new drill bit through the steriliser, then tightened it in place in the chuck. As calmly and clearly as he could, he tried to explain to the OIM what he planned to do. Snakey's reaction did not surprise him.

'Jesus Christ, laddie! You've got to be fucking kidding me. You want to drill a hole in the poor bastard's head? And I'm supposed to just let you get on with it.'

'I don't think we have an option. It's the only way to relieve the pressure on his brain. If this were a hospital, then they'd have an MRI scan to see what was going on inside. But they'd probably end up doing something similar.'

'It's like trepanning,' Gemma added. 'Back in the day, they used flints to cut open people's skulls if they had a nasty brain ache. Some of them survived.'

'And plenty of them didn't, I'll bet. Well, if you're telling me, hand on heart, there's no other way, you'd better get on with your damn Stone Age surgery. I don't have to be here, do I? It's bad enough watching that shit on TV.'

Snakey looked like he might need medical attention himself soon, so Stevie offered to escort him down to the mess. He looked relieved, but insisted he'd come back when the procedure was over.

Danny positioned the drill bit just above Scott's left ear. The jig gave some stability, but not enough. In his trembling hands, the drill was rotating randomly. He was in real danger of drawing a figure of eight on Scott's scalp.

Danny took a deep breath and tried again. His eyes were fixed on the area of Scott's head he'd shaved earlier, but the drill had a life of its own. Callum put a friendly hand on his shoulder.

'Let me do it,' he said. 'This looks like a precision job. Just like tapping into a pipe, or whatever. Right up my street.'

Danny wanted to argue, but Callum's hand was as steady as any surgeon's, so he let him carry on. As the drill bit touched Scott's scalp, blood trickled from the wound. Danny switched on the suction unit and concentrated on keeping the area clean. Then the drill began cutting into bone. The whining noise reminded Danny of dentists and fillings.

Gemma had a tight grip on the head restraint, but she couldn't keep Scott totally still. Danny shuffled round to check that the makeshift stop was fixed in place. It was all that was preventing Callum from penetrating the brain if his hand slipped.

After what seemed like an age, the noise changed in tone. A stream of bloody fluid poured onto the tray below. After a few seconds, the flow became a trickle, and the team breathed a sigh of relief.

'What do we do now?' asked Gemma. 'Bandage him up?'

'God knows. I don't want to risk infection, but we can't just leave him with a hole in his head. We need to keep the wound clean.'

In the end, Danny settled for fixing a sterile absorbent pad over the entry wound. He examined Scott's eyes again. Was the dilation reducing? He couldn't be sure.

'His heart rate's dropping,' Gemma said. 'That's a good sign, right?'

'Yeah, but not that low. That looks like bradycardia.'

Scott's blood pressure and oxygen sat levels were dropping too. After a few seconds, the alarms on the monitor started going off. His patient was crashing and Danny stood frozen to the spot.

Gemma leaped for the defibrillator, yanking the unit off the wall. She unzipped the cover, and it opened like a book. The pads were already plugged into the box and Gemma quickly ripped them out of the sealed bag. As soon as she handed them to Danny, he snapped out of his fugue and switched on the shock box. He was relieved to find that this was one of the idiot-proof models. It gave instructions in an emotionless digital voice.

APPLY PADS TO THE CHEST

Four coloured ECG electrodes already surrounded Scott's heart, cluttering the areas where he needed to attach the palm-sized de-fib pads. He stuck one up by the left shoulder and another on the right-hand chest wall so that the charge would cross his heart.

ASSESSING RHYTHM

Danny took a deep breath. Gemma looked ready to leap into action. He waved her away to give the shock box time to analyse Scott's heartbeat, assuming he still had one. It could have only taken ten seconds at most, but it felt like forever. He stared at the readout, willing it to hurry.

SHOCK ADVISED

Danny pressed the flashing charge button.

UNIT CHARGING

He waited for a few more agonising seconds until the shock button lit up, then shouted out a warning.

'Stand clear. About to shock!'

Gemma was behind him; nothing was touching the pads, so he pressed the button. There was a thump, like the sound of a breaker snapping open. Scott's chest went briefly into spasm.

CONTINUE CPR

'Continue? Why didn't you tell me before? You useless piece of shite.'

Gemma muttered and dragged a box over to the bed. She stepped up onto it and started giving Scott chest compressions to the tune of "Stayin' Alive". She sang at the top of her voice while pounding rhythmically on Scott's ribs with the heels of her hands. It was every first aider's go-to song for CPR. Danny wondered if anyone had told the Bee Gees. The lyrics were perfect, as was the beat, but possibly no one had ever sung it as badly as Gemma.

Danny's gaze flicked between the ECG monitor and the shock box, waiting for a response, but none came.

After twenty seconds of heart-pounding effort from Gemma, the shock box cut in.

Assessing rhythm

Gemma stepped back and leaned against the wall, desperately trying to catch her breath before the next attempt.

Shock advised

Danny charged the shock box and fired again. This time, the ECG trace blipped twice before returning to its deathly flat line.

Continue CPR

Gemma jumped back on the box and sang with gusto. After a few seconds, there was a dull crack. One of Scott's ribs had snapped.

'Get tae fuck! I've broken him. What now?'

'Keep going, Gem. You're doing fine. Better a few broken ribs than a broken heart.'

The shock box prepared the third charge. Scott's chest twitched, but there was no reaction from the patient or the monitors.

Assessing rhythm

Danny had a feeling he knew what was coming next.

Shock not advised

It was as he feared — they were nearing the end.

CONTINUE CPR

Gemma's face was purple, and she looked ready to burst. She threw herself into the rhythm of the song again, but "Stayin' Alive" was only coming out in gasps now. Thinking she might be about to fall off her box, Danny readied himself to step in, but then he saw blood and straw-coloured fluid pulsing out of Scott's head wound with every compression.

He put his arm around Gemma and pulled her away.

'I'm not finished yet. What about the drugs, adrenaline and all that? We canna give up.'

He shook his head and gestured at the wound and the silent monitors and called it.

'Time of death: 4.37 a.m.'

Chapter Eight

DANNY FELT DRAINED. HIS first emergency and he'd failed. A man was dead. His fault.

He cleaned up while Gemma called Callum, Stevie, and the OIM. They agreed to meet in the mess. Danny tried to break the news gently, but the shock was etched on their faces. Stevie sauntered away and came back with mugs of tea. Callum waved him away. He looked in need of something stronger.

'What did I do wrong?' he asked.

'Nothing,' Gemma said. 'You were rock steady. You must have nerves of steel, pal. I couldn't have done it.'

'The swelling must have been far worse than we thought,' Danny added. 'He would have crashed soon enough, probably. It was my call. It didn't work. There's nothing more we could have done.'

There was not much of the night left and no one expected to sleep. After they'd sat in the mess in near silence for an hour, Snakey ordered them all back to their cabins.

In the morning, Danny hobbled down to breakfast with the aid of a crutch. It wasn't entirely necessary, but it earned him a few sympathetic glances on the way. He sat down in the mess. After a while, a few crewmates came by to offer an encouraging word or a pat on the shoulder. Danny wasn't sure he deserved it, but there was a feeling of solidarity about the Alpha that hadn't been present before Scott's death.

Before Danny could go back to regular duties, he needed to tackle one problem. The ever-practical Gemma went through the platform's procedures and, sure enough, found a grim document titled: "Actions to be Taken in the Event of a Fatality".

'Told you,' she said. 'There's a procedure for everything. I guarantee it tells you how to wipe your arse somewhere in here.'

For once, Danny was happy to follow due process and began filling out the paperwork. There was no way of calling Scott's next of kin until Callum fixed the phones. Gemma radioed their support vessel, the Viking Protector, and the skipper promised to pass the news on to Aberdeen and the operating company, International Oil.

Whoever had written the procedure seemed principally worried about the effects of a tropical environment on the deceased's remains. In the middle of the North Sea in winter, that was the least of Danny's concerns. With Stevie's help, Danny wrapped the body in a couple of large hessian sacks and loaded it onto the stretcher.

They had to pass the gym first. Vladimir Kovac, the shaven-headed power technician, lumbering along on the treadmill, came close to causing another accident by crossing himself mid-stride. A couple of grunting drillers stopped pushing weights and turned towards the pall-bearers, their shoulders slumped and eyes downcast. Another abandoned a swinging punchbag and, without taking off his boxing gloves, fumbled open the heavy door and held it back as they exited the accommodation module.

Fortunately, there was no one outside to watch their slow descent to the cellar deck. Wrestling the stretcher down the narrow stairwells felt disrespectful, but it was the only way to get Scott to his resting place.

Neither man wanted to go back and ask for help, but as they reached the final flight, the wind made carrying the stretcher nearly impossible. After several attempts, they rested it on the deck and dragged it down, one step at a time, clattering into the warped and rusted railings as they went.

Eventually, they reached the cellar deck and shuffled along the exposed walkway until they came to a disused pump room. By now, they were drenched with salt spray. Stevie forced open the door and they manoeuvred their charge into a suitable position on a raised dais strewn with abandoned valves and flanges.

Without really knowing why, Danny picked up a handful of grimy disk-shaped seals. He lay them on top of the body in the crude shape of a flower. The two men bowed their heads, then left Scott to rest in peace and battled their way back up to an eerily empty sickbay.

Shortly after the morning break, Jack Blake gathered all the crew together. He stopped short of calling it a memorial service since Scott had been an outspoken atheist. Cameron Law, the Camp Boss, said a few words.

'Laws is a lay preacher for the Wee Free,' Gemma said, who had worked with him for longer than she cared to remember. 'He's never shown me much of the Christian spirit, mind. He's teetotal; maybe that explains why he's such a misery.'

He had a soft Shetland accent which sounded almost Scandinavian to Danny's ear and he could barely make out half of the man's words. Scott's workmates in the front rows were visibly moved. There were a few tears shed, though the guys did their best to hide them as they shuffled out in silence.

Callum still looked shell-shocked, but Danny had a job for him. Maybe keeping busy would help.

'Did you manage to fix the phones?'

'Sorry, I checked the phone system this morning, but it's completely dead. There's no internet either. I was about to break the bad news to Trev.'

'What's the problem? Can you fix it?'

'Oh, I figured out the problem quickly enough. As far as fixing it is concerned, it's probably better if I show you.'

He grabbed Danny and steered him down the corridor and through the control room to a recess behind the main control desk. Hidden around the corner was a locked door labelled "Communications Hub". Callum fumbled with the key and led Danny inside. The room was about the same width as the corridor outside. Along one side was a row of dark green electrical cabinets. The last one was labelled "Network Switches", and its door was open, revealing a rat's nest of loose wiring and fibre optics.

'What am I supposed to see?' Danny asked.

'It's what you're *not* seeing that's important. There's no fibre-copper converter. It's gone. And someone's cut through the optics.'

'I thought you said there were supposed to be two cables.'

'That's right. It's dual redundant. But both fibre optics end up in the same room. The other one was mounted on this network panel. Shite design, of course, but there you are. It's obsolete tech, like most of this platform.'

Callum showed him the second cabinet, which looked even more of a mess than the first one.

'Don't you have a spare converter or whatever?'

'I did. There were two spares in the IT stores.'

'And where's that?'

Callum pointed at the racks of electronic components in the corner. Several boxes were open and there was packaging strewn over the floor.

'So this is sabotage?'

'I'm guessing someone got hold of the key last night while we were seeing to Scott. They sneaked in here and trashed our main communications link to the beach.'

'The beach?' Danny was picturing golden sands and maybe a bar or two.

'You know. Aberdeen, onshore, anywhere. No more phones, internet, nothing. Without the fibre optics and the satellite, we're nicely cut off from the world. Apart from the radio, that is.'

'Who knew that all the fibre gear was in this one room?'

'All the technicians, the operators, and Gemma, I guess. You can discount the drillers or the scaffs, I suppose, since they didn't smash up the place with a sledgehammer.'

Chapter Nine

Danny left Callum trying to salvage something from the detritus that the saboteur had left behind, and climbed the stairs in a daze. He headed back to the gym. The medic's locker was down the far end, nestled between the dartboard and emergency exit. There was something he needed to check; he didn't want to share his suspicions with anyone, especially Snakey, until he was sure.

Under the pretence of checking the lifeboats, Danny pulled on his overalls and headed outside. The wind had strengthened overnight. Danny had to cling to the handrail just to stay on his feet. Because of his bruised foot, he slowly climbed the steel-grated stairs up to the drill deck. There was no one around. It was far too hazardous to continue drilling operations in the teeth of this gale.

He made his way across to the gantry where the satellite dish had been, and climbed up the vertical ladder to the mounting frame. Six of the heavyweight bolts that held the dish in place were bent and the threaded ends had broken off. The rest looked intact, but the threads had been scraped clean where the wind had torn the dish free.

Danny scrambled back down the ladder and started a painstaking search of the deck below. It took him more than an hour, and he was losing the feeling in his fingers. Eventually, he retrieved all sixteen nuts that should have held the dish in place. Some were still joined to the fractured end of their bolts. Others showed no sign of damage, other than the marks of the wrench that a saboteur might have used to remove them.

The storm was worsening, but Danny felt he had to continue his rounds, in case whoever had done this was watching. He stood under the shelter of a guano-splattered compressor module and stared out towards the Cuillin Charlie. It was only a kilometre from the Alpha, but barely visible through the horizontal veils of rain and the black thunderclouds. Gales were whipping the North Sea swell into fearsome grey mountains, trails of spindrift swirling from each towering crest.

Every time a wave hit one of the four massive steel legs that supported the platform, the entire structure flexed and then sprang back into place. It may have moved only a few centimetres, but it was enough to send Danny staggering from one handrail to the next. The motion was unpleasant and disconcerting. This was his first taste of bad weather offshore. It seemed like the sea might swamp this tiny iron island at any moment and send them all plunging into the icy waves.

Danny had one last lifeboat to inspect, down on the machinery deck. The wind was howling between the equipment modules and the maze of pipework. His laminated checklist was coated with salt and virtually unreadable. He carried on, surveying each lifeboat as best he could, and hoped to God he'd never have to set to sea in one of these appalling orange tubs. Even during his survival course, the lifeboat bobbed around like a cork in a cauldron. And that was on a flat, calm lake. The thought of being crammed inside that airless cocoon with forty crewmates during a storm was enough to make his guts heave.

Checks complete, Danny scurried back up to the main deck and hauled open the heavy airtight door into the heli admin. A squall of icy North Sea air followed him inside, swirling around the room, sweeping up a stack of reports from the reception desk and strewing them over the floor.

The L-shaped area that acted as briefing room and departure lounge was deserted, so Danny leaned furtively over the counter and took a peek at the weather station. Seventy-knot gusts and a six metre swell. No one was leaving the Cuillin field any time soon.

On the plus side, whoever was responsible for Scott's death wasn't going anywhere. Danny couldn't figure out why someone would sabotage the communications between the platform and the beach. Had Scott been deliberately targeted? Maybe he was just the victim of a tragic accident.

Of course, it could be a straightforward murder. During his brief career in the military police, Danny had come across one or two suspicious deaths on deployment. It wasn't entirely surprising in the powder keg atmosphere of Camp Bastion, but it was rare on home soil and even rarer in a civilian workplace onshore. It seemed almost inconceivable offshore. Besides, it was an extremely unreliable way to arrange a killing, particularly if you had a specific target in mind.

Whatever the motive, Danny was determined to get to the bottom of this. Investigating crimes, he thought grimly, just what he needed. If only he were good at it.

Until he found out what was going on, no one was climbing to the helideck and flying away from *his* scene of crime.

That meant he was trapped indefinitely on Cuillin Alpha with a perpetrator, determined to isolate them, even at the risk of their colleagues' lives. Danny had no idea what the endgame was, or to what lengths they might go to achieve their goal.

The door beside the radio console opened, and Gemma bustled in, letting it slam behind her as she took up her usual perch behind the glass screen. She leaned over and shook her head at the mess. Under Gemma's disapproving gaze, Danny crawled around gathering up her scattered paperwork.

'What are you doing in here, Danny?'

'What do you think? I'm waiting to find out when I can get Scott's body to the mainland.'

'And hitch a lift home yourself, I expect. Well, you've got a long wait. Like I told the other nineteen boys I've had hanging around this morning. I may be the goddess of this shitpile, but I canna control the weather.'

'How's the forecast?'

'It's looking shite. You'd better get yourself back to your sickbay. You're going to have a few more customers if this keeps up.'

'They're not going to send the guys out to work in these conditions, surely?'

'No, but having a bunch of bored drillers and deckhands confined to the accommodation is trouble enough. And you just wait until the fresh grub runs out. There'll be food riots in the mess.'

Gemma turned her back on him and started fiddling with the radio console, their one remaining link to the outside world. Danny reluctantly trudged down the accommodation stairs to the mess.

Putting Scott's death to one side, the offshore life wasn't exactly living up to his expectations. That initial flush of excitement had worn off after the first days, to be replaced by the feeling that he had chosen the wrong career. Again. *I'm getting good at that*, he thought.

As soon as this was all over, he needed to get back home. He yearned to see a bit of greenery and breathe some air not loaded with hydrocarbons. He needed to talk to the few friends he still had and to his soon to be ex. Most of all, right now, he needed a stiff drink.

Instead, Danny sat by the serving hatch, supping Irn-Bru from the can, wondering what to do next. A few of his new colleagues passed by and nodded. No one stopped for a chat. Danny had to admit that he hadn't made friends so far, but his twin roles as offshore medic and safety coordinator didn't help.

There wasn't much help he could offer. He'd had a couple of informal complaints about rusty handrails, which he'd passed on to Trev Sinnott, the Scouse maintenance manager. For the medical emergencies, all he could do was patch them up and hand out pills. So far, all he'd had to deal with were a few cuts and bruises. Apart from Scott, his only client had been Mickey Walters, the paranoid deckhand, complaining that the chef was trying to poison him.

Ewan Haver was the head chef on the day shift. He was a sour-faced man with a permanently jutting lower lip, and he was currently sitting in the mess, glaring at the crew. He clearly disapproved of them cluttering up his mess room outside of mealtimes. For all Danny knew, he might try to poison them. Eventually, Haver lumbered back into the kitchen to give his cauldron another stir.

Danny decided it was time to make himself scarce. He finished his drink, made sure he dumped his can in the correct colour-coded recycling bin, and trudged off reluctantly to the OIM's office to talk to Jack Blake.

'Sabotage?' Snakey sounded sceptical. 'Don't you think you're overreacting? I can believe it was gross negligence, more likely. I'll have Trev's balls in a sling if one of his lads forgot to tighten up those bolts.'

'But what about the fibre optics?'

'That's a different matter. The only time we ever have thefts on the Alpha is when some new contractor turns up. There's only one of those on board at the minute, isn't there? I can't prove anything. No more than you can prove your crazy sabotage theory.'

Danny left in disgust, taking the scratched nuts and mangled bolts with him. *There's none so blind as those that will not see.* Clearly, that one of his team would sabotage his platform was too much for Snakey to stomach. He'd rather believe it was petty theft or plain stupidity. Danny wasn't sure *who* to trust, but at least his own judgement was sound.

He decided to warn Trevor Sinnott that Snakey was on his case and sound out his opinion. He scurried down the three flights of stairs, past the smoker's locker room, to where Trev and his maintenance team had their office.

A few slackers sat in the corner, watching football on the TV while taking an age to fill out their risk assessments. Trev wasn't around but, unfortunately, Mickey Walters was. Danny smiled and nodded and tried to make a break for it. Too late. Mickey was a big, lumbering guy, deceptively quick when he wanted to be, and he got between Danny and the door in two giant strides.

'I'm glad you're here, Danny. Do you have a minute?'

'Hi, Mickey. Good to see you. I was just. . .'

'I wanted to talk to you about what happened to Scott. Everyone's saying it was an accident, but I know different. I'm afraid it may be my fault.'

That stopped Danny in his tracks. Reluctant as he was to encourage Mickey and his conspiracy theories, he thought he'd better let him say his piece.

'You remember I told you what those satellites were really for, right?'

Danny remembered. According to Mickey, the government was using communication satellites to beam thought-control waves at everyone, to prevent them from finding out that the royal family were aliens. Or was it reptiles? Some crazy crap like that.

'I told Scott to be careful with them satellite dishes, but he wouldn't listen. Should have dealt with it myself. I was walking down Glossop High Street when one of them things started tracking me. So I bought myself one of those tree loppers from B&Q. They were on special offer. I used it to cut the cable and smash the wretched thing off the wall. I got into a bit of bother about that, but they let me off with a caution in the end.'

'And what's that got to do with anything?'

'You see, if I'd done the same to the one here, Scott would still be alive. I was too scared of getting into trouble again and losing my job. I should have disconnected it, at least.'

'You didn't mess with the Alpha's satellite dish, did you, Mickey? Try to undo the bolts, maybe. . .'

But conversations with Mickey were one-way traffic. If he had anything to do with yesterday's incident, he wasn't saying. Danny thought it highly unlikely. Mickey might suffer from paranoia, but he was hardly dangerous; on the platform, he was a stickler for the rules. He was a guy who wouldn't blow his nose without a work permit.

'I don't need to worry about satellites myself. I'm immune to the beams, you know.' Mickey rapped his knuckles on his hard hat.

'Lined it with tinfoil, have you?'

'Don't be daft. I'm not crazy.'

'No, of course not.'

'Tinfoil is far too thin. I've made a proper Faraday cage for mine.'

Mickey tipped off his hat and showed Danny the layers of fine wire mesh inside.

'I can make you one. It's aluminium – lightweight. You won't even notice it's there.'

Danny declined the offer and made a rapid exit, shaking his head in disbelief. It was no wonder most people smirked every time Mickey's name was mentioned. "Taking the mickey" had extra meaning on the Cuillin Alpha.

Back on dry land, Mickey's oddball views would probably have cost him his job. Offshore, they were just an amusing distraction. He was a good, hard-working deckhand. He didn't seem to mind being the butt of everyone's jokes and, according to Gemma, he wasn't even the weirdest bloke in the Cuillin field.

Chapter Ten

DANNY WOKE FROM A deep sleep. He fumbled for his alarm clock, but he couldn't stop the persistent pulsing beeps. Eventually, his befuddled brain realised that the sound was all wrong and far too loud, and he rolled out of bed, swearing under his breath.

'Shit! General alarm. What the hell now? Alright, alright, you can shut the bloody thing off. Is this some kind of conspiracy to stop me from getting a decent night's sleep? Bastards!'

It had to be a real alarm. Even Snakey wouldn't drag the entire day shift out of bed for a muster practice. Danny struggled into his clothes by the dim glow of the emergency lighting. It wasn't until he'd flicked the main light switch on and off that the cause of the alarm dawned on him.

'Power outage. Bollocks! Why in the middle of the night?'

Danny rummaged through his survival grab bag for the torch and stuffed it in his breast pocket, then he slung the fluorescent yellow sack over his shoulder and headed out. The emergency lighting sufficed to see where he was going, but it gave the corridors in the accommodation module an eerie, forsaken feel.

Hordes of bleary-eyed men began tumbling, two by two, out of their rooms on the floor below. Now the scene was decidedly like *The Walking Dead*. Each shuffling zombie worker was carrying the same yellow bag over their shoulders and heading for the muster point in the messroom. He was halfway down the stairs when he heard the cheerful chimes of the PA.

ATTENTION ALL PERSONNEL. ATTENTION ALL PER-
SONNEL. THIS IS THE OIM. THE PLATFORM IS ON GEN-
ERAL ALARM FOR A POWER OUTAGE. THIS IS NOT A
DRILL. ALL CREW REPORT TO MUSTER STATIONS AND
AWAIT FURTHER INSTRUCTIONS.

'Yeah, yeah, I'm coming,' Danny grumbled as he made his way to his muster station in the far corner of the mess. He was moving in the opposite direction to most of the crew. He put his best shoulder forwards and forced his way against a weary tide of muttering men. Just as he reached his muster station, there was another brief announcement.

MEDIC TO THE CONTROL ROOM. MEDIC TO THE CON-
TROL ROOM.

He cursed and turned round to push back through the crowd.

———

As the captain of this immovable vessel, Jack Blake took alarms and drills seriously. The crew were supposed to stay off the PA system and the phones unless they had vital information to report. So Danny was surprised to hear the chimes yet again and a strangely robotic voice make its own announcement.

ATTENTION ALL PERSONNEL. ATTENTION ALL PER-
SONNEL. FOR ALARMING, FOR ALARMING. THIS IS THE
PIED PIPER CALLING. THE LIGHTS ARE GOING OUT.
SOON THE RATS WILL SCRABBLE AROUND IN THE DARK.
WHAT WILL YOU DO THEN, CHILDREN?

It sounded like HAL's artificial voice in *2001: A Space Odyssey*. Obviously, whoever it was didn't want to be recognised. That sort of prank could easily cost the perpetrator his job and maybe a hefty fine to boot.

Danny hurried to the control room to see what those in charge made of it. A group of grim faces greeted him upon opening the control room door. He shuffled in behind the operator's console.

'Not funny, eh?' Danny said.

'I'll have him dragged off the Alpha by his bawbag when I find out who it is,' Snakey replied. 'He's lucky that we've got bigger fish to fry right now.'

Next to Snakey stood the pillars of his management team: Cameron Law, Blair Scorgie, Adam Chinaka, and Trevor Sinnott. Trev was talking to Vlad, the power tech. Trev was an outwardly genial Scouser, with long, black comedy sideburns, but today, he looked worried sick. He was new to the job of Maintenance Manager, according to Callum, and he didn't seem to cope too well with the latest crisis.

'Mickey Walters is missing,' he said. 'I called the night shift back inside at about eleven o'clock when the wind really picked up. Mickey was talking shite, as usual, so I gave him a bollocking. He went off in a huff and now he's not shown up for muster. Crazy bastard could be up on the helideck feeding the seagulls for all I know, but given the weather out there, we have to assume the worst.'

'What's this got to do with the power outage?'

Trev wouldn't meet Danny's gaze. Instead, he turned to Vlad, who shrugged.

'Someone does not like my turbine. He breaks the overspeed unit. Turbine cannot run unless the overspeed circuit is okay.'

'We can't be sure, but it looks like sabotage,' Trev said. 'They tripped one of the turbine generators, then the other one overloaded and tripped out. That shouldn't have happened either, but it did. And of course, the third unit is in bits awaiting an overhaul.'

'So, you think Mickey had something to do with it?'

Trev nodded.

'But you've got no proof?'

'No. And this goes no further than this room, right?'

'I'm not sure Mickey has the skills to sabotage complex electronics, has he?'

Vlad held up a mangled lump of plastic and circuit boards and handed it to Trev.

'Yes, thank you, Vlad. Looks like someone smashed it with a hammer. Even Mickey could do that. It's not that hard to stop the generators if you've got a mind to do it. Starting them again, that's a different matter.'

'Got any of these overspeed whatnots going spare?' Danny reckoned he knew the answer.

'What do you think? We'll bypass the unit if we have to, but that deviates from the safety case. Under normal circumstances, we'd need authorisation from the beach and that would take days, even if we *could* contact them.'

'Everywhere there is too much safety shit,' Vlad said. 'You want me to fix it? I fix it good. One big switch. I bypass everything. You want turbine stop, you off the switch. Easy.'

Snakey was hovering around at Trev's elbow and elbowed his way into the discussion. 'Thank you for that helpful suggestion, Vlad. Christ, it might even come to that, but if Trev authorises your bypass, he'll be in deep shit if the turbine overspeeds. Blades flying everywhere and God knows what else. It's a risk analysis from hell. I guarantee someone's job will be on the line.'

It won't be the OIM's job. No way Snakey was going to sign away his career. He was infamous for his liberal use of the blame-thrower, so Danny decided to mention his conversation with Mickey before he got caught in the cross-fire. His description of Mickey cutting down the satellite dish in Glossop had Snakey spitting feathers.

'The ungrateful bastard! To think of the number of times I've listened to his lunatic conspiracy theories. I know he's had a hard time of it in the past, but I should have got him sectioned off the platform years ago. I'm too soft by half, that's my problem.'

'Well, if we want to know what he's been up to, we're going to have to find him first,' Danny said, trying his best to calm his boss down. 'If he's missing from the muster, we'd better send out the search parties.'

Unsurprisingly, Trev didn't fancy going outside to look for a crazy deckhand, at night, in the middle of a gale.

'Surely it's worth hanging on until the morning, eh Jack?'

Snakey was having none of it.

'Get your lazy arse out there, Sinnott. We're looking for a saboteur. While you're having your beauty sleep, Mickey could have smashed up half the platform. Start with the cellar deck. Take Danny and Adam with you and a couple of the night shift lads.'

Danny groaned. Adam Chinaka was nominally in charge of the plant operators, though they paid him little heed. He was on a training exchange from International Oil's Ghanaian subsidiary. The operators didn't get on with him, partly because they were racist and partly because he was a strict timekeeper and a stickler for the rules.

Trev was already kitted up and headed down to round up volunteers. Adam followed Danny up to the gym, where they scrambled into fire retardant overalls, hard hats, ear defenders, boots, glasses, and gloves. Danny grabbed his emergency medical bag and they headed outside.

———

As soon as Danny stuck his head through the heavy sliding door, the wind plucked his hard hat from his head and sent it bouncing along the deck. Adam niftily trapped it with his foot before it disappeared overboard and into the sea. Danny stuck it back on his head and snapped the chin strap into place, expecting a telling off from Adam, but the Ghanaian just smiled and patted him on the head.

'We go downstairs. To north truss. You must hang onto your hat. Otherwise, it will become a fishbowl!'

Straining to hear garbled instructions through ear defenders and the howling gale, Danny followed Adam into the pipework maze below.

Danny figured the wind would be less fierce on the lowest tier of the platform. But as he clattered down four flights of rusting steel stairs to the cellar deck, he rapidly revised his opinion. The waves were huge. Every time one struck one of the platform legs, spray jetted up through the open-grated walkway. The bottom half of his overalls were soaked and the water was dripping down into his boots.

The rest of the search team didn't look any happier. They spread out across the deck and Danny found himself squeezing through a matrix of vertical pipes off to the north truss. He wasn't a tall guy, but, being broad-shouldered and stockily built, he feared getting stuck among the pipework, left to the mercy of the sea.

A great gull sitting on the guardrail seemed to have the same idea. It stared at him and made no attempt to move out of his way. It looked hungry. Danny shuffled past its foul-smelling perch and hoped the bird's vicious hook of a beak wasn't as sharp as it looked.

Someone was calling him on the radio. Presumably, it was Trev. All Danny could hear was a distorted howl. He glanced around for a phone to check in. It was always possible that Mickey had turned up and they could all go back to the tea shack. *Fat chance of that.*

The gull stretched its wings and took off, diving towards the sea, then wheeling around the underside of the deck in search of a meal or a perch that was better sheltered from the wind.

Danny watched it fly past with grudging admiration until something caught his eye. A lump of dull orange debris was dangling from the twisted remains of an old escape to sea ladder. It could be just stray cladding, of course, or a torn tarp.

As he got closer, the crest of a huge wave caught the debris and it swung back and forth. It looked like a scarecrow hanging on the scaffold. A scarecrow wearing company-issue overalls.

Chapter Eleven

A BODY WAS HANGING right underneath his feet. Danny leaned carefully over the railings. He felt sick.

The emergency call station was a few metres further on by the stairwell. He bobbed his head under the gull-splattered yellow canopy. Fortunately, the emergency phones were still working. He called the control room to update Snakey.

'It's Mickey Walters, most likely, though I can't see the face. He's caught up on that broken escape ladder on the north leg, but I don't see how we can get to him. It's too risky.'

'Is there any chance he's still alive?' Snakey sounded concerned.

'His head's well out of the water, and I can't see any blood. Worst case, he's been down there an hour. Assuming the fall didn't kill him, I don't suppose there's been enough time for hyperthermia to finish him off.'

'Then we have to attempt a rescue. I'll get hold of Trev and tell him to fetch the rope access kit.'

A few minutes later, Trev arrived, breathing hard and cursing between every breath. He was wearing a full-body harness. With him were a couple of lads with biceps bigger than Danny's thighs. Between them, they were carrying enough rope to tie up an elephant.

'It's not safe to go climbing down in this wind,' Danny said. 'You don't have to do this.'

'Yes, I do. It's probably my fault the bastard's down there. I'm his boss and I told him to fuck off, and so he did. I tipped him over the edge. Literally. I mean, we all knew he was crazy.'

'Maybe it was an accident.'

'You mean he tripped up and threw himself over a two-metre-high safety fence? Not even Mickey's *that* much of a fool.'

'Are you sure you know what you're doing?' Danny didn't know precisely how old Trev was, but he wasn't a young man and he didn't look in the best of health, not to mention his heavy smoking.

'I might not have been over the edge for a while, but I've had a rope access ticket for over thirty years. I know more about abseiling than the rest of these muppets put together.'

He motioned towards his team, who were looping wire strops around a couple of anchor points and tying off the lines. Trev checked his harness and clipped on another length of rope to use as a restraint and looked around.

Danny held out his hand, but Trev passed the line to Adam, who was a good head taller and maybe twice his weight. He shouted a few last instructions and stepped over the edge. 'Keep the tension on this, alright? These gusts are bloody lethal. I don't want to end up knocking the bastard into the drink.'

Trev swung his legs over the railings, carefully planted his feet on a suitable stanchion, leaned back and lowered himself slowly. His feet slipped a couple of times, sending him swinging away from the structure. Trev never panicked. He waited until the rope stopped swinging and carried on down as if nothing had happened.

Finally, he reached the casualty, stopped his descent and shouted up. He seemed puzzled, staring at the body, but then he became agitated pulling off the man's hard hat and throwing it into the sea. It was hard to pick out the words over the roar of the wind, but there was a lot of swearing, and his free arm was waving like he was drowning.

'Haul him up,' Danny hollered in Adam's ear.

'Something's wrong.'

Adam pulled on the restraint, trying to swing Trev back towards the deck. Danny made a move to help, but before he could reach him, there was a twang and the working rope gave way. Trev dropped a good ten metres, and then the safety line caught him. The rope snaked and shuddered until his weight stretched it taut, leaving him dangling like bait on a hook.

Adam still had hold of the restraint line. He tried to let go, but it coiled around his hand. The coil tightened and the momentum of Trev's fall jerked Adam straight over the rail. For an instant, he was tumbling headfirst towards the angry sea.

As luck would have it, his end of the line was threaded between the railings. He dropped a few metres and jerked to a halt. With Trev hanging on the other end as a counterbalance, Adam was dangling one-handed with the coarse rope flaying his wrist red raw.

He yelped with pain. After a few desperate lunges, he managed to reach up with his free hand to grab the deck plate. He hauled himself up just enough to relieve the pressure on his wrist. When the swaying stopped, Adam flexed his strong shoulders and tried to pull himself back onto the deck. His excess body weight and the trailing rope made it impossible. Every time the line went taut, he slipped back towards the drop.

Danny leaned over the rail and tried to help. Adam was just too heavy. He waited until the rope went slack and slipped it off Adam's wrist. It was a risk, but without it, Adam could pull himself far enough up for Danny to get a proper grip. He tucked his hands under the big man's arms. With one mighty heave, Adam launched himself onto the deck like an orca onto the ice.

Danny lurched back to the railing and peered through the spray at Trev hanging far below. Somewhere out there, among the mist and mountainous waves, was the standby vessel. He doubted they could get close enough for a rescue in these conditions. If Trev ended up in the North Sea in wintertime without an immersion suit, he would be lucky to last more than fifteen minutes. Danny needed to find a way of reaching him.

He looked across the cellar deck and saw someone grappling frantically with Trev's safety line. One of the rope team, he assumed, but he couldn't make out who.

Maybe if they got enough hands helping the man on the rope, Danny thought, they could haul him up and out of harm's way. He shouted for the rest of Adam's team to follow, and they staggered along the wet steel decking into the teeth of the storm.

Another wave struck; the wall of spray blinded him. As he wiped away the salt splatter, he saw the man holding the safety line had a saw-bladed hunting knife. The rope in his hand was frayed almost halfway through. Danny assumed he was trying to cut a tangled line free.

The toe of Danny's steel-capped boot clanged against the uneven grating and the man looked up. He was wearing a standard issue smoke hood which completely obscured his face. Then, he started to run.

The distance between them didn't look that far. It was far enough for the man to make one last cut. He dropped the knife and bounded away. He was a tall man with a long stride, but there were plenty of tall guys on the platform.

Danny heard a frantic cry of distress and looked back to see two bodies tumbling off the tiny ledge and into the sea. The wind in the wires and the crashing waves almost obscured the sound of the splash as Trev and Mickey hit the water. Part of Danny's consciousness registered their predicament, but the sight of his prey just ahead kept him focussed on the chase.

The knifeman scaled the vertical ladder into the void under the machinery deck and disappeared from view. Danny clambered up and peered inside. It was an oily black catacomb in there. He could continue the pursuit in the darkness with an unknown assailant waiting for him, or he could go back and help the others to reach the men in the water.

Danny climbed back down the ladder and jogged back to the severed rope. It was the only sensible decision to make. The medic's place was with the rescue party. No one would blame him. But, right choice or not, it felt like cowardice.

There were two figures in the water directly below. One was waving for help, but the other appeared lifeless, face-down in the water. Adam Chinaka held a lifebelt on the end of a long orange rope. With his good hand, he threw it towards the casualties. When it hit the water, he manoeuvred it using the line, as if he was fishing for giant crabs.

Danny peered down through the railings and watched as Adam flicked the rope again. The lifebelt moved ever closer to the swimmer in the water. It had to be Trev. Even if Mickey had survived the initial fall, he was almost certainly dead now.

It looked like Trev could grab the floating lifebelt. In these rough seas, things were never that simple. The wind was blowing the belt away from him. The strong tidal flow between the platform legs was taking his body in the opposite direction.

Adam swung the rope once more and dropped it neatly into the trough between two waves. The lifebelt was now only a few metres from the man in the water. Trev made one last heroic effort to swim towards it in a wildly thrashing doggy-paddle fashion.

His waterlogged overalls and heavy boots hampered him all the while. He finally got one hand on the orange and white ring. A rolling wave swept him back under the water. His head broke the surface just long enough to take a gulp of air before he disappeared under the waves again. This time, he surfaced right in front of the lifebelt. With two manic butterfly strokes, he clasped it in both arms.

By now, the entire team had hold of the rope. Their attempts to haul Trev up nearly sent him tumbling back into the sea. Adam's thunderous bass voice stopped them before they could try again. With much shouting and gesturing, he persuaded Trev to duck under the lifebelt. As he resurfaced, he stuck his head and arms through the centre of the ring.

The lifebelt rope wasn't long enough to reach up to the block and tackle overhead. The team had to dead- lift him, using the railing as an impromptu pulley.

More crew arrived on the scene. Even with the extra hands, it took all their strength to get the casualty high enough to connect the winch.

They hauled their sodden colleague over the edge and laid him out on the deck. Trev was gasping like a fish out of water. The left side of his face was grazed and bleeding. He gave his rescuers a weak thumbs-up as they wrapped him up, strapped him onto a stretcher, and carried him off to the sickbay.

Chapter Twelve

ADAM WAS SEVERELY BRUISED. Danny cleaned the wounds and put some ointment on the man's wrist before bandaging it. Adam winced but declined a bed in sickbay.

'It reminds me of hospital. Many people die in hospital. I will rest in my cabin. It is safer.'

Trev had a lot of visitors once Danny declared him fit enough. However, the only ones who seemed genuinely interested in Trev's welfare, were Callum and Gemma. Most of them, like Snakey, seemed more interested in *what* he knew.

'Did you see who did it?' the OIM wanted to know.

'Who cut the rope? Did you see anything at all?'

'Sorry. No. I was too busy hanging on for dear life. I can make a good guess, though.'

'Oh, yes? Who?'

'Mickey bleeding Walters.'

'But he was in the water with you. Wasn't he?'

'No, he bleeding wasn't.'

'So who was dangling from the leg if it wasn't Mickey?'

'A dummy.'

'A what?'

'A safety dummy, used for emergency drills. The bastard dressed it up to look like himself. It even had "Mickey The Dummy" written on the chest with a marker pen.'

Danny couldn't believe what he was hearing.

'So our saboteur's taking the piss now? How did I not see that it was a dummy?'

'It was dark, and he laid it face down,' Trev said. 'Not your fault, mate. We all thought it was the real Mickey down there.'

Gemma was less forgiving.

'You'd think you'd learn the difference between a corpse and scarecrow at medical school, but there you go. They'll take anyone these days.'

'Thanks a bundle,' Danny said. 'I feel much better now.'

'Just availing you of the facts.'

'Isn't it me you're supposed to be making feel better, Gem?' Trev interrupted. 'Where were you when I was dangling over the edge?'

'Hey! I was on the radio, coordinating. If it weren't for me, those boys would've wandered off for a tea break halfway through the rescue.'

'And I was guarding the galley,' Callum added. 'Making sure no one stole the cakes. I'm not good in the cold and wet.'

Snakey let the banter run on for a while longer before his patience finally ran out.

'Well, if you think of anything, Trevor, come straight to me, okay? I know Danny here's ex MP, but this is not a war zone, not until I say it is. If there's an investigation to be done, it has to be done via the proper channels. And that's me, understood?'

Danny's time spent in war zones as a medic had been mercifully brief. As a military policeman, he'd spent most of his time in army camps. He bit his tongue. The less they knew about his military police career, and particularly the ending of it, the better. He was more concerned about the speed of any investigation that Snakey might run. By the time he'd filled out the paperwork to arrest someone, they could have rowed halfway to the Shetlands.

Having said his piece, Snakey patted Trev on the arm and wandered off. Danny hated to risk making a sick man worse, but he had a few more pressing questions for Trev.

'So now Snakey's gone, you can tell me if you saw anything else, right? Are you sure it was Mickey who cut the rope?'

'Had to be him, didn't it? I can't say I saw much of him. He wore that damned smoke hood. You must have seen it, right? I was too busy with my little bungee jump to notice much else. That's all I know, honest.'

Danny wasn't finished with him. Or with Gemma and Callum. Things were preying on his mind, and he wanted to talk to people he could trust. Right now, that didn't include Snakey and his management team.

Finding some private space on the platform was never easy. Even the wall between his cabin and the sickbay was only thin. He motioned to Callum and Gemma, who followed him reluctantly up to the gym.

There was one solitary driller in the corner who looked like he was trying to cycle home on a fitness bike, but they could hear tinny music coming from his earphones and he paid them no attention. There was a stretcher and a couple of rescue dummies propped up in the corner. They didn't even look vaguely convincing.

How could I have been so stupid?

'I'm starting to think someone targeted Trev deliberately,' he said. 'Who would know that he was still qualified to attempt an abseil rescue?'

'Plenty of people, I guess,' Callum said. 'Trev was always going on about how fit he was and how he was still the best rope man in the field. He was desperate to be one of the lads, despite the promotion and all that. You're getting as paranoid as Mickey. Why wouldn't they just bash your man over the head and be done with it?'

'I think the killer is enjoying this. He wants to keep us guessing. He pulls the strings, then stands back and watches us dance.'

'Conspiracy theories and cod psychology all in the same shift. That's all too much for me,' Gemma said.

'Alright, so forget the whys and wherefores for now. Let's concentrate on the basics. I can't see how anyone could have planned for Adam to be holding onto the rope like he did. If it was a targeted attack, they had to be after Trev. Who do we have on the Cuillin Alpha who might have wanted him dead?'

'If you'd asked me that six months ago, Danny boy, I'd have said no one. But since Trev got his promotion, I reckon half the crew would like to push him over the side. Me included.'

'Why? Did promotion change him that much?'

'Oh, aye,' Gemma said. 'Insecurity, I suppose, if you want the psycho babble. He's a truly crap manager and tries to cover it up by blaming everyone else. He's even reading policies and procedures instead of watching the footie. It's like he's found religion and the manuals are his bible. I tell you, he's got himself a personality bypass into the bargain. He's in line for "the most annoying guy on the platform" award and believe me, there's some stiff competition.'

'Well, I suppose that could be something. There's plenty of simmering resentment going around. When you're cooped up with a guy you hate for two weeks, it wouldn't be surprising if it occasionally spilt over into violence.'

'Except that it never does,' Gemma insisted. 'Well, hardly ever. Guys just put up with it, think about the money, and go bash seven bells out of the punchbag in the gym of an evening. The guys who work out here long term might do plenty of simmering, but they don't boil over. You get the occasional hothead, but they never last.'

'What about Ewan Haver then?'

'Ah, he's special. He's a chef and you know what they're like. The only guy officially allowed to carry a knife onto the platform and the one you'd least want to own an offensive weapon.'

'What do you mean?'

'Let's just say I've seen his HR file, and it doesn't make pretty reading. The boy's certainly got a temper, but he's never murdered anyone, as far as I know. And he's a damn fine cook.'

Danny wasn't convinced the chef was a likely suspect.

'These aren't hot-bloodied violent attacks. It's pre-meditated sabotage, and perhaps the fact that someone got killed was just collateral damage. There's something else going on, I'm sure. As for Trev, I just wondered if he knew or saw something. You know, maybe it wasn't his winning personality that made him a target after all. Seems like we're at a dead end.'

'Maybe the guys on the support vessel saw something,' Gemma suggested.

'Christ, you're right! I've got to talk to them before the radio packs in as well.'

Danny was up and out of his chair, but Gemma waved him back down.

'Wheest, laddie. I'll go call the Viking Protector. The skipper keeps a sharp lookout. Goes with the job. He's a Norwegian; his English is pretty good, but they're a touchy lot, the Scandies.'

'I'll come with you.'

'No, you won't. Diplomacy, Danny. That's what's needed. You're about as diplomatic as that blondie bawbag Trump.'

Gemma stomped off down the stairs.

'God, this is a mess,' Danny complained. 'When I was a military copper, I ended up hating the job, couldn't wait to get out. But ever since Snakey told me to back off, my copper's nose is twitching like a rat in a restaurant.'

'Got any other suspects?' Callum asked.

'Too many,' Danny replied. 'Apart from the four guys I had in my line of sight, it could have been anyone.'

'I reckon it was Trev.'

'Oh yeah, and how did he manage that while he was free-falling into the sea?'

'Well, he's recovered a bit quick, considering how far he fell. Smoke and mirrors, that's all I'm saying. Smoke and mirrors. Besides, he's a scouser. They're always up to something shady.'

'That's a load of old cock, Cal. It's more likely to be you, I'd say. I don't think eating cake in the mess is much of an alibi. Did anyone see you stuffing your face?'

Callum ignored the slight and hit straight back. 'What about you, fella? You're always around when trouble kicks off. And nobody trusts a medic. They're always taking drugs and feeling up their patients.'

A silence fell. Callum broke it.

'I've just realised I'm missing my tea. Don't want Weevil's shortbread going to waste.' James 'Weevil' Weaver was the Night Baker, Haver's right-hand man and expert maker of bread, cakes and fancy biscuits. Unsurprisingly, he was popular on the platform, despite frequent reprimands for hygiene violations.

While Callum loped off to the tech station, Danny walked back to the sickbay to see how Trev was getting on. He looked bright enough and his breathing and heart rate were normal.

'Give it another hour and you can go.'

'What, no lunch in bed?'

'If you can get Haver to provide room service, I really would be worried. That would take serious extortion, not to mention physical violence. I'll give you a sick note, though. You can spend the rest of your shift in the TV lounge.'

'I might just take you up on that. Some other twat can keep that team of muppets in check. I've had it up to here.'

Danny looked up at the wall clock. It was a good hour since Gemma left. He had hoped she would have talked to the skipper of the Viking Protector by now. He tried to call her, but there was no answer. Then the PA fanfare struck up again.

ATTENTION ALL PERSONNEL. ATTENTION ALL PERSONNEL. THIS IS THE PIED PIPER. ALL SWIMMING LESSONS ARE NOW COMPLETE. ALL DUMMIES ARE ACCOUNTED FOR. PERSONNEL ARE REQUESTED TO MIND THEIR HEADS AND WATCH THEIR BACKS.

'Bastard!' Trev fairly spat the word out. 'I could have died from hypothermia. I'll send this gobshite Pied Piper for a swim in the North Sea. See how he likes it.'

The last part of the announcement sounded like a threat, Danny thought. If the Piper was responsible for Trev's fall, they could all be in danger.

'Look, Trev. If you're still feeling okay, do you mind if I nip down and see what's keeping Gemma? I need to talk to the support vessel before they disappear out of comms range.'

'Yeah, no problem. But I wouldn't mind one of Weevil's bread puddings if you're passing?'

Danny promised to do what he could and trotted down the stairs towards heli admin and the radio room. The heavy airtight door leading to Gemma's domain was even stiffer than usual. When he finally got it open, he realised why. There was debris on the floor and two oily tracks leading from the radio room to the emergency exit and out onto the main deck. The fireproof door was wedged open by a heap of laundry, or so it seemed.

It was only when Danny got right up to the exit that he realised it wasn't a bundle of discarded clothes. It was Gemma.

Chapter Thirteen

BEFORE CHECKING GEMMA FOR signs of life, Danny looked round to make sure his own was not in danger. He couldn't help Gemma if he ended up lying in a pool of blood next to her. There weren't many places to hide in heli admin; Danny checked them all before stepping over Gemma's body and putting his shoulder to the door.

He burst out onto the main deck. There was no one around except for Ailsa Troup, the steward, sweeper-upper, bottle washer, and Gemma's cabin mate. She was battling her way against the wind with an overstuffed bin bag in each hand. When she saw Danny standing over Gemma's inert body, she dropped the bags and ran.

At least that solved the problem of how to get a message to the control room. Danny had no idea if the emergency phones were still working. They were supposed to be independent of the regular phone network. Danny was losing faith in the platform's resilience under this sustained and deliberate assault. God knows what Ailsa would tell them, but they were likely to come running. He could sort out any misunderstandings later.

Happy that he wasn't about to be bashed over the head by an unseen assailant, Danny got to work. From the way Gemma was lying, it looked like someone had put her in the recovery position. Another puzzle among many. If he'd had a camera to hand, Danny might have taken a quick photo. The Health and Safety Executive took a dim view of people using flash photography in an explosive environment. Snakey viewed carrying cameras or phones outside the pressurised accommodation as a major crime.

Danny dropped to his knees, pressed his cheek close to Gemma's lips, and stared at her chest. He felt the warmth of her breath, but the howling wind just beyond the door was creating sporadic drafts, and he couldn't be sure. As he watched, he saw the gentle rise and fall of her ribs and breathed a sigh of relief. The pulse in her throat was strong, if rather rapid. There was no blood and nothing obvious to explain why she was lying there unconscious.

He examined her neck, but there were no bruises or marks he could see. Had she been injected with a sedative? He made a cursory check of her exposed skin, but it was a lot harder to spot foul play than all those ludicrous crime programmes made it seem.

Danny scrambled back to his feet and took another look round the radio room. Someone had given the central radio console quite a battering. They had ripped a few of the front panels. Smashed circuitry lay on the floor. A paper cup was lying on its side on the desk, its contents forming a thin brown rivulet which was dripping onto the floor. He took a sniff. It smelled like cold sweet coffee; no hints of anything untoward added. The chloral hydrate he kept locked in the drug safe had a bitter aftertaste, but some sedatives had no distinctive taste or aroma.

He wondered what was taking the first aiders so long. The reason soon became apparent when the main door to the accommodation burst open. Snakey waddled in flanked by the two biggest guys on the platform: Blair Scorgie and the drilling foreman, Erik Halcrow.

'Come along with us, Mr Verity,' Snakey said. 'Looks like we've got a lot to talk about.'

'I'll be happy to talk to you all day once I've seen to Gemma and got her settled in the sickbay.'

'I think Ms Gauld's had enough of your attentions for one day. Step away from her, if you will.'

'Look, I don't care what you think you know about what happened here. I had nothing to do with this. She's unconscious, and she needs treatment. I can't leave her unattended. You recall what happened to Scott, right?'

'Yes, I do. You got Callum Jarvie to drill a hole in his head and then he died. I thought it was a crazy idea. Now it looks like it was your perverted way of getting someone else to kill him for you.'

'Oh, piss off Snakey, you moron, and just let me treat Gemma, will you?'

'No, I will not. And you can mind your tongue, laddie. There are people here who can look after her better than you.'

He motioned at the furtive first aid team lurking behind his minders. They included Ailsa, who was staring at Danny like he was Hannibal Lecter. Stevie the sparky at least had the decency to shrug his shoulders and look rather sheepish.

'Oh, for Christ's sake, I'll come with you if it means Gemma can get some treatment. Keep a check on her vitals, Stevie. Breathing and circulation seem normal, but I don't know what's been done to her. You okay with that?'

Stevie nodded and started checking her over, while Ailsa and another member of the catering crew readied the stretcher. As they led him out of heli admin, Danny pointed to the chaotic scene in the radio room.

'I suppose you've noticed that little lot?'

'Bastard!' Snakey said. 'What are you trying to do to us? Cut us off completely? Well, you'll not get far. Blair, you get that lazy twat Jarvie down here to fix this mess, pronto. I want to get a message to the beach tonight to tell them I've caught our Pied Piper. Cuillin Field Ops were having kittens. They thought we had terrorists on board. Next thing you know, they'll be sending in the SAS. I want them to know that I have the situation under control.'

Danny thought Snakey looked like he was scarcely in control of his bowel movements. He decided he had better go along with this charade until they all calmed down. Not that he had a choice, with Big Erik, who was much taller than him and a martial arts expert, holding his arm. Danny was worried he might lose the use of his left hand.

Erik and Blair escorted him along the corridor to the Bond, the platform's tiny tuck shop and duty-free emporium. Snakey locked the door, and Danny was pushed onto a small wooden bench next to the storeroom. A single emergency light lit the room. He presumed the main generators were still offline.

'What's your game?' Snakey sneered at him.

'Game? You think this is some kind of game? There's someone on this platform who is determined to do us all harm. I don't know what his plan is, but he's almost certain to strike again. And all you've done so far is get in the way. You're interfering with my investigation when you know full well that I'm the only guy on this platform who has the first idea of how to track down a perpetrator. And now you want to lock me up for trying to save another life. Talk to Trev, talk to Callum, talk to Gemma when she comes round. They'll tell you. I had nothing to do with what happened to her. Or any of the other crap that's been going on.'

'I spoke to Trev earlier. He told me that you abandoned him in the sickbay without supervision, while he was still in a fragile state. He says you went off with some flimsy excuse about having to talk to our radio operator. And we all know how that conversation turned out, don't we? Ailsa certainly does. She caught you in the act.'

Danny suspected Snakey was twisting Trev's words to suit his personal agenda. *What was the OIM's problem?*

Jack Blake looked like a man weighed down by the responsibilities of leadership. Danny had a list of the prescription drugs on board and who was taking them, so he knew Snakey was on anti-depressants. His wife was ill, so Gemma said. She was having chemo after a breast cancer operation.

Suppose Snakey had finally cracked under the strain and decided to take the rest of the crew down with him? He didn't strike him as a man of action, but he was ex-navy, so would know about unarmed combat. He certainly knew his way around the platform, and he was in the ideal position to cover his tracks. Was that what he was doing?

'As for Callum Jarvie,' Snakey continued. 'I wouldn't believe a word that man says. He might well be your accomplice. And, yes, I will talk to Gemma, though I have a feeling you've made sure she won't regain consciousness. I ordered a twenty-four-hour guard on the sickbay. I don't know what you did to poor old Scott, but if you've done the same to Gemma, I'll give you a head injury myself.'

Snakey ordered Erik to shut Danny in the storeroom.

'You can't do that,' Danny shouted as Erik pushed him in the room. 'It's false imprisonment. You don't have the authority to lock me up.'

'I have responsibility for the safety of the men and women on board this platform. I also have complete authority to do whatever I see fit to ensure their safety. You, Mr Verity, are a danger to my crew and under maritime law, I can restrain you until we reach port. Since we're not moving, I believe that means I lock you up and throw away the key.'

Danny lunged at Snakey, but Erik wrapped one giant arm round his head and pinned him to the wall. He tried to break free, but he was no match for the big driller. Snakey removed his belt and his watch and emptied his pockets.

They left Danny a mattress, a couple of bottles of water, a bucket to pee in, and padlocked the sturdy steel-barred door. All of the bond stock remained locked away behind wire grills. The combined aroma of hundreds of chocolate bars drifted into Danny's nose, but there was no way he could get to them.

He should have been hammering on the walls, or pacing the floor, worrying about Gemma. But having missed both breakfast and lunch, his focus was solely on the chocolate. The aroma was becoming nigh on unbearable and pushed every intelligent thought to the back of his brain.

Danny began creating a list in his head, starting at the top of the organisation with Jack Blake, OIM. Guilty or innocent, he wasn't sure he cared anymore. Some people on this platform were going to pay for this.

Chapter Fourteen

With no watch or phone and only a single dim bulb illuminating stacks of inaccessible sweets, Danny found it hard to keep track of time. The place was almost silent, a novelty on any oil platform. With no generators, pumps, or fans running, the creaking of the platform's superstructure as each storm-driven wave struck, and the relentless howling of the wind echoed through the ventilation ducts.

Danny dozed off eventually, hypnotised by boredom. He awoke with a start when the fluorescent lights flickered into action.

'Nice one, Vlad.'

Danny assumed the ever-resourceful technician had restored the power. He seemed to be the only one who understood the intricacies of the gas turbine generators. How long they kept running was a different matter. Snakey must have let him bypass any damaged components with his "big switch". Danny made a mental note to stay away from the turbine module, assuming he ever got out of here.

Vlad's fixes were notorious. They were ingenious but conformed to no codes of practice. When a pipe sprang a leak, he'd filled the hole with sealant and wrapped it up with duct tape and jubilee clips. When a bracket broke, he just bodged it back on the wall with tie-wraps and bloody great nails.

He seemed blessed with the inability to worry about anything for more than five seconds, driving Snakey and Trev mad. They knew if they sacked Vlad, it would only take a few minutes, and the platform would be in darkness. Not to mention several irreplaceable generator control cards that would have disappeared over the side.

Danny struck him off his list of suspects. Vlad's fixes might one day prove fatal, but if he was the saboteur, most of the platform would be out of order by now.

There weren't too many others he could cross off the list, and even fewer he felt he could trust. Gemma, who had hopefully regained consciousness by now, was alongside Vlad at the bottom of his suspect list. She would hardly have smashed up her own radio room and was even less likely to have hauled herself up the comms tower and unbolted the satellite array.

Trevor Sinnott, after his swim in the North Sea, was obviously in the clear, despite Callum's harebrained suspicions. Even if he had somehow faked his "man overboard" routine, he was in sickbay when Gemma was attacked.

Danny still wasn't sure what to make of Callum. He liked the man, but he had a history of run-ins with the platform's management, and pretty much anyone in authority. Was that motive enough?

Then there was Adam Chinaka and the rest of the abseil team. When Trev's rope was cut, all of them were clearly in his line of sight. There was no way any of them could be the Pied Piper. That was assuming the idiot on the PA was also responsible for the attacks and the sabotage. Those PA announcements showed too much foreknowledge to be just a hoax, surely?

The most obvious suspect, Mickey Walters, was still missing. Someone had gone to a lot of trouble to fake his death. Mickey himself? Or did someone else use his disappearance as a smokescreen?

The first task would be to find him, since it was clear he wasn't floating face down in the North Sea. Danny wondered if Snakey was searching for him, or had conveniently decided that Mickey was presumed dead.

Somehow, Danny couldn't see Mickey as a cold, calculating murderer. Blind faith in his judgement of character was one of the many downfalls that led to Danny's early departure from the military police. He vowed not to make that mistake this time.

He needed to get out of here. He would never solve this mystery if he stayed locked in the storeroom. And even if Snakey let him out, he was hardly going to let him interview the crew and continue his investigations.

Another sinister PA announcement interrupted his train of thought.

> ATTENTION ALL PERSONNEL. THIS IS THE PIED PIPER. PLEASE BE INFORMED THAT THERE WILL BE NOTHING ON THE RADIO TONIGHT. OR IN THE FUTURE. PERSONNEL SHOULD TAKE CARE ON THE LOWER DECK BECAUSE OF AN EXCESS OF DIRTY LAUNDRY. THIS WILL BE WASHED IN PUBLIC AT THE EARLIEST OPPORTUNITY.

Danny wondered what it was supposed to mean. Perhaps there'd be a reveal of some unpleasant secrets. Or maybe trouble brewing in the actual laundry room?

The access to the laundry room was down a short flight of stairs opposite the bond. As far as he could tell, no one had been up or down them during his incarceration, but there had to be an emergency exit or some other way of getting in.

The follow up on the Pied Piper's taunts came shortly after. Danny heard distressed shouting, though he couldn't make out the words. A few minutes later, several pairs of feet were jogging down the stairs. More footsteps and something metallic clattered against the door. It sounded like someone was dragging a cumbersome load along the corridor.

All fell quiet and time passed slowly again. It was maybe a couple of hours before the main Bond door opened and Blair Scorgie edged in, closing the door behind him. He unlocked the cage door on the storeroom and stood back to allow Danny out of his tedious, chocolate-scented cell.

For a moment, Danny considered jumping the Ops Manager, taking the keys from him and making a run for it. With the element of surprise, Danny was confident he could take him down.

But where exactly could he run to? Even if he stole a lifeboat, he didn't fancy his chances of launching it single-handedly in storm conditions. And his stomach did cartwheels at the mere thought of trying to cross a hundred miles of ocean in such an unstable craft. He had at least one patient in need of his attention, probably more by now by the sound of it.

'How's Gemma? She come round yet?'

Blair nodded.

'Was she drugged? Did she see who did it?'

'She doesn't remember what happened. Apart from a headache, she's back to her usual self. They found drugs from the sickbay, you know. You're not in the clear by any means.'

Danny stared at Blair expectantly, but the big man seemed unsure how to continue. He took a deep breath and cleared his throat. 'I'd like to help you, Danny, but I'm not sure I like your attitude.'

'My attitude? I thought you and Snakey had me down as a psychopath. What sort of attitude do you expect from a psychopath?'

'I don't think you're one. But Jack Blake is under a tremendous amount of pressure at the moment. Your constant attempts to undermine his authority are making things worse.'

'He doesn't need me to do that. He's putting himself under enough pressure as it is. Burying his head in procedures and hoping the crisis just fades away. And locking me in isn't going to solve anything.'

Blair said nothing. He appeared to be in the throes of making a difficult decision. Danny thought he should at least give him a nudge in the right direction.

'I don't think you came down here to talk about my attitude, did you? I admit I may have overstepped the mark, and yes, I questioned the OIM's authority. But we're all on the same side. I'm just trying to find out the truth. And I can't do that shut up in a store cupboard. If you want my help, you need to trust me. You're going to have to get me out of here.'

'You know Derek Cochran, the scaffolder?'

'Cocky? Yes, of course. Everyone knows Cocky. Why? What's happened?'

'He was assaulted in the laundry room at the end of shift. He was taking his overalls down for washing. Someone knocked him to the floor and kicked him repeatedly.'

'Did he see who did it? No, forget that, no one ever sees the Pied Piper. He's the bloody invisible man. How bad did he hurt Cocky?'

'He's a bit bruised and battered. Stevie Dunn thinks he may have cracked a rib or two. And if Derek knows who his attacker was, then he's not saying.'

'And what does Snakey have to say?'

'He says it is not related to the other incidents. Just a workplace dispute that got out of hand, probably because of the strain of the last few days.'

'But you don't?'

'No, of course not. We all heard the Pied Piper on the PA. I mean, Derek is not the most popular man. He isn't called Cocky for nothing. There are plenty of people who would like to see him taken down. But if this was just someone settling a score, why wait until now? Derek has made a twenty-year career of upsetting people. It seems unlikely that anyone would wait that long to get their own back.'

Several of the crew had threatened violence against Cocky even in the short time Danny had been on board. The guy certainly had a nasty habit of getting on everyone's nerves.

'So you agree?' Danny said. 'It's too much of a coincidence for it to be unrelated to the other attacks. Does that mean Snakey's decided to release me?'

Blair shrugged.

'Most of the crew thought you were the saboteur. Since we locked you up during the latest attack, I expect they will have to find a new scapegoat. Mickey Walters most likely, assuming he didn't fall into the sea. It's almost like the Pied Piper wants to give you an alibi. Doesn't that worry you?'

'Yes, it does. I'd rather worry about it in sickbay than locked up in the Bond though.'

'The OIM still seems to think you're involved somehow.'

'So are you planning to follow his orders? Or are you going to let me out of here?'

Danny desperately wanted Blair to release him from this chocolate prison.

'Can I rely on your discretion?'

'That's the least of your problems. If there's another attack, we'll both get the blame. Unless you're sure about the crew, I'd be safer locked up. I don't want a lynch mob coming after me as soon as I'm free.'

'Just give me a while to talk them round. You're new here. People don't know anything about you or your background. As soon as they hear you were a policeman, they'll understand why I had to release you. And Jack is no fool. Even he will need to use your expertise.'

Danny doubted it, but if he was to carry on his investigation, he needed an ally; it looked like Blair Scorgie was his best option.

'I wouldn't go telling them I was just a corporal in the military police. Let them think it was something cool, like Special Branch or CID. Give me free rein. I can only find out the truth if I have evidence. If anyone is prepared to talk to me, or give me access to the scene of the crime, I might work out what's going on before anyone else gets hurt.'

'That's fair enough. I don't think you'll have much difficulty accessing the laundry. But I might struggle to cordon it off for long. If the crew run out of clean underwear, things could get very unpleasant.'

'Let's get on with it then.'

Blair unlocked the bond's outer door and checked to see if the coast was clear. Danny followed him cautiously. There were many people he wanted to avoid right now. Fortunately, no one was around, and Blair was able to escort him to the laundry without incident.

The only steward inside raised an eyebrow when he saw Danny stroll in but kept silent. Danny made a show of searching through the racks for his laundry bag. If there was some order to this chaos of clothing, he'd never figure it out. It was a good idea to put your most gaudy boxer shorts in with every wash, so you had a chance of finding your bag among the piles of monochrome work wear.

After a while, the steward got bored and wandered off with an armful of sheets. Blair led Danny past the row of upright washing machines and industrial dryers, which could turn XL clothes to XS overnight. Around the corner were the racks of overalls waiting to be collected. Some had red tabs clipped to the collar to indicate that the wearer had left something undesirable in the pocket, such as a screwdriver or rusty nuts.

Danny didn't think that even the most gormless crew member would have left a murder weapon in his pocket, but you couldn't be sure. The racks had been pulled forward and four safety signs placed in a rectangle around a dried pool of blood on the floor.

Danny examined the walls and found a crescent-shaped indent in one of the insulating tiles. He mimicked someone swinging a cudgel at the head of a standing victim, and deduced the mark could have been caused by the attacker's forceful back-swing before striking Cocky's head. A hollow pole of some sort, then, maybe a small pipe? There was no trace of paint, so presumably bare metal. That was as much as Danny found out. Anything he'd missed would probably be washed away by the morning.

Feet were clattering down the steps to the laundry. It was the steward returning, but Blair ushered Danny hurriedly out through a door marked "No Access. Authorised Personnel Only". They went through a narrow passageway full of electrical switchgear, up a dimly lit flight of stairs, to a door which opened out in the main corridor next to the gents' toilets.

'What's Jack Blake going to say if he sees me strolling past his office?' Danny asked. 'He'll have a fit.'

'I'm sure he would, but I asked him to talk to the drillers about a problem with the new wells. I'm not sure I should tell you this, so please keep it to yourself. I've arranged an emergency meeting of the senior managers. After that, I think we'll all need to speak to Jack. I've discussed the state of Jack's mental health with Trevor and Oliver, and we are very concerned. If the rest agree, I will ask Jack to step down temporarily. As his deputy, it's my duty to tell him when he's no longer up to the job. I believe that time has come.'

'Christ! He will not like that. Suppose he refuses? Are you going to lock *him* up in the storeroom? One in, one out.'

'I don't believe it will come to that. Jack's a sensible chap. He's just been under a great deal of pressure lately. I'm afraid you haven't seen him at his best. He's a fine OIM under normal circumstances.'

'I'll have to take your word on that one.'

Danny wondered what "normal circumstances" looked like on the Cuillin Alpha. If Snakey was Blair's idea of a good installation manager, he'd hate to meet a bad one.

Chapter Fifteen

INVESTIGATING A MURDER FROM inside the sickbay would be no easier from inside the bond. Danny had promised to be discrete, not to hide in his cabin.

Fortunately for both Danny and Blair, the first interviewee was right in front of them as they entered the sickbay: the bandaged and decidedly un-cocky Derek Cochran. He was being tended to by Stevie Dunn, who startled when he saw the men enter.

'It's alright, Stevie, carry on. Danny is back in the fold, but he'll need a rest before he resumes his duties. And in case you're worried, I think he is innocent and am taking personal responsibility for his release. He couldn't have had anything to do with Derek's injuries, could he?'

'I never said he did,' Stevie agreed. 'I never thought he had anything to do with any of it. Load of baloney. I don't know what's got into Snakey lately.'

'Nice of the old fud to lock up the doc, just when I needed him most,' his patient said, raising his head. 'If ya see him, tell him Cocky says he's a doaty auld bawbag.'

'Blair is going to do something soon,' Danny said, holding the door open for the operations manager. Blair hesitated before marching out, shoulders back and chin held high. Danny figured he might regret his act of clemency already.

'Where's Gemma?' Danny asked, having expected to see her lying on the bed instead of Cocky.

'She discharged herself. She's back in heli admin, giving everyone a hard time. Situation normal. Though she thanked me for looking after her, so she can't be fully recovered.'

'And what about our new patient?'

'Not dead yet,' Cocky said. 'No thanks to you and that pompous wanker, Scorgie.'

'Sounds like you're on the mend,' Danny suggested.

'Aye well, takes a lot to keep a solid laddie like me down. Nothing broken, Stevie says. As if you can believe anything a sparky tells you. Just a bit of rough and tumble. I've had worse.'

'I bet you have.'

'You mean a little gobshite like me is bound to get a kicking from time to time?'

'Something like that.'

'Har, bloody, har. That's tough talk. I hear you let that great jessy Scorgie put you behind bars. I'd have nutted him one. And his big blond boyfriend.'

'Strange you didn't try that on whoever beat you up today.'

'Well, I got hit from behind, didn't I?'

'Surely you must have seen something? The colour of their overalls? The make of their watch? Anything?'

'Nar. Only saw the bastard's boots. Wearing them indoors, he was. Scorgie would have hated that. He couldn't give a shit if some scabby scaffolder gets a kick in the nuts, so long as the bastard wipes his feet first.'

'Size and make?'

'The boots? You taking the piss? Usual zip-ups like every wanker wears. Normal size. It wasn't a lass or one of them pixies from the control room.'

'Upset anyone in particular lately?'

'Only the usual. Snakey and his bum-chums, of course. Trev Sinnott interrupted my tea break, so I told the scouse jobsworth to go fuck himself. There's Ewan fuckface Haver, but he'd start an argument with his own shadow. And then there are the techies. The lot of them were having a go at me yesterday. Cheeky fuckers.'

'What did you do to upset them?'

'Trev told me to rig up a fucking scaffolding platform alongside the fucking power turbine. So then the tech boys wanted to get at their fucking overspeed gizmo and they said it was in the way and to take it down again. I said, "no fucking way without Trev's say so".'

'Who are "they"?'

'Oh Jesus, I don't remember; Vlad the Impaler, Cal, Stevie, and a whole bunch of skiving fuds. Even the black fella, Adam Chinky-Knackers, or whatever his name is, comes down to stick his two penneth in. Fuck knows what it's got to do with him, the nosy fuckwit.'

'Did you take the scaffolding down after all that?'

'Nope. Still there. I'm too sick to do it now, right?' He winked. 'That fat fuck Tommy Barnwell will have to do it on the night shift. He needs something to keep his massive fucking arse out of the fucking galley.'

Danny took another look at Cocky's wound. It was similar to the mark on the laundry wall. He wondered if the attacker had used a scaffolding pole in a sadistic sense of irony. It would have to have been a pretty short pole to have swung it with sufficient force in the close confines of the laundry room. And small enough to be concealed about their person after the attack, as Danny had not found a weapon in the laundry.

It was time to leave the sickbay and see if Blair's reassurances were worth anything. He wasn't planning to risk leaving the accommodation module just yet, but he needed to talk to the Pied Piper's previous victim.

First, Danny went to the medic's storeroom to see what was missing. Blair had said they found drugs from the sickbay in the radio room, but the lock on the drug cabinet was intact, with no sign of forced entry. He retrieved his keys from Stevie, opened it, and started working his way through the stock list. Everything was in order until he reached the sedatives and the anaesthetics; a bottle of chloral hydrate was missing and two of the boxes of temazepam were empty.

'Shit!' he swore, rushing back to the sickbay. 'Stevie, did Gemma have any adverse reaction? Any side effects?'

'Nope. She was complaining of headaches, but I didn't dare give her any pain relief in case she'd been drugged. She recovered quickly enough, even if she doesn't have as thick a head as Cocky here.'

'Aye doc, she was hoping you'd give her a thorough examination, but you never turned up. I offered to show her what a real man could do, but she ran away screaming.'

Danny chuckled. 'No way you said that.'

'Ach no. Me head hurts enough already. Just tell her I'll be thinking about her when I'm back in me bunk. And no getting it on with her in heli admin, eh? We've got to sit on them seats. That's if that fucking chopper ever turns up to fly us off this shithole. . .'

Danny left Stevie listening to the rest of Cocky's misogynistic nonsense and walked away, shaking his head. He was no great fan of political correctness, but there were limits. Sometimes it felt like the Lost World out here, including cavemen and dinosaurs, cut off from modern civilisation.

Some women he'd met on his offshore survival course could swear and curse worse than your average squaddie; it was a man's world offshore, and that was one way of fitting in. Gemma dealt with it differently. She was unfazed by the foul language, the inappropriate remarks, and the occasional outbreak of blatant sexism. God help those who overstepped the mark, though. She had a good line in withering sarcasm, as Danny had already discovered. According to Cal, repeat offenders often found themselves bumped off flights or sleeping in the dilapidated cabin next to the bilge pumps.

Gemma was sitting on her usual perch behind the counter in heli admin. She had hung a sign over the sliding window, which said:

WELCOME TO HOTEL CULLIN – WE'LL MAKE
SURE YOU CAN NEVER LEAVE!

'You're bad, Gem,' Danny said.

'What? If you canna have a laugh when you're about to be murdered in your bed, when can you?'

'Gallows humour, eh? I'm not sure Snakey'll find it funny.'

'Then the miserable old bastard can lump it.'

'That's the spirit. He can't sack you when you're dead.'

'I wouldn't put it past him.'

Danny wondered if she ever took anything seriously.

'So they let you out? Shame. A long spell in pokey would have done you good.'

'I'm sure. Can I just look at your eyes, Gemma?'

'So no "how are you" or "how's your day been" then. I suppose I'm lucky it's only my eyes you want a look at. I've seen you staring at my tits often enough.'

Danny wasn't sure how to respond, so decided to not even try. She glowered at him as he shone a light into her pupils.

'So what happened, Danny? Somebody tried the date-rape thing on me?'

'Something like that. A sedative of some sort. Did your coffee taste funny?'

'Are you joking? When did we ever have coffee out here that tasted anything but funny? I usually put three sugars in, so you could fill the machine with crude oil and I wouldn't notice.'

'Did you see anyone coming into the radio room before you conked out?'

'Ailsa came into heli admin to empty the bins, that's all. I didn't see another soul. If anyone spiked my drink, they did it on the sly. While I was in the mess, maybe?'

'Take it easy until we're sure your system is completely drug free. At least you didn't get whacked over the head like Cocky. He took a serious beating, but your attacker even put you in the recovery position. It was as if he didn't really want to hurt you. He wanted to get to the radio equipment, and you were just in the way.'

'Oh aye, he was a gentleman mugger and no mistake. So why did he give Cocky a good thrashing? Apart from him being such a knob?'

'I'm not sure. Cocky wasn't near any critical bits of machinery; he was just in the laundry picking up his overalls. If that was part of some grand plan, I'm not seeing it.'

'It got you out of jail, didn't it? Maybe that was the plan. The mugger is your new best pal. I mean, he's had plenty of chances to bash you over the head, and he's not done it yet.'

'Maybe he enjoys having someone following his moves. Some blundering copper, always one step behind, never quite grasping the big picture. Do you know anyone who reads detective novels?'

'Blair's a big Agatha Christie fan, but don't let him know I told you. He wraps them in car magazines.'

'Like I said before, I reckon this Pied Piper is getting a kick out of this. Maybe Scott's death was what it seemed, an accident. But now he's enjoying the power trip. A few broken heads and even the odd death are all part of the fun.'

'You might have something there, Sherlock. But if this guy works on the Alpha, then he's no Moriarty. You might just be the smartest bloke on this dump and that's not even a compliment.'

For all her bluster, the drugs seemed to have knocked some of the wind out of Gemma's sails. Or maybe it was the feeling of being powerless. She leaned back against the long bench seat. The cushions had been flattened by years of wear. This was where her outgoing passengers usually gathered to watch the briefing video before boarding the helicopter home.

Danny didn't want to say anything, but he was concerned to see her throw her head back, look up at the ceiling, and puff out her cheeks.

'Are you sure you're okay?'

'No. Not really. My headache's about gone. Getting there anyway. But to tell you the truth, my head's still spinning with everything else that's going on. Like it's all spiralling out of control.'

'How do you mean?'

'I'm no weatherman, but I'd say this storm will be on us for a while yet. So long as the wind keeps blowing, we can't escape and we can't contact the beach, nor will our support vessel be close enough for radio contact let alone help. There's no SAS coming to our rescue, whatever our genius management team might think. We don't even know what the psycho looks like or what he plans to do. And our best hope is some failed ex-army copper, who's no more idea what's going on than the rest of us.'

'Sounds about right.'

'But listen here, Danny. If you tell anyone I'm fretting, you'll be the one laid out on the floor next, and I won't be putting you in no recovery position.'

The accommodation door opened, fluttering the safety notices on the wall, and in walked Tommy Barnwell, Cocky's scaffolding comrade. He was as Cocky had described him: seriously overweight with a round, jowly face and a gut that sat precariously on his overstressed waistband. He smiled, or rather leered, at Gemma, and gave Danny a quick nod.

'How's old Cocky doing? I saw the "Do Not Disturb" sign on your sickbay door, so I figured he's either recuperating or dying.'

'Not dying, I'm pleased to say.'

'That's alright then. I've never liked the little tosser, but I wouldn't wish him murdered all the same. Dumb maybe, but not dead.' Tommy edged over to Gemma.

'You've got a bit more colour in your cheeks now, love. Looks like you're on the mend.'

'Aye, I'm all the better for seeing you.' Her voice dripped with irony, but Tommy appeared oblivious and sat down beside her, his hairy stomach peeking out from under his shirt.

As appalling as Danny found the spectacle, it was an ideal opportunity for a witness interview.

'Whereabouts were you when Cocky was attacked, if you don't mind me asking?'

'Oh, I'm not so sure. Hanging around the galley, I suppose.'

'Did anyone see you?'

'Well, I usually have a wee chat with Ailsa if she's not busy. I'm sure she'd remember. Why do you want to know?'

'I'm just eliminating people from my enquiries, that's all. And there's always a chance somebody saw something useful. I mean, the galley and the laundry are pretty close. You might have seen his attacker go past without even realising it.'

'I doubt it. There was no one really, apart from Ailsa and the stewards. I just popped in to nick a few of them cheesy rolls for my supper. Oh, and I handed a couple to Mickey when he dropped by.'

Chapter Sixteen

IT TOOK DANNY A while to register what Tommy was telling them. Gemma was far quicker on the uptake. She leaped to her feet and squared up to the big scaffolder.

'Mickey? As in Mickey Walters? The missing loon that every man and his dog have been searching for these past days?'

'But then they gave up looking,' Tommy said. 'I assumed everyone knew where he was. I mean, he doesn't come in for meals because he's hiding from aliens or secret agents or some shite like that, but he pops in for a bite when there's no one around.'

'Who else knows he's alive? And that he's been strolling in and out of the accommodation like the Scarlet Pimpernel?'

'Not sure, really. He's paranoid. I offered to bring some food out to him, but he was worried someone might follow. Sometimes, I get a coffee and cake from the tea shack on the main deck and leave it around the back for him. And I got some clothes from his cabin and left them in the locker room.'

'How come he trusts you, Tommy?' Gemma enquired.

'Oh, we go way back. We started together in the Piper field back in the eighties, Mickey, Cameron, Snakey and me. It was a good craic offshore back then. None of this health and safety shite. Then Snakey got all serious and left for a supervisor's job in the Cuillin field. I got laid off a couple of years before the Piper Alpha disaster. So I was a jammy bastard really. Should have seen it coming. They made a bunch of cutbacks when the oil price dropped. A bit like now. Turns out they were cutting back on more than just the workforce. After the fire, Cam found religion and Mickey lost his.'

'Aye, the fates were kind to you and Cam, Tommy? But Mickey wasn't so lucky?'

'Mickey was offshore when the Piper Alpha caught fire. Cameron had swapped his shift so that he could go to his old man's funeral. He's only alive now because his dad died. Ironic, eh? Mickey survived by diving off the side and swimming for it. He was never one to do as he's told. I guess that's what saved him.'

'That accounts for his craziness, I suppose. I thought he'd dodged the disaster like his pals.' Gemma was taking it as a personal affront that someone had kept a secret from her.

'Mickey never talks about it. Snakey knows, that's one reason he cuts Mickey a bit of slack, even when he acts up. Mickey swore he wouldn't go back offshore, but there was no work in town for lads like us back then, so what do you do? Mickey was sitting in his flat, hitting the bottle and getting depressed. Snakey got the company to give him a job and even then he had to more or less drag him onto the chopper.'

'I'll bet he did.'

'We were all a lot different in them days. You shoulda seen us. Snakey was a class act. Loyal to his pals, and a good laugh too, not a jumped-up fandan like he is now. Cameron was always getting into fights. He had a wicked temper. And Mickey didn't use to be so weird. I mean, don't get me wrong, he was always strange. He used to go to that happy-clappy church in Rosemount. His family joined some oddball religious sect, but he never talked about it much. That all went out the window after the fire. Hard to believe in heaven when you've seen hell.'

'So Cameron figured that the Good Lord saved him, and he comes over all religious. Meanwhile, Mickey thinks that God's abandoned him, so he loses his religion and finds conspiracy theories instead,' Danny said. 'Has he said anything to you about why he went AWOL?'

'No. And I didn't ask. I'm never sure what's fact or fiction with him anymore.'

'Could he be behind the sabotage? Is he the Pied Piper?'

Tommy was silent. Danny realised he was on the verge of tears. He hid it well, resting his head in his hands. When he spoke again, his voice was steady, with only the odd pause betraying emotion.

'Could be, I suppose. I mean, if anyone's got cause to hate the oil industry, it's Mickey. Did you know that some buckos who cut lumps out of the safety budget for Piper Alpha business are working at head office for International Oil now? Probably earning a big bonus for shaving money from this rust heap, too. If I wanted to get back at them, I'd hit them in the pocket. Trashing one of their rigs, and their precious bonuses.'

'What about the attacks, though?' Gemma asked.

'Mickey never struck me as a violent type.'

'I've never seen him hurt anyone, but he gets pretty angry sometimes. You know, with things on the news about government cover-ups. He's been in trouble with the law now and again. The cops caught him damaging stuff and spraying paint on CCTVs. He's a good pal of mine, and I don't like to think about it, but maybe he's getting worse.'

'Have you any idea where I might find him?' Danny asked.

'Not a clue, pal. Even if I did, I'm not sure I'd tell you. Not till I'm sure if he's gone postal on us. Maybe he's just hiding, staying out of trouble. He already thinks the world's out to get him. With this sabotage business going on, he knows he's the prime suspect. Snakey's ready to lock up anyone. I don't think Mickey would fare too well locked up, waiting for a storm to break. He's got this fear of being trapped. Always knows where the emergency exits are. Not surprising really.'

Tommy had a point, Danny decided. Snakey would certainly lock Mickey away if there was even a hint of suspicion pointing his way. If he prevailed, he was going to have to find a seriously large lock-up for all his suspects and enemies. If, on the other hand, Blair and his cronies were successful, the outcome would most likely be the same for Mickey.

There was nothing he could do about Blair's problems, but he could at least search for Mickey. The problem was where to start. The number of POB on the whiteboard again read ninety-four, ignoring the one lying in dead in the cellar deck storeroom. Nearly a hundred on board the Cuillin Alpha and the platform itself was only about 150 metres square. Where in this crowded steel labyrinth would a paranoid and allegedly claustrophobic deckhand hide?

Danny's task was that much harder because of the screaming gale outside. Gemma wanted to know where he was heading, but since he wasn't sure. Even if he didn't come back, what was she going to do about it?

'I'm coming with you,' Tommy said. Danny tried to argue with him, but the big lad had a point. Mickey was more likely to come out of hiding for his old pal.

'All outside works cancelled 'cos of the wind. I'm supposed to get permission from my supervisor.'

'Don't be daft,' Danny said. 'What are you going to tell them? That you're off on a wild goose chase, looking for a missing lunatic, with the help of an alleged saboteur. That should go down well. Who is your supervisor now?'

'Trev in theory, but I can't see him getting back to work anytime soon. Meantime, we're supposed to report to Blair Scorgie.'

'Well, that settles it. He's very busy today; literally tied up if he's not careful.'

To avoid getting him into unnecessary trouble, Danny got Tommy to fill out and sign a generic risk assessment. Aside from the wind, the most significant risk appeared to be having someone crack you over the head with a scaffolding pole. He ticked the "dropped objects" hazard box, as that seemed to be the nearest fit, and wrote that they would wear hard hats with chin straps. That was about the best "risk mitigation" Danny could offer under the circumstances.

For want of a better idea, Danny decided to start the search down on the cellar deck. It seemed like a decent place for a fugitive to hide out.

Conditions down on the bottom deck were no better than the last time he was there. The swell was higher, and the spray was coming over the top of the rails, as well as up through the grating floor. Even with both hands on the rails, it was a struggle to stay upright.

When they rounded the south corner of the platform and stepped into the teeth of the wind, it got even worse. The cold salt spray scoured his skin, and the sheer power of the storm took his breath away. Where there was a break in the railings, they were forced to crawl on hands and knees as the intense gust swirled around the superstructure.

Eventually, they reached the vertical ladder that his suspect used to make his escape. The ascent was equally perilous. At least the wind was now blowing them against the ladder. There were bars to grab on all sides. The trickiest part was climbing off the ladder. This involved scrambling over the safety gate, and into the void between the decks and the equipment modules above.

There was a waist-high yellow barrier across the entrance to the void where Danny last saw his fugitive. Years of rust had firmly shut it. That didn't bode well for their search, but Danny refused to brave the return journey until they had at least looked round and caught their breath.

Chapter Seventeen

DANNY ASSUMED THAT THE howling wind would cover the sound of their approach so they could sneak up on anyone hiding out in the void. However, the amount of noise Tommy made climbing over the low gate soon scuppered that strategy.

Perched at the top of the ladder, Tommy attempted to get his leg over the gate, but got his foot caught in the framework. He wobbled for a while, then fell over backwards in a sort of fat man's Fosbury flop, and landed heavily on his shoulder. His other steel toe-capped boot struck the module wall, making a tremendous booming sound that echoed through the void. He might as well have brought the Band of the Scots Dragoon Guards with him to announce their arrival.

They perched on the narrow ledge and he unlatched the access hatch. It opened with a metallic screech but moved freely enough.

'This hatch was definitely open last time I was here. Otherwise, I would have caught up with the bastard before he crawled into the void,' Danny said.

'It's not supposed to be left open, in case seawater gets in. Same with all the hatches. There's a sign on the outside.'

'But it was open. And now someone's closed it again. One of your lads, maybe?'

'Not likely. Nobody goes looking for work offshore. And you can't see the sign when the door's open.'

The hatch and the space beyond were barely waist height. The void, used occasionally to access the underside of the gas compressors and the generators on the machinery deck above, was filled with obstructions: bulkheads and baffles, pipework and cable trays. Not the ideal environment for an overweight sixty-year-old scaffolder, so he suggested Tommy stay behind and guard the entrance.

Tommy sounded relieved. 'Got to have a man outside when you go into confined spaces. You need someone to go for help when you're dying from hydrogen sulphide poisoning. They made us watch that bleedin' DVD again last week.'

Danny didn't find this reassuring and checked his gas detector was still working, then switched on his explosion-proof head torch and crawled into the void. It was damp, cramped, and stinking of oil. Even the powerful head torch could not penetrate far into the gloom. Low-hanging pipes blocked the beam, and Danny had to get down on his stomach and crawl like a snake to get under them.

Not only was there a fair amount of seawater on the floor, but every flange in the void also seemed to have sprung a leak over the years. Crawling under them involved dragging his crotch through pools of cold, oily water. At least he hoped it was just oil seeping into his boxer shorts. There were plenty of other fluids pumping around the platform, which could do severe damage to his chances of ever fathering a child.

Even if Mickey had overcome his fear of confined spaces, it seemed unlikely that he would have lived down here, no matter how many cakes and cups of coffee Tommy smuggled out to him. In places, the void opened out and Danny could stand if he crouched slightly. These open areas were all directly under running machinery. The noise was at an uncomfortable level even with earplugs and a set of padded ear defenders.

The radio crackled and whooped; the sound echoing around the void. Startled, Danny stepped back and struck his hard hat against a galvanised cable tray. The hat survived, but his head was still ringing as he turned down the volume and tried to pick up what Tommy was yelling. The only things he could make out was compound swearing, interspersed with his name.

'What are you doing Danny? ... It's bastard freezing... '–king move on. Snakey's called a meeting. ... in the shit if we don't...'

'Tommy, this is Danny. Can't hear you, but I get the drift. I'm heading back. Did you get that? Over.'

'...Hurry the ...uck up. My nuts are... and I'm starving. Out.'

Danny ducked under a beam and found himself in a chest-high space. He was just about to retrace his steps when he saw a hatch in the ceiling. Someone had scraped the rust off around the catches and had opened it recently. He levered open the catches and applied his shoulder to the hatch door. It was heavy but clanged open with a little persuasion.

Danny put his arms through the hole and hauled himself up like a gymnast on the parallel bars. He found himself in what looked like the air intake for a turbine. There was a circular mesh screen but no turbine, just an empty plinth with a few rusting valves and pipes that led nowhere. This had to be part of Vlad's generator module. The tech station must be close by.

In the corner of the intake, someone had collected all the loose pipe insulation and made themselves a lumpy but well-padded bed. There was a hessian sack next to the bed containing a few clothes and a wash kit. Danny lifted the sack. It was a lot heavier than he'd expected. He rummaged inside and pulled out a supermarket carrier bag. In it was a steel tube.

He would have to check with Tommy, but it looked suspiciously like a roughly sawn-off scaffolding pole. There were stains on one end, which Danny strongly suspected were blood.

The radio burst into life, but all Danny could hear were bursts of static. There was no way he was going to crawl back through the void and fight his way back around the wuthering Cellar Deck when he only had to walk past two modules and out through the airlock to reach the steps to the accommodation. He called Tommy to tell him to make his own way back, as best he could. He didn't sound happy.

'Tommy here... You could have told me before... you wanker. Out.'

Danny picked up the weapon and stuffed it back into the bag. There was no possibility of tracing the blood, of matching any fingerprints out here, but he could at least try to maintain the chain of evidence.

Things were looking bad for Mickey. He was with Tommy on this. He'd hoped to catch up with Mickey and hear his side of the story.

He didn't even know what to do with the evidence. If he just presented it to Snakey or Blair, a lynch mob would look for Mickey. He didn't want to have *that* on his conscience.

Suppose he withheld the evidence and then Mickey went off and killed someone. Suppose he killed Gemma? Or came after Danny himself?

Danny was tired of being out on a limb, fighting authority. Once the current power struggle was sorted, he would present the evidence to whoever was in charge and let them make the decision. He was just a medic, not a detective. It wasn't his job to decide how to manage this situation. Nobody was going to thank him for taking it all on, especially if he made the wrong call.

With that decision made, he darted out of the abandoned module and made for the steps up to main deck. There was a little more shelter here, but not much.

Surely this storm can't go on much longer?

At the top of the first flight of steps, an oily and smelly Danny met a cold and wet Tommy. He looked pissed off. Danny smiled and nodded, but Tommy just glowered at him and they reached the accommodation door together in silence.

Chapter Eighteen

CREW MEETINGS ON THE Cuillin Alpha were always held in the mess room, the only place with enough space to accommodate the entire crew. You had to turn up early to guarantee a seat. To encourage attendance and improve team spirit, there was usually a good spread of tray bakes. The majority of the crew would show up, even if most of them dozed off after the first half hour. There were the occasional arguments about pay and conditions or the state of the facilities, but they were mostly dull affairs.

It would not be that sort of meeting. Danny eased himself out of his filthy overalls and dumped them by the bins at the entrance. He slipped a couple of plastic covers over his boots and pulled them back on his feet.

Everyone had been summoned to the meeting, and the mess was packed. No tray bakes this time, just a few packs of digestives and only a lucky few had managed to fix themselves a coffee before the meeting started.

People were shouting in a variety of thick regional accents. Danny could pick out strange Doric vowel sounds of Aberdeen booming over the PA, but what was Snakey bawling into his microphone? Blair Scorgie was also keen to get his message across, but a phalanx of scaffolders rebuffed his attempts to seize the microphone from Snakey. A shoving match ensued between the scaffolders and Blair's small band of supporters.

Danny sidled up to Callum, who was lurking by the hot food counter, more in hope than expectation.

'What's going on, Cal? Is Snakey still in charge? It sounds like the world swearing championships in here.'

'You're not far wrong, fella. It's the Great British Fuck Off. I'm not so sure anyone's in charge at the moment. Scorgie decided the best way to depose Snakey was to call a meeting. It's revolution by committee.'

'Nice strategy. How's that working out for him?'

'Not well. Blair's been working on the platform for less than a decade. It probably seems like a lifetime to him, but the old fellas on here still see him as a young upstart. Snakey's been part of the management team for over thirty years. He's practically oil rig nobility. They might think he's an eejit, right enough, but he's the eejit they know. Blair's the outsider, and they're giving him a hard time.'

'What about Cameron? Did Blair get him on his side?'

'Hard to say. Old Cameron was preaching love and peace, but he's moved on to the fiery pits of hell now. I think if push comes to shove, he'll back the status quo unless Snakey starts wearing his pants on his head saying he's the King of Siam.'

'And Trev?'

'He's the sort who'll stand on the sidelines until he's sure who's going to win, then tell them how he supported them all along.'

'Suppose there's no winner?'

'I think you've hit the nail on the head there, mate. This looks like the battle of the losers to me. I'm firmly on the side of Callum Jarvie. You'd better keep your head down and look after yourself.'

Danny was no student of history, but his teacher had forced him to read Julius Caesar for English GCSE. If nothing else, it had given him insight into the pitfalls of regime change. He had also watched the remake of *Mutiny on the Bounty*, mostly for the topless South Sea women, but some of the story had stuck.

'If you're going to start an uprising, aren't you supposed to put the captain in a boat and cast him adrift? Or maybe you just all stab him to death?'

'That would be my plan. And then I'd be getting the boys to polish off his family and friends quietly. Just like the Bolsheviks did in Russia. That turned out well, eh?'

'So, what happens now?'

'Well, Blair's got a few pals, too. Olly's boys are up for a scrap. The techies and the stewards will side with him. Let's be honest. There's plenty of folk pissed off with the way Snakey's been handling this whole sabotage business. Not to mention the ones who just think he's an arrogant little twat.'

'You're expecting a fight? Who's your money on?'

'Hard to say. And no one's taking bets, always a bad sign. Snakey's got the scaffolders and the deckhands, but Blair's got the drillers. Short and vicious versus big and strong. It's a tough call.'

'It's not always the strongest that wins. It's the ones who are prepared to get violent the quickest. If Blair's boys aren't ready to stick the boot in, they're going to lose.'

'It looks to me like the scaffs have come tooled up. Either they're pleased to see us, or they've got a few homemade weapons in their pockets. Bad business.'

'You're not wrong. People could get properly hurt if it kicks off,' Danny said, temporarily forgetting that he was supposed to be staying out of platform politics.

'Well, you're the safety coordinator. Are you not supposed to be preventing injuries as well as fixing them afterwards?'

Callum gestured towards the ceiling. It took Danny a while, but then the penny dropped. He squeezed his way to the back of the crowd until he reached the wall by the muster board. In the centre of the room, a flurry of pushing and shoving broke out. It looked like Cocky and Ewan Haver were squaring up to each other. It was only a matter of time before someone would throw the first punch.

Nobody seemed to pay him any attention. They were all too wrapped up in the developing brawl in the middle of the room. Danny balled his fist and punched the red fire alarm box, smashing the thin plate of glass and depressing the button.

A pulsing whoop sounded immediately, followed by a deluge of cold water spraying down from the sprinklers on the ceiling. Within seconds, everyone and everything in the room was soaked.

Danny quickly edged back towards the hot food counter before anyone realised who was to blame. Callum gave him a furtive fist bump, then grimaced and pulled up his collar as the water began trickling down his back.

Through the spray and confusion, it took Danny a while to realise that the fight was continuing. Cocky and Haver were grappling on the floor in a growing pool of bloody water, while Asim Holroyd and Owen Shives, the diminutive control room operators, were trying to keep an enraged Tommy Barnwall in a restraint hold. What Danny knew, and Tommy presumably didn't, was that Asim practised Kalaripayattu, an Indian martial art. It was surely only a matter of time before he elbowed Tommy in the balls.

The flow of water trickled to a halt and some of the fire went out of the fight. Adam Chinaka moved from his sheltered position in the corridor and strode across the room, parting the struggling mass of bodies like Moses the Red Sea. He jumped up on the food counter, his deep booming voice cutting through the angry babble.

'Stop this nonsense. This is an emergency! There is a fire! Report to muster stations immediately!'

Danny couldn't say if it was Adam's commanding voice, or that he was the only dry person in the room that gave him the aura of authority. The angry shouts died down, and the combatants began shuffling to their assembly points.

This was a routine ingrained into the soul of every member of the crew and repeated each rotation ad naseum. They all were aware that one day, the routine and repetition might save their lives. Even Danny and Callum felt the Pavlovian urge to join the queue at the muster board.

Adam seemed to have a few words with both Snakey and Blair. There was no way for Danny to eavesdrop, but the two managers had the look of naughty schoolboys caught fighting in the playground. The leadership struggle was not over. At least the fight had fizzled out of the two main protagonists for now.

Adam strode off to take control of the emergency drill and soon his garbled instructions were being relayed over the PA system to a confused and disheartened crew. Eventually, the general alarm was tuned down.

> FIRE ALARM IS INVESTIGATED. IT IS FALSE. STAND DOWN. RETURN TO YOUR DUTIES. AND IF THERE IS MORE FIGHTING, THERE WILL BE NO DINNER. I MEAN IT, PEOPLE.

The crew sloshed back toward the locker rooms for a change of clothes and a cup of tea. Most of them had no duties to return to, so they sat in rows on the hard slatted benches to chat and bicker and await further developments.

Ewan Haver was standing by the door of the mess, plucking the main troublemakers from the crowd and ordering them to help him clean up the mess. In his eyes, this included Danny, who wasn't sure if Haver had seen who broke the fire alarm, but didn't dare argue with him. Ewan wasn't a martial arts black belt, but he had a comprehensive collection of sharp knives, and a temper like Mount Vesuvius. It seemed best just to pick up a cloth and get on with it.

Danny was eventually rescued from this drudgery by Gemma, who wandered through a few minutes later, dry as a bone.

'I need the medic. There's been an incident in the gym.'

Haver swore, but even he withered under Gemma's gaze, and he waved them away with the back of his hairy hand.

———

The gym was a small square room, usually packed with sweaty bodies. Today there was just Vlad, relentlessly cycling the Tour de North Sea on a creaking exercise bike.

'So where's your incident, Gem?'

'Some numpty's unhooked the punchbag. I'm not tall enough to reach and Vlad says he won't do it without a work-at-heights permit.'

'Is not my job,' Vlad puffed. 'Is steward job. I am too busy.'

'So how come you weren't at the meeting, Vlad?'

'I never go to meetings. Nobody gives any shits about me, so I am not giving shits about them. I am a worker. They are bullshitters. I go to muster if I smell fire. I do not smell fire. I smell shit. Was there fighting at this meeting?'

'A bit of handbags at dawn, nothing much.'

'Pity. I enjoy fighting. If there is proper fighting next time, I will come to watch.'

The punchbag was heavier than Danny expected. He struggled on manfully for a while, but it wasn't until Gemma put her shoulder under the base that he managed to hook it back in place. Danny perched on a weight-lifting bench until he got his breath back.

'Are you sure you're okay, Gemma? I thought you'd have been in on the action.'

'I've got more sense. You're a Yorkshireman, right? Did they not teach you about Dickie the Third and the Battle of Bosworth? The smart guys sat on the sidelines and waited to see who'd win before they joined in. I saw which way the wind was blowing. And a gal in my position can't be seen taking sides.'

'And what position is that?'

'Chief mediator and headbanger. Since I'm clearly the only person on here with an ounce of common sense, I figure it's down to me to stop the whole place descending into anarchy.'

'Good luck with that. You ought to talk to Adam. He seemed pretty good at that sort of thing.'

'Aye. He did alright. He's got the voice for it. But he'll never be the boss of me; he won't listen to anything a mere lassie has to say.'

Gemma pulled on a pair of well-worn boxing gloves and began pounding seven bells out of the bag. Danny picked up the least offensive mat he could find and, laying it down in the space behind the rowing machine, he launched into a Pilates routine. Gemma paused to give the defenceless punchbag a rest.

'You realise everyone thinks yer gay, Danny.'

'What?'

'Poncing about with yer yoga and all that.'

'Yoga is for gays,' Vlad added, staring fixedly out through the single tiny salt-splattered window. 'And also women. And men who dress like women.'

'It's not yoga, it's Pilates. It builds up your core strength and improves flexibility.'

'Looks like yoga to me. I notice you never start on that stuff when the drillers are working out.'

'I'd be scared of sticking to the mats if they'd been using them.'

'Aye, you have a point there. Well, it's nice that you're in touch with your feminine side, you big fanny. I've not been on speaking terms with mine for years.'

'You are a lesbian, yes?' Vlad said.

'Only for you, Vlad. Only for you.'

Vlad grunted and carried on pedalling.

'All oil women are lesbians. Offshore is no place for proper women. Offshore is no place for gays.'

'Thanks for that, Vlad. Nice to see you keep up to date with all the latest LBGTQ issues. Sure you don't lean that way yourself?'

'I do not. I shower with many naked men at sauna and I am never hard. I watch video of naked women in shower and I am hard like wood.'

'Jesus, Vlad. Too much information. If you come anywhere near my shower, that's the last hard on you'll ever get. I promise you.'

Vlad ignored Gemma and increased the resistance on the bike.

'Drillers are also gay; that is why they work out so much. Last time I was in Aberdeen I see Halcrow go to gay bar.'

'Well, he's kept that pretty quiet,' Danny said. 'But if you're a gay driller, you probably would keep shtum. Maybe he was just curious.'

'He talks to gay man with studs in eyebrows. I tell OIM, and I think he talks to Halcrow because Halcrow is very angry. He makes big threats. Maybe OIM is scared of him. I say what I think. I am not scared of anyone.'

'So the idea of antagonising a six foot five muscle-bound driller doesn't worry you at all?'

Vlad shrugged and wiped his forehead with his off-white T-shirt, exposing a large, hairy belly.

'I also have plenty muscle. It is well hidden.' He laughed and slapped his swollen stomach to Gemma's obvious disgust.

However much Danny might dislike Vlad and his antediluvian attitudes, the man had a point. If Erik was gay, he would have reason to be unhappy with a good number of people on the Cuillin Alpha. The oil companies were keen enough to publicise their diversity policies, but the offshore world was not a very diverse or tolerant place. It was hardly a motive for murder, though, and he wasn't about to provoke the big driller by asking him about his sexual orientation.

Chapter Nineteen

'JACK SAID HE WOULD stand down,' Blair said. 'He said he'd been under a lot of pressure and that he'd made some bad decisions. But *he* wanted to announce it to the crew. Make it clear that it was his decision.'

'And you believed him?' Danny's voice betrayed his disbelief.

'He sounded upset. It seemed the honourable thing to do. I thought there would be a smoother transfer of power if we discussed everything out in the open.'

'But we just ended with no transfer at all. A power vacuum. Mob rule.'

'Look, I've never had to deal with anything like this before. None of us has. It's not in my nature to rebel against authority. But this situation is intolerable. Just because Jack was clever enough to trick me into that fiasco in the mess, doesn't make him a fit and proper person to run this platform.'

'We can agree on that,' Danny said. 'I'm surprised he hasn't had me arrested again. Or locked you up.'

'Well, whatever he may think, his power is weakened. The crew know where I stand now. I had plenty of support at that meeting. Jack only held on to power by the skin of his teeth. If some idiot hadn't triggered that fire alarm, who knows what might have happened.'

Danny had a fair idea. A mass brawl, which Snakey's mob would almost certainly have won. Shortly followed by a night of the long knives in which Blair and his mates would have found themselves bundled into a lifeboat and dropped into the North Sea. As for himself, he would almost certainly have had to walk the plank with the rest of them, while whoever was responsible for Scott's death would have been left alone to continue his campaign of sabotage.

He had hoped that Blair might have concocted a better plan to restore order, but he remained sitting in his comfy chair in the control room. Admittedly, that was the seat of power on any platform, but with no means of communication, other than shouting over the PA system, it was just another chair.

'Do you think Snakey had a hand in the attacks and the sabotage? I mean, judging by the way he's been acting, he's not exactly in a stable frame of mind.'

Blair shook his head. 'As much as I am tempted to blame Jack, I can't see how he could be responsible. I was with him when Trevor fell overboard. He was coordinating the rescue. As for the other incidents, I'm not sure, but it would be hard for him to wander around attacking people with no one noticing.'

'I suppose so, but could he have ordered other people to do them? He's obviously been expecting a threat for a while. That wasn't a spontaneous show of support in the mess. That was planned. Could he have persuaded some of his heavies to rough up the opposition?'

'Why would he want the platform cut off from the outside world? His bosses on the beach have always supported him. And why would he want Scott dead?'

'Maybe things got out of hand. Maybe the company wants to pension him off. I'm still prepared to believe that Scott's death was accidental. I mean, someone intentionally sabotaged the satellite comms, but they may not have meant to hurt anyone.'

'Danny, I know Jack commands a lot of loyalty on the Alpha, but not that much. I find it hard to believe that the people supporting him would consider violence and sabotage acceptable just to keep him in office.'

'Ah, but not everyone needs to be in on it. He only had to find one willing volunteer. He'd know if one of them had violent tendencies.'

'I suppose so. But just because he's conspiring to stay in power, doesn't mean that everything that happens is a conspiracy. Honestly, you're sounding like Mickey.'

Perhaps he *was* becoming as paranoid as Mickey. Danny tried to put his concerns about Snakey aside and concentrate on the task at hand. He needed to get hold of Mickey and find out what he was up to. Finding the culprit was far higher up his list of priorities than Snakey and Blair's power struggle. They weren't endangering the crew. A mentally unstable saboteur with a grudge against the entire oil industry, that was a different matter.

Danny promised Blair his support, with his fingers firmly crossed, and left the operations manager considering his options. The platform was a pretty small place and it wouldn't be possible to avoid confrontation for long. Blair had better come up with a plan before Ewan Haver started dishing out this evening's meal, or else it would be Armageddon after dinner.

Danny snuck into the mess while the stewards were out cleaning the cabins. There was the usual clanging of pans, the clattering of cutlery and the sizzle of hot fat coming from the galley. Danny reflected on how everyone was going about their daily routines as if nothing had happened. He hadn't expected such devotion to duty. He realised that out here, everyone depended on each other for their health and wellbeing. Whatever the conflicts and calamities, there was no one else to turn to, so they just got on with it.

Just to be on the safe side, he snaffled some cheese out of the chiller cabinet and a handful of bread rolls from the breakfast bar, then headed to heli admin to talk to Gemma. She had similar concerns about food supplies and was sitting in the radio operator's alcove with a cup of tea and a stack of ginger nuts.

'At least the biscuits survived your little stunt,' she said. 'Nice work, by the way. But if the word gets around, you're in deep shit. Half the platform's caught a chill. I had to kick Cal out of here for sneezing and coughing over the monitors.'

'So where's Cal now?'

'With the rest of the lads in the tech station. It's probably the safest place on the platform now. You should join them.'

'I might just do that. You started your shuttle diplomacy yet?'

'Just as soon as I've finished my wee snack. Have you seen anything of those two balloon heads lately?'

'I don't know about Snakey, but Blair's hiding in the control room.'

'I'm not surprised. Fancy falling into Snakey's bear trap like that. I'll go talk to him. And I'll have a word with our glorious leader. Then it's just a matter of bashing the doaty bastards' heads together.'

'Are you sure that's going to work?'

'It'll have to. I had a laugh at you giving the bastards a cold shower, but this is no joking matter, Danny. They cannot piss around with our safety like this. I will not stand for it, you hear me?'

Danny heard her loud and clear. There was steel in that voice. He felt sorry for the two managers. It was hard to imagine Snakey trying to lock Gemma up in the bond. As for Blair Scorgie, he might be big, but he was likely to fall hard if he rejected Gemma's peace proposal.

'Done lots of head-bashing before, have you?'

'Aye. I learned young. Where I grew up, it was bash or be bashed. Anyway, I like a good scrap now and then.'

'I guessed you wouldn't be the sort of girl to spend her childhood pushing dolls around in a pram.'

'I had dolls. Who do you think invented Ultimate Doll Fighting, eh?'

'Big in Aberdeen, is it?'

'Not anymore. They all lost their heads, so to speak.' Gemma finished her cessation of hostilities declaration and strolled over to pick it up from the printer. Presumably, Snakey and Blair would be expected to sign it — in blood. Danny left her to it, climbed up the stairs, and marched through the gym to the medic's locker. Once suited up, he headed out to find Callum.

He tried the tech station door, but it wouldn't open. He kicked the framework a few times with his boot until there was some movement from within. After a lot of swearing and clattering, the door opened a fraction and Iain Carr, the second mechanic, peered out through the crack.

'Piss off,' he said. 'We're closed.'

Danny could hear Callum's voice coming from inside.

'Who is it, fella?'

'The bleeding medic. I'm no sick, so he can piss off.'

'He's alright. Let him in, will you?'

'Aw bugger it,' Iain said, and wrestled with the door until it opened sufficiently for Danny to squeeze through.

'Preparing for a siege?' Danny asked, as he took in the pile of tinned food and tea bags in the corner by the washbasin. There were some heavyweight wrenches stashed by the bar, plus the long-handled crowbar that the techs called the persuader.

'Something like that,' Callum said. 'Or are you here to tell us that war is over?'

'Gemma's working on it. Heads will be bashed, apparently.'

'That's great. Peace in our time. We decided to stay out of the way until the dust settled, but it's boring as hell in here. Can't even get Norwegian radio.'

'Fancy joining me on a wild goose chase, then?'

'Sounds like fun. Should I bring the shotgun?'

Chapter Twenty

As they were heading out, they heard the PA chime, followed by the guttural sound of Gemma clearing her throat and making an announcement in her best BBC Scotland voice.

> Attention all personnel. This is an important announcement...

'That was quick,' Danny said. 'Do you think she's knocked them both out and seized control?'

'More than likely,' Callum said.

> ...In light of the recent threats to platform integrity, the OIM has declared a platform-wide emergency. All non-essential work is suspended. A platform evacuation plan has been agreed. All personnel are to be on standby to evacuate the platform once helicopter flights are resumed. If the "Prepare To Abandon Platform Alarm" is sounded...

'Oh, crap! You know what that means?' Danny said,

'He's going to sound the PAPA and send us bobbing across the ocean in those flaming lifeboats.'

...OPERATIONS MANAGER BLAIR SCORGIE HAS BEEN APPOINTED AS EMERGENCY COORDINATOR. HE WILL PREPARE CONTINGENCY PLANS AND ROBUSTLY RE-SPOND TO THE RECENT OUTBREAK OF DAMAGE AND ASSAULTS ON PERSONNEL.

'How the hell did she get the big eejit to agree to pick up that particular poisoned piss-pot?' Callum asked.

...ADAM CHINAKA WILL TAKE CHARGE OF BOTH OPER-ATIONS AND MAINTENANCE UNTIL THE EMERGENCY IS OVER. FULL DETAILS WILL BE PRESENTED AT A SPECIAL MEETING AT NINE O'CLOCK TOMORROW MORNING IN THE MESSROOM.

'Good old Adam,' Callum said. 'Whoever shouts loudest gets the job, I suppose. Of course, since we're not doing any maintenance work and the process is off line it's not exactly the toughest task in the world for yer man to cope with.'

'Are we still pumping oil back to the mainland?'

'We were until the latest outage. Since then, we've not generated enough power to restart the main pumps. Not sure anyone's trying too hard, to be honest. We've had a few other things on our minds lately.'

'So all he has to do is keep the lights on, then?'

'That's about right.'

From somewhere far below, they heard the descending whine of a turbine as another generator shut down, a final gasp of air escaping from its valves. They were plunged into darkness again. After a few seconds, the emergency lights flickered on and the dimly lit tech station was filled with multi-lingual profanities, as Iain and Vlad collected their tools and headed out.

'I'd better go with them,' Callum said. 'In case it's a controls issue. I'll have to take a rain check on that goose chase, fella. Have fun without me.'

Danny wondered if the mechanics really needed Callum's help. Maybe he just didn't fancy crawling through the void, or maybe Tommy told him how he stood freezing his balls off in the cellar deck wind tunnel for hours.

Danny didn't want to crawl through the void either and made his way to Mickey's probable hideout in the air intake, using the route down from the main deck. He shimmied down the last set of ladders and surveyed the scene.

If he hoped Mickey had left him some clue as to his whereabouts, he was out of luck. Mickey might be crazy, but Danny felt sure that he wasn't spending his days lying in a pool of oily water down in the void. He assumed Mickey hadn't jumped overboard. *Where could he be?*

Danny left the abandoned module and made his way to the walkway that circumnavigated the machinery deck. As he stepped out onto the grating, he braced himself, expecting to be tossed around by the wind, but it was sheltered here. Was it too much to hope that the storm was subsiding and rescue might soon be on its way?

That wishful thinking was dispelled as soon as he rounded the south-west corner of the platform and the full force of the gale stopped him in his tracks. Danny turned back, planning to go anti-clockwise instead. As he turned, he saw the number three and four lifeboats dangling from their davits. Lifeboat Four was his designated means of escape in the unlikely event that a PAPA ever sounded, and it was good to see that it hadn't left without him.

Now there was a thought. Could Mickey be hiding out in a lifeboat? Sneaking on board would be straightforward enough since there were few people outside in these conditions.

The side of the lifeboat rested up against the walkway, but the only way to access the entrance hatch involved striding over the exposed gap onto a narrow ledge, followed by the steep descent down the short ladder inside. That might be fine in an emergency, but Danny wasn't desperate enough to scramble into every lifeboat on the platform on a hunch.

His boat and the one adjacent looked predictably grimy and unused. It didn't look like anyone was having a crafty snooze inside.

There were two more identical boats on the north side, equally untouched. That left the secondary boats on the deck below. Danny checked Lifeboat Five carefully, leaning across the rear davit as far as he dared. It looked no different from the other two. But Lifeboat Six had smear marks on the stern and the hatch clasps weren't fully in the closed position. What's more, a trace of an oily bootprint was visible on the tiny ledge by the hatch. Someone had taken the trouble to wipe away all traces of their activity.

It was a little more sheltered here, but climbing out to the stern of the vessel was still a dangerous task. The hatch opened with suspicious ease and Danny lowered himself into the belly of the boat. He imagined himself sitting in here with forty other terrified crew, so tightly packed that you had to interlock your knees with the poor sod opposite, thrown around by the towering waves, as the smell of diesel fumes filled the vessel. He felt sick at the thought of it.

There was no one on board and no sign that anyone had been sleeping on the narrow bench seats. A few boxes were piled up at the bow. Danny opened the top one. It contained bread and fruit, biscuits and cheese, water, and a sizeable cellophane-wrapped pack of Irn-Bru, the iconic Scottish beverage.

The lifeboats were all provided with limited emergency rations, but whoever had stocked this boat felt they needed additional supplies. *For an impromptu voyage across the North Sea?* The pirates or deserters who were intending to flee in this vessel were obviously taking no chances.

None of this looked like the work of Mickey Walters. How would he have smuggled the food past the eagle eyes of Ewan Haver? Even with Tommy's help, it would have been nigh on impossible. This smacked of an inside job. Danny wondered if Haver himself was responsible. Maybe the entire catering crew was planning to sail away and abandon the rest of them.

Another mystery to be solved, and Danny was no nearer to finding his missing deckhand, or determining if Mickey was the platform's bogeyman. He decided to return to the accommodation module, grab some lunch, and maybe have a snoop around the food stores while Haver was busy.

The main lights were back on and the galley seemed to be open for business, but before he even reached the messroom door, strong hands grabbed his shoulders from behind and slammed his face into the wall.

'You knew the bastard was still alive, didn't you? When were you gonna tell the rest of us? After he'd thrown a few more poor sods over the side, is that it?' The gravel-voiced Glaswegian accent could have belonged to any of half a dozen guys. He had the impression that his assailant wasn't alone. Danny could hear people passing by, but no one stopped to help.

'I don't know what you're on about,' Danny said, trying to sound calm. That earned him a slap on the back of the head, pushing his face harder into the metal bulkhead.

'Mickey. Fucking Mickey. As if you didn't know. Missing, presumed mad as a fucking hatter. You want to tell us where he is? Or shall we just chuck you overboard to save him the bother?'

'Look, I don't know where he is. I've been looking, you're right. But if he's still on the platform, he's doing a good job of hiding. There's no sign of him as far as I can see.'

The pressure on his face eased. As he began to relax, he was swung round by the neck and was dealt a hard kick to the backside, which sent him sprawling to the floor. He lay there for several seconds before he felt a hand loop under his arm and help him to his feet.

'Dirty wee bastards,' Gemma said. 'It's handy you've no good looks to ruin, eh?'

'Do you know who that was?'

'Aye, I do. But it won't do you any good chasing after them. They'll give you a proper pasting next time. And I dare say Snakey would let them.'

'They're his cronies, then?'

'You might say that. Amazing what crawls out of the woodwork when the ship's sinking.'

'Sinking?'

'Not literally, you muppet! It's a metaphor. I can do a good metaphor. I got an English Higher. Only thing I did pass, mind you. Now let's sit you down and get you some food before you fall down. I had my lunch already, but a treacle sponge wouldn't go amiss.'

As he staggered into the mess, Danny spotted Tommy in the corner and he guided Gemma towards the injured deckhand's table. He was sporting a bruised and swollen lip and the beginnings of a black eye. Danny tried to commiserate but Tommy wouldn't even look at him. He stood up and took his tray of half-eaten food over to the washing-up hatch.

'Don't mind him,' Gemma said. 'I know he's a bit of a perv, but he's as soft as shite. As much use in a crisis as a tampon in a tsunami. I'll look after your seat while you get your scoff. And don't forget my treacle pud.'

Chapter
Twenty-One

DANNY PUSHED HIS FOOD around his plate, feeling his developing bruises with every mouthful he scooped into his mouth. Gemma gave him a rundown on the shortcomings of each of the diners remaining in the mess. At least it took his mind off his injuries. After a while, Danny gave up and deposited the leftovers in the bin. With no supply vessels able to get close, meal options were becoming severely limited. Apart from some meat encased in ice at the bottom of the freezer, it was mostly dried or tinned food, and Haver's galley staff were losing the will to do anything creative with it.

Today's offering was Aberdeen Stovies, a traditional beef stew, ideal for keeping out the winter's cold. There was little beef in it, and Danny didn't like the look of the unidentifiable lumps sticking to his fork. He reckoned he'd have got more nutrition from boiling up his boots.

Mealtimes were the main distraction from tedium offshore. Now, most of the crew were sitting idle. The fresh food was running low. It didn't bode well for morale and discipline.

The emergency lighting came on again. A few seconds later, the general alarm sounded. Everyone groaned.

Most people stoically lined up by their muster stations, but a gang of four headed out without waiting for the roll call. After a couple of minutes, Callum rolled up. He plonked himself down between Danny and Gemma. He looked drained, but managed a weary grin while giving Danny the latest bad news. 'I hope you had some hot food. That's the last you're going to get until we hit the Shetlands. The main power grid is well and truly screwed.'

'I thought you boys had fixed those generators. If I'd ever had any faith in your electrical skills, I'd be losing it about now.'

'We fixed them. Well, one of them anyway. But then the main export circuit breaker went bang and now it's welded shut. There's no getting anything online unless you know how to hot-wire an 11,000 volt breaker.'

'More sabotage?' Danny asked.

'Maybe. We'd have to take everything apart to tell. But it would take balls of steel to throw a spanner into the high voltage equipment. Unless you had some clever way of doing it remotely, you'd probably end up as a stain on the wall.'

'What about the emergency generator?'

'Yeah, that's on a separate breaker, thank God. So long as we don't run out of diesel fuel, we have enough power for essential services, but the operators will waste none of it on home comforts. You might be allowed the odd bowl of soup, but regular hot food is probably off the menu.'

'A bunch of guys left here as soon as the lights went out. You must have seen them. Who are they?'

Gemma put a finger to her lips, but Callum ignored her.

'Archie Grier and his pals? Snakey's new best friends. The guys who put the nightmare into the night shift.'

'I reckon they're the ones who did this to me.' Danny showed him the graze on his face.

'Nice. What did you do to upset them? Not that it takes much.'

'They know Mickey's alive, and think I'm sheltering him. I told them I don't know where he is, but I'm not sure they believed me.'

'I guess they've gone to find him then. I don't rate Mickey's chances if they catch hold of him.'

'You think they'd do him serious harm?' Danny asked.

'I think he might have an unfortunate accident while resisting arrest. Very easy to be man overboard. I'll bet you know all about that sort of thing from your army days. They're thugs with a grudge and now they have carte blanche to deal with Mickey.'

'Then we had better find him first.'

'Easier said than done. I thought you'd checked every nook and cranny on the platform?'

Danny was sure he had. But Callum's question made him think. He'd checked everywhere on the platform, but not *underneath* it. He needed to find out, but they were still officially at muster and he didn't want to wind up Snakey more by walking out.

Fortunately, it was a brief affair. Adam Chinaka showed up and told them that there was no point hanging around in the mess, waiting for the power to come back on. It would not happen. Then Snakey poked his head out of his office and told them to piss off and go back to whatever they were doing.

The day shift still seemed worried that Snakey would dock their pay if they wandered away from the worksite. Most of them sat in the locker room in their overalls playing cards and chewing the fat. Others hung around the tea shack. Typically, the night shift guys would have been sitting in the TV lounge, rotting their brains in front of *Bargain Hunt*, or *Homes Under the Hammer*. Today they were staring at the blank screen or leafing through outdated newspapers.

Once they were dismissed, Danny grabbed Callum's arm and led him out onto the main deck. Gemma shouted for them to wait while she pulled on her outdoor gear. When she joined them, Danny explained what was on his mind.

'What I was wondering is, can anyone get into the south leg? I know there's an access hatch, but is it locked? Do you need abseiling gear? And what about the other legs?'

'That's not such a crazy idea,' Callum said. 'Anyone could get in there. Only the south one is properly accessible though. We use the rest for storing fuel.'

'But you could get inside? If you needed somewhere to hide.'

'Aye, you could,' Gemma agreed. 'It fair gives me the creeps. Stevie let me in one time. You don't need to do any abseiling. There's a sort of spiral staircase. But you're meant to wear a harness. It'd be one hell of a drop if you tripped.'

The access hatch was hidden away behind a scaffolding tower on the machinery deck. There was barrier tape and a work permit lashed to the scaffolding. Someone must have been inside to service the equipment before the storm struck. Callum climbed up and tried to wrestle the hatch open. Danny made to join him, but Gemma elbowed him out of the way.

'My granny's got more muscles than you. You couldn't wrestle your way out of a wet paper bag. Just you keep watch and leave this to the workers.'

The hatch opened easily once they finally released all the catches. Inside, there was a small platform leading to a narrow spiral staircase bolted to the inside of the superstructure. Only the first flight was visible by the wintry light filtering in through the hatchway. A handwheel and a worn ratchet mechanism were on the inside of the door. None of them felt like locking themselves inside this underwater cavern. Callum settled for hanging a tarpaulin over the entrance to hide the gaping hole.

'I don't want anyone knowing we're in here. There's only one way in and out. Let's hope Archie and his mates don't take it into their heads to come and lock us in.'

Callum found a switch mounted on a panel by the entrance, and a string of shrouded lights flickered into life. Danny took an involuntary step back and scrabbled for something to cling onto. Now he could see the whole of the space below, and it was a disconcerting sight.

The Cuillin Alpha platform was mounted on four giant steel legs, each about ten metres in diameter. The legs rested on the seabed around two hundred metres below the waves. Faced with the view from the inside of one of those legs, Danny felt like he was aboard a submarine diving vertically into the Mariana Trench.

A spiral of dim lights drew his gaze towards the seabed and a sudden attack of vertigo made him feel as if he was being sucked into the abyss. He had to fight the urge to lean over the rail and let gravity do the rest. Despite the sulphurous smell and the grease and grime, it was an awe-inspiring sight. Terryfing, but inspiring nonetheless. Danny could easily imagine the paranoid Mickey Walters hiding in this subterranean world.

'At least it's not as claustrophobic down here as I thought.' His voice sounded weak and lost in the cavernous space. 'How come we've still got regular lighting?'

'It runs off the emergency generator. Can't have people stumbling around in the dark. Imagine sliding all the way down this oversize helter-skelter. You wouldn't have much flesh left on your arse, would you?'

'Any sign of life?'

'No, but there's a fair amount of machinery in the way. We'll have to climb down a long way before we can be sure.'

'I was afraid you'd say that.'

There were plenty of pipes and pumps mounted on the thick steel walls, but precious few flat surfaces. If Mickey was sleeping in here, he'd need a hammock suspended in mid-air and a mountaineer's head for heights. They gingerly descended about a third of the way before Danny realised how Mickey had solved that problem.

On the opposite side of the spiral stairs, a good twenty metres below, was a series of scaffolding platforms. They were ingeniously cantilevered off the stair mounts and bolted to pipe brackets. The whole edifice stretched nearly a quarter of the way around the inside of the leg. It was a labour of love. Mickey's personal underground kingdom.

The only thing missing was Mickey. Then Gemma spotted him cowering beneath an overhanging valve.

'Mickey, it's Gemma. Stay put, you little wanker. I'm coming down.'

'Leave me alone!' Mickey shouted. 'Any closer and I'll jump.'

He stepped out from under the valve and clambered up onto his home-made veranda. Mickey was wearing a tatty old harness. In his hand was a grey metal box and his thumb hovered over two red buttons. Danny panicked, thinking it was a suicide vest, then reminded himself that he wasn't an MP on the lookout for terrorists anymore. He'd be as paranoid as Mickey soon if he wasn't careful.

'It's okay, Mickey,' Gemma yelled. 'I've told everyone you're not the Pied Piper. I know you had nothing to do with Scott getting smashed up. We're just here to talk. Maybe you know what's really going on.'

'Oh, I know plenty. Too much. That's why they want to silence me. That's why they've been sending agents after me. But I'm no fool. I turned the tables on them. I've been spying on the spies.'

The first strip of lights on the steps ahead was on the blink. Mickey paced across his underground home, so intent on his paranoid fantasy that he was no longer concentrating on whatever his uninvited guests were doing. As the lights flickered off for a few seconds, Callum took his chance and padded down the stairs, darting from one patch of darkness to the next, while Danny tried to keep Mickey talking.

'Good for you, Mickey,' he said. 'What spies would these be? Do you have any names you'd care to share?'

'Don't be daft. They're spies. They don't use real names.'

'No, of course not. But what about the fake names they're using? Can you tell me that?'

'Why should I trust you? They probably sent you down to trick me.'

'Now then, Mickey, why would you think that? I'm a medic. I'm here to save people, not harm them.'

'I know what you are, and I know what you have been,' Mickey said. 'But even if I trusted you, I could never trust him.'

He pointed at Callum, who was now only a dozen metres away from the platform. Callum halted, caught in the twin headlights of Mickey's head torch and his obsessive gaze, then jumped down the remaining steps. He landed a few metres from where Mickey was standing.

There was no fear or anger in Mickey's expression, just a look of defiance. He took one deep breath and calmly stepped off the platform into oblivion.

Chapter Twenty-Two

IT TOOK A FEW seconds for Danny to realise that Mickey hadn't plunged to his death on the dark and oil-pooled concrete base far below. Only when Callum came charging up the steps towards him, Danny realised the truth.

The relentless waves, crashing against the outer wall of the south leg, were masking the whine of the electric winch motor, mounted a few metres above the entrance hatch. When Danny looked up, Mickey was staring down at him, dangling by his harness from a barely visible wire, and using the pendant buttons to control his ascent.

'No, you bastard!' Callum screamed, taking the treacherous steps three at a time. 'Get after him, Danny. Don't let him get to that hatch first, or we're all screwed.'

Danny followed as fast as he dared, his fear of falling battling his fear of being trapped in this cylindrical cavern. The winch was slow, but Mickey was still ascending vertically, while his two pursuers were spiralling around the circumference of the leg. It was no contest and Mickey reached the top well ahead of Danny, with Callum still on the opposite side of the leg.

Mickey climbed out of his harness and glanced over at Danny. Making sure Callum was still out of view, he held up a gloved hand. There was something small concealed in his palm which he slipped into the harness, then he swung it and the winch out of the way and climbed through the hatch.

An ominous metallic clang sounded. They were trapped.

Danny staggered up to the top step, gasping for air, and surveyed the entranceway. Callum followed shortly behind and aimed a savage kick at the hatch. It stayed resolutely shut. The handwheel on the inside spun freely. Danny wasn't even sure if it was connected to the latching mechanism.

The clank of boots slowly trudging up the steel steps echoed around the south leg until, at last, Gemma reached the entrance. She slumped down on the top step, purple-faced and panting.

'I hope you weren't expecting me to join the chase, Danny. I'm not built for speed. You catch 'em. You kick 'em. That's the way it goes. But you couldn't even manage that much, could you?'

'Hey, Gemma. Glad you could make it. I don't suppose you thought to tell anyone that we were heading down the leg for a shufti.'

'Sorry, pal. I was too busy jogging after you two athletes.'

Callum crouched down by the hatch. There was panic in his voice when he finally spoke.

'Jesus fecking Christ, Gem! It's no joke. How are we going to get out of here? Even if the rescue chopper comes, how are they going to know where we are? It's not like Mad Mickey is going to tell them.'

So much for not suffering from claustrophobia, Danny thought. It was a strange feeling when you knew there was no way out and the lights might fail at any time.

He tried to reassure Callum. 'Look, Mickey's bound to have left a stock of food and water behind. When you're that paranoid, you always have plenty of supplies to hand. We might eat better than we would in the mess. Why don't we go look?'

'Yeah, yeah. I'll be right with you.' Callum was still clinging to the rim of the hatch. He shuffled to one side of the top step to let Danny pass.

A few steps further down was the harness, dangling just out of reach. Danny searched around the stairwell and found an improvised hook and pulled the harness towards him. Tucked in the front neoprene pouch was a slim blue notebook. Not sure why he was being so secretive, he palmed it from the harness and slipped it into the breast pocket of his overalls.

'Nice idea,' Callum said. Danny flinched, thinking his sleight of hand had been spotted but Callum was more interested in the harness.

'Why walk when you can winch?' he suggested.

Callum was still breathing hard, but whether from the effort of the climb or out of fear, it was hard to tell. He stepped into the harness, tightened the straps and swung out over the abyss, giving a manic 'whoop' as he did so. Danny steadied the hoist as Callum lowered himself down to Mickey's hideout.

'How am I going to get the harness back up?' Danny called out to him.

'You'll have to fetch it!'

'Lazy bastard,' Danny muttered.

'I'll guard the entrance, alright,' Gemma said. 'I'm not climbing back down those stairs. You boys go organise the escape plan. Don't forget to come back for me, eh?'

Danny patted her on the hard hat and trudged down the stairs after Callum. By the time he arrived at the lashed-up balcony, Callum was already out of the harness and rummaging through Mickey's stuff.

'What are you looking for?'

'A way out of here.' Callum sounded desperate. 'When we got here, the hatch was shut and Mickey was already inside, right? He didn't lock himself in, did he?'

'No, but someone else could have. Some tidy-minded deckhand, maybe.'

'I don't believe it. For one thing, I've never met a tidy deckhand, and for another, Mickey's paranoid about confined spaces. He would never have risked setting up camp in here if he thought they might shut him in. He'd have unbolted the latches or wire-locked the door open. He might be crazy, but he's not stupid.'

Callum had a point. Surely there should have been a release mechanism on the inside of the hatch. Maybe there was some kind of opening tool. Had Mickey removed it?

As Callum continued his search for an "open sesame" device, Danny looked around for another exit. He concentrated on the area around the hideout. Why had Mickey picked this precise spot? Why carry those heavy scaffolding poles and planks further than you had to?

From his perch, there was nothing to see but blank, curved walls, so Danny lay down on the loose scaffolding boards and edged forward until he could crane his neck over sufficiently to see underneath. There, nestled directly under their feet, was a small round hatch, its access ladder rusting away to nothing. The boards Danny was lying on cast a shadow over the hatch; it was hard to tell if anyone had used it recently.

Danny called Callum over.

'Holy fuck! How are we going to get out through that? Do I look like an orangutan?'

With his wispy ginger hair and long wiry limbs, that was precisely what Callum looked like to Danny, especially in this eerie subterranean light. He didn't respond but shone the torch down on the hatchway. As he swung the torch's powerful beam around, light reflected off a grey-coated length of electrical cable, leading from the bottom rung of the decaying ladder to the steps over to the right. Although the line sagged alarmingly, it ought to be possible to get to and from the hatch safely, but Danny didn't fancy monkey-climbing over the abyss without something to catch him if he fell.

'Was there any abseiling kit in Mickey's stash?' he asked Callum.

'Could be. Some bits and bobs that look like climbing gear. Why?'

He showed Danny a couple of snap-hook karabiners, a clasp and some loop-ended fabric straps. Danny picked up the gear and the harness and led Callum down to where the cable was lashed to the steps. Callum's mood improved considerably when he realised what Danny was showing him.

'Dead on, man,' he said. 'That's mains incomer cable. Should be plenty strong enough to take your weight.'

'So I'm going first, am I?'

'You're the lightest. And you know about climbing and all that malarkey.'

'I recognise a karabiner when I see one, but that doesn't make me a mountaineer.'

Seeing that Callum wasn't budging, Danny scrutinised the cable. It was looped securely around one of the supports for the steps using a solid-looking steel clamp. He fixed the karabiner to the harness, using the longest straps to avoid having to lean too far over the edge, then clipped himself and tugged on the line.

Danny slowly sat himself down on the step, feet dangling over the edge. He wrapped one leg over and swung himself sloth-like onto the cable and swayed there for a while.

'Hold on a sec,' Callum warned. 'I'm not stopping in here a minute longer than I have to. I need to get that harness back when you've done with it.'

He trotted off to the other end of the hideout. Danny was just about to swing himself back onto the steps when Callum returned and threaded a length of twine through the impromptu strop and waved him on his way.

As he began his slow shuffle across to the hatch, Danny tried not to look down, but looking up was as bad. The height of the chamber reminded him of how much further there was to fall.

It wasn't until his foot struck the outer wall that he realised he had been descending with his eyes shut. To lower himself down to the manhole-sized hatch, he needed to look where he was going and put his faith in the harness. There was no ledge, so Danny gripped a rusty rung in one hand and hauled on the handwheel with the other. After much heaving, the wheel spun free, and the hatch swung open.

Water came pouring through the open hatch and for a terrifying moment, Danny thought he was below sea level. The flow subsided. He wiped the salt from his eyes and peered out through the hole. He wasn't below the waves, but at eye level with the highest of their spray-topped crests. While he was surveying the state of the external access ladder, a huge wave struck the south leg and forced him to pull the door shut.

'What are you playing at, you eejit?' Callum shouted.

'We can get out, but the waves are coming right over the top of this damn hatch. I'm going to climb out when there's a trough, but I need to time it right, otherwise I'll be surfing all the way home.'

'Can we climb up to the cellar deck from there?'

'Yeah. I think so. The bit of ladder I saw was rusty as hell, but it looks solid enough. Wish me luck.'

Danny waited until he felt the leg shudder under the impact of the next wave, then counted to three and pushed open the hatch. With his good foot perched on the rim, he used his free hand to unclip the karabiner and clambered up the ladder, kicking the door closed as he went.

He could hear Callum, still trapped inside, calling for the harness in a panic-filled voice. Danny ignored him. He wasn't about to stand on one leg, taking this overgrown nappy off while the waves broke over his head. Callum would have to understand and not pull too hard on the twine. He climbed well above the spray, stepped out of the harness in relative safety, and released it to dangle freely from the hatch.

He was still a long way below the cellar deck, and the more time Danny spent hanging onto the ladder, the tougher the ascent would become.

He took a deep breath and began the long, uncertain climb to safety.

A solitary figure leaned over the railings and watched him scale the rusty ladder. Danny was about to call out for help, for a rope, or a safety harness, but something made him bite back the words. As he got closer, the figure stepped back, and the strobe of the navigation beacon above illuminated the face. The brief feeling of relief engendered by his climb to freedom ebbed away and that ever-present gnawing fear gripped at his guts.

It was Mickey Walters. He had a knife in his hand.

Chapter Twenty-Three

DANNY KNEW HE COULDN'T hold on to the decaying ladder. Despite the cold, his hands were sweating and several times, he nearly lost his grip altogether. He was breathing hard and tiring fast. He had to reach the safety of the deck soon. There would be no miracle rescue for him. No one knew he was here except Mickey and Callum. Mickey was hardly likely to call for help, and Callum might find himself in a similar predicament.

The only thing to do was keep moving. Danny was no expert climber, but knew enough to keep his body close to the ladder and let his legs to do most of the work. That was easier said than done. Many rungs were broken or missing. It was a case of feeling for bolts and rusting spurs of metal with his toes while maintaining his body's upward momentum. Whenever his ascent stalled, the climb became immediately harder and more treacherous.

Danny pushed himself onward, step by step, without thinking of the remaining distance or what Mickey's reception would be. He vaguely remembered there were metal beams sprouting from the leg's superstructure at an acute angle, and a welded grating deck somewhere above his head. He wasn't sure if this was the cellar deck or an access platform somewhere below. Either way, if Danny could drag himself up to the deck, he could take a desperately needed a break from this relentless climb.

He reached up. A hand grabbed at his arm. Danny nearly fell. His impulse was to pull away with all his remaining strength. In his precarious situation, that could have proved fatal. Fortunately, he kept his primitive instincts in check and instead, put all his energy into one final upward motion.

Danny pushed off from an intact rung and hurled himself through the gap in the grating onto the deck above, clawing for some kind of hold as he landed, chest first, on the hard iron deck. He took one wild south-paw swing before he realised that the man grasping his right arm wasn't Mickey; it was Cameron Law, the camp boss.

'Steady boy. Steady. I'm only trying to help.'

'Sorry,' Danny apologised and slumped down on the deck. 'Thanks for the helping hand. We weren't expecting much of a warm welcome.'

'We?'

Danny pointed down at the figure of Callum, steadily climbing the broken access ladder.

'Does he need assistance? I can call the control room.'

Danny watched as his fellow escapee continued his climb. In his desperation to free himself, Callum seemed to make considerably better progress than he had. Danny was reluctant to get any more people involved or to call undue attention to their recent escapades.

'I think he's okay. By the time anyone can get the gear together to mount a rescue, he'll be back on deck.'

Cameron Law shouted down a few words of encouragement and began praying. Even if the prayer didn't do the trick, at least Callum wouldn't be haunted by the spectre of a knife-wielding maniac during the climb. Danny decided to keep his fears to himself.

'Was Mickey around when you got here?'

'Would that be the living and breathing Mickey Walters that you were expecting to see? I thought he was on his way to a better place.'

'He's very much alive, though he might not be for long if I catch hold of him. He had us trapped in the south leg. I'm sure I saw him standing up here as I was climbing. That's why I panicked when you grabbed me.'

'So he didn't drown? I thought I saw him a couple of days back, but I told myself I was seeing ghosts.'

'If he had jumped overboard, I wouldn't put it past him to haunt the platform.'

'You shouldn't joke about such things. I've seen plenty of strange sights out here. Only the Good Lord knows what becomes of us when we pass on. Maybe departed souls linger awhile before they meet their maker.'

'So what brought you down here to the cellar deck in a howling gale? Not that I want to appear ungrateful, I just wondered.'

'There's too much turmoil inside at the moment. I came down here to clear my head and to seek the guidance of the Almighty.'

'Have you tried asking God to strike Snakey down with the odd lightning bolt?'

'I have not. I gave Blair Scorgie moral support when he asked Jack to stand down, but I wouldn't countenance any violence. I have been praying for peace and reason to prevail ever since. For all our sakes.'

'Amen to that,' Danny said. 'But I don't think there will be much peace on this platform until we abandon it to the seagulls. I guess that's going to happen soon enough.'

'You may be right. But I've spent too long on this old platform to leave without a fight.'

'I thought you said there'd be no violence.'

'No violent struggle between the good folk on this platform, that's what I meant. Whoever is causing this mayhem and turning the crew against each other has the taint of evil upon him. He is doing the devil's bidding. And if I find out who it is, I won't stay my hand. You've not seen me angry yet, Danny, but I've got a mind that you will before long.'

A plaintive voice from below interrupted them.

'Are either of you feckers going to give me a hand, or what?'

Cameron reached down to grab Callum's collar and he and Danny dragged him onto the deck, where he lay on the rough grating, gasping for air like a shark out of water.

'Jesus, I'm banjaxed running up that fecking ladder,' he exclaimed. 'I figured the faster you climb, the less time you have to fall off.'

Danny gave him a quick medical once over. Callum's biceps and quads were still quivering with the effort of the climb and there was no need to take a pulse, Danny could see the blood throbbing in Callum's throat at a hundred and fifty beats per minute or more. The wild staring eyes were standard for Callum. He always looked on the verge of a panic attack. Maybe that was a legacy of growing up in Northern Ireland in uncertain times. A certain level of nervous tension was probably a useful survival tool during the Troubles.

After a while, he appeared to have recovered, and Danny helped him to sit up. He backed away again smartly as Callum slumped onto his elbow and vomited through the grating.

'That's better,' Callum said, once he'd finished retching. 'Sorry about that, man.'

'Good thing there's no more decks below. With any luck, you might have hit a shite-hawk or two on the way down.'

'Ach! Leave them poor seagulls alone. They crap everywhere, but they're the only ones that belong out here in the middle of the fecking North Sea. We're the vermin, not your feathered friends up there.'

'So you're feeling alright now, David Attenborough? Because we ought to be getting back to let Gemma out of the hole.'

'Jesus, the poor girl, will be beside herself. Let's go. I'll be staying right behind you, just in case she's not so pleased to see us after all this time.'

It was disheartening to have to climb back up to the machinery deck to find the south leg's access hatch, but at least it was only a couple of flights of well-maintained stairs, rather than a long and rickety ladder. The scaffolding tower had been taken away without any sign of the promised repairs to the access steps. Considering none of the scaffolders were supposed to be working outside, it was slightly suspicious.

There was a wooden electrician's ladder propped up against the nearby turbine package, so Callum lifted it over to the leg and crawled up to the hatch. He seemed to have difficulty opening the catches without tipping the ladder beyond the point of no return.

Danny held onto the bottom rungs as best he could, but there was no way he could support Callum's weight if it started to topple over.

He was about to tell him to come back down when Callum released the final catch. There was still the tricky task of dodging the door as it swung open, but then Callum shinned up the last few rungs and ducked inside.

Danny was expecting Gemma to come bursting out and scold them for taking so long about her rescue, but Callum poked his head out through the hatch, his face a picture of confusion.

'She's gone,' he said, and held out a shiny white helmet with Gemma's name inscribed on the front.

Chapter
Twenty-Four

DANNY SCURRIED UP THE short access ladder and stared through the hatch. Callum stepped to one side and let him in. He did not see any bloodstains or signs of a struggle. Everything was just as they'd left it, except for Gemma.

He peered over the edge. The base of the leg was a long way down, and it was hard to pick out details. Something was lying among the pools of oil and the detritus of the years of haphazard repair work. It was body shaped. His stomach knotted up.

'Look,' he pointed. 'We *have* to go down again!'

Calum swore. 'Do we have to? Could we not just check the accommodation first in case she escaped? She might be in the TV lounge sipping tea as we speak.'

Danny shook his head. 'We're wasting time. If your claustrophobia is still a problem, you just stay here and I'll go.'

'Hey, I'm not scared of confined spaces, just of getting myself shut inside them. I'll guard the entrance in case that mad fecker comes back.'

The harness was back up by the entrance, so after careful inspection, Danny put it on and descended slowly, looking out for booby traps and hidden hazards. There were shadowy areas caused by blocks of equipment and pipework, apparently randomly distributed throughout the structure. Danny paused at each one, looking for signs of Gemma's presence. Eventually, he realised he was just putting off the inevitable descent to the concrete base on which the entire platform's weight rested.

The closer he got, the more the shape looked like a body lying face down on the floor. Once he reached seabed level, Danny splashed across to the body and turned it over.

He stared at an expressionless face. Inscribed on the front of the orange overalls, it read: "DANNY THE DUMMY". Anger surged through him, followed by sudden panic.

How could he have been so stupid? Again! The last time, two men had fallen into the sea and nearly drowned. Mickey had failed to lock them out of the way, so maybe he had decided on a more permanent method of keeping them quiet.

He pressed the up button, but nothing happened. There was some kind of commotion above. He ran up the narrow and greasy steps. One slip convinced him that this was not a good idea. He was a good thirty feet from the base and he came very close to tumbling headfirst over the edge.

He broke into a steady jog, but even that was hard to maintain. For the latter stages of the climb, he settled into an increasingly weary uphill march. The hatch was still open; a rectangular slab of daylight gave him the incentive to keep going as fast as his tiring legs would take him.

The light was fluctuating intermittently and Danny soon realised that the pattern was in sync with the rise and fall of the wind's lupine howl. The door was being blown open and closed with force, but it never slammed shut entirely.

The reason for this soon became apparent. Danny saw Callum's body lying slumped across the threshold. He grabbed hold of his friend and, as gently as he could, tried to haul him back inside. The continuous dribble of blood from his scalp was picked up by the wind and strung out in a fine thread across the machinery deck. Danny braced himself; on the third attempt, he managed to roll Callum onto the tiny entrance ledge.

The semi-circular cut on his forehead was not deep, but it was immediately recognisable and sent a chill down Danny's spine. The original murder weapon was hopefully still locked away, but the platform was full of identical scaffolding poles. No doubt the killer had obtained another one just as effective.

There was barely enough space to get Callum into the recovery position, but Danny tried to keep him comfortable. The wooden ladder had gone, of course, and would be impossible to lower him single-handedly down the remains of the tattered access steps. Nor could he afford to leave his casualty and go for help. He had to stay and hope that someone crazy enough to go for a stroll in a hurricane passed by close enough to hear his cries for help.

At regular intervals, he kicked the door open with both feet and let it bang shut. Once he'd perfected the timing, he banged out a full SOS signal and repeated the message until his bruised foot became too sore to continue.

No one came. He undid his overalls and took off his T-shirt to staunch the blood flow. The makeshift bandage worked well enough, but Callum was shivering with cold. There was little Danny could do. After a few minutes, he decided to go for help before they both died of hypothermia. As he carefully laid his patient's head on the remains of a reel of high voltage cable, Callum came round.

Danny could have cried with relief. Within a few minutes, Callum was fully awake and trying to piece together what had happened. It was a good sign, but Danny knew the consequences of concussion, especially with such a long period of unconsciousness.

At least now he could climb out, check the coast was clear, and recover the ladder. With great care, he guided the wobbly-legged Callum, rung by rung, down to the deck floor. Together, they staggered drunkenly towards the accommodation where they ran into a couple of Snakey's men minding the entrance, like a couple of scruffy nightclub bouncers.

A piggy-eyed thug with tattooed hands barred their way, but when Danny showed him the state of Callum's head, he reluctantly granted them entry. His colleague, a vacant-looking, neckless knuckle dragger with forearms thicker than Danny's thighs, helped him get his patient up to the sickbay. Danny resolved once again to avoid rash character judgements.

He lay Callum down on the examination bed and strapped an array of instruments to his chest and arms. His patient kept asking for a hot cup of tea and a biscuit, but had to settle for a warm blanket and a glass of lukewarm water.

Danny studied Callum's pupils and checked pulse and blood pressure. He relaxed. There seemed nothing to worry about.

'Either you've got an amazingly hard head like Cocky, or the bastard only gave you a friendly tap on the skull.'

'Ain't that the cure for water on the brain?'

Callum didn't even laugh at his own feeble joke.

'Stupid question, but did you see who hit you? Was it Mickey?'

'I think so, but I only caught a quick glimpse before I passed out.'

Danny desperately wanted to set out in search for Gemma, but he did not know where to start, and his duty was here with his patient until he was sure Callum was out of danger.

'Look, I'm fine,' Callum said. 'At least take a scan round the accommodation and see she isn't just in her cabin catching up on her beauty sleep.'

Danny reluctantly agreed, once Callum had promised not to unplug himself and start his own search.

Chapter
Twenty-Five

DANNY TOOK A GRAND tour of the accommodation. It didn't take
long. There were few places to hide. He held his breath and checked
the smoking TV lounge and was met with blank stares and resentment.
The tiny fetid sauna next to the gym was empty, as were the bond store
and the steward's store cupboard.

A carcass in the meat freezer looked suspicious but, although it might
have been horsemeat, it was definitely not human. For the umpteenth
time, Danny resolved to go vegetarian. His willpower usually gave out
at the next breakfast. The smell of bacon frying always lured his inner
carnivore out of hiding. An irate Ewan Haver caught him examining a
frozen lamb chop and threatened him with a meat tenderiser.

He left the mess and went looking for Cameron Laws. The camp boss
took some persuading, but eventually loaned him the master key for
the cabins and printed off Gemma's latest room allocation list. Danny
hoped that Gemma might have secreted herself in one of the vacant
rooms.

There were quite a few, mostly down on the lower level of the
auxiliary living quarters, below the mess. It looked dark and dingy in
the ALQ. Some crew members preferred it because of the better shower
heads. Plus, the cabins were out of earshot of the PA system and nice
and handy for the smoking lounge.

The first two were empty. The third showed signs of recent occupation.
He removed the key. Someone had tampered with the lock and it was

spinning freely in the door. The duvet on the lower bunk had been pushed aside and there was a human-sized indent in the mattress.

He peered over the edge of the upper bunk and realised someone was lying there, with their socked feet peeking out from beneath the duvet. Judging by the size of the feet, it couldn't be Gemma. Realising he'd been rumbled, the bunk's occupant sat up sharply and banged his head on the ceiling.

'Shitting dogs!' a familiar voice cried. It was Cocky. He blinked and stared at Danny like an overgrown dormouse emerging from hibernation. 'Oh. It's only you. Fuck off, will you? And turn the light off when you go.'

'So this is your regular hidey hole?'

'No scaffolding allowed. Too windy. Gaffer said so. The rules only say I can't go back to my bunk when I'm on shift. They don't say nothing about taking a nap in some other bugger's bunk. What's it to you, anyway?'

'Nothing. But we have some people missing, not just skiving off.'

'Well, if I see them, I'll let you know. Now fuck off.'

Danny left and slammed the door behind him. He didn't bother switching the light off.

Gemma's cabin was on the floor above. Danny tapped on the cabin door and a soft voice told him to come in. Gemma's roommate, Ailsa Troup, sat in the corner on the only chair, gawping at him like a rabbit in the headlights. She was a bonny lass. Big-boned, as his mother would say, and there didn't seem to be a lot going on behind her vacant gaze.

'Have you seen Gemma, Ailsa?'

'Aye, yes, well no, not so much.'

'When did you see her last?'

'Mebbez yesterday, or mebbez it was the day before. Ma head's in a whirl with all this strife. I'm too feart to leave ma cabin now.'

'I'm not surprised. Are you getting enough food? You can't just sit here and starve to death.'

'Aye, that Tommy just brought me some bread and cheese and a pork pie or three. I've not much of an appetite.'

'I hope Tommy's behaving himself. He's a bit of a one for the ladies I heard.'

'Oh aye, he's a bit touchy feely. Sometimes I ha' to tell him to sit away on the bed and keep his hands in his pockets. He's a good lad though.'

Danny hated to think what Tommy was doing with his hands in his pockets, but he was glad someone was looking after Ailsa.

He made his way back to the medic's cabin and lay down on the bed. Ailsa wasn't the only one whose head was spinning. He needed some time to reflect on what had happened and to formulate a plan. Somehow, he knew he would not have time to do any of those things.

He still had Mickey's little blue book stuffed in his back pocket. He pulled it out to see what words of wisdom might be inside. It held a random collection of observations, some banal, some profound, and some just downright bizarre.

There were dates next to entries, mainly ones relating to his crewmates' actions. He'd listed things that people had done to upset him, like strapping a dildo to his hard hat. He recorded things they'd said: insults, jokes, nuggets of homespun philosophy. Interestingly, he'd also recorded suspicious behaviour.

This is the diary of a paranoid fantasist. That Mickey thought someone's movements suspicious was hardly substantial evidence of wrongdoing. Anyone following Mickey around would surely have found the same.

Startling, however, were the predictions, dated the day before the storm struck. Mickey had written it as though they were God given prophesies. It was hard to know if this was his view or a cunning code to throw his enemies off the scent. Whatever the motive, making sense of the damn thing was a tortuous business. There were eight pages filled with archaic phrases and pretentious blank verse. It was like reading the prologue to a poorly written fantasy novel.

Some had already come true. They were undoubtedly "alone in silent desperation" on "the isle of death; creation of man's greed" where "strife and chaos holds sway". No one could deny that they were "without light or warmth or comfort".

However, he didn't think that eating salad and cheese and cold frank-furters counted as "scraping the last remnants of a failed harvest from the dead earth". And he fervently hoped that Mickey's apocalyptical vision of "flaming sulphurous towers sinking beneath the angry waves" would never come to pass.

Instead, he wondered if Mickey had more than a seer's hazy knowledge of forthcoming events. Another way of reading his notes was to consider them as a plan, rather than a prophecy. It's not hard to make accurate predictions if you are the one creating the chaos...

Chapter Twenty-Six

HELI ADMIN WAS EMPTY. There were a few cake crumbs on the floor, but no sign of Gemma. Her booth was locked, but the admin hatch was open and he could clamber over the desk and slide feet-first into the tiny radio room beyond.

Although the radio was out of order, there was a VHF handset sat in its charger on the desk. Danny wasn't sure if it would work without the main transmitter, or who he would call.

Surprisingly, the weather station was operational. Though it could no longer receive data from the Met Office onshore, data from the last few days was still available. It seemed to Danny that the wind and the wave height were dropping gradually. There were still some horrendous gusts coming through, but perhaps the storm was finally beginning to blow out.

Danny took another look at the handheld VHF radio. There was a label stuck over the display. It read:

IN CASE OF MEDICAL EMERGENCY CALL NURSE ON CHANNEL 7.

It took Danny a while to realise that it was a direct message for him. He ripped off the label, changed channels and held down the Press-to-Talk button.

'Nurse. Nurse, this is Danny Boy. Call back.'

He heard nothing but pulsing static for several minutes. Then a faint and distorted voice replied.

'Danny Boy. This is Nurse. What's your location? Over.'

'I'm in your domain. And you? Over.'

'Here, there and everywhere. I'm on the air. See you out there. On the helideck in five. Nurse out.'

The access door to the helideck was two floors above the medic's cabin. First, he popped his head in the sickbay to see how Callum was doing. His patient was sitting up, reading a motorbike magazine. Danny said nothing. He didn't feel like passing on any news until he was sure Gemma was okay.

The access door opened readily enough, but slammed into the module wall as the wind caught it. So much for the storm dying down. He clung onto the handrail and fought his way up to the helideck.

Gemma was standing in the exact centre of the landing marks, with her feet apart and her toes hooked under the safety netting. Her bushy brown hair fanned out around her face like an unruly halo. She looked for all the world like a rather squat goddess of the sea, defying the storm.

He lurched across the deck and enveloped her in a bear hug. She seemed surprised. He thought he saw her blush, but it could have just been wind-burn.

'Hey! No groping. There's a company policy against that sort of thing, pal.'

'I'm just pleased to see you. I thought you were dead.'

'Aye, well, that's an original chat-up line, I'll give you that, but I'm not so easy to kill. I am not "weak and feeble" and I can kick like a mule.'

'Did Mickey come back, or did you just boot the door open?'

'I would have kicked Mickey where it hurts most if I'd seen him, but no, it was the preacher man that showed up.'

'Cameron Law? How did he know you were there?'

'Must have heard me hammering. He likes to snoop around, like the big creep he is.'

'But we saw him on the cellar deck. He didn't even mention you. What's he up to?'

'Blowed if I know. I've given up trying to work out what the old God botherer wants. I thought he wasn't even letting me out to start with. Said I deserved to be locked up and I should repent my sins and all that shite.'

'What particular sins are these?'

'Ach, well, I shagged his son. Just the once, mind. He's a bonny lad if a bit wet behind the ears. We had a Christmas get together down the town, and his old man brought his eldest along. He got completely shit-faced and the old fool asked me to look after him. He kept saying how gorgeous I looked, so he must have been well gone. Anyway, we ended up doing it in the cloakroom at Kirk's nightclub. I think that's what upset his dad the most; it used to be a Wee Free back in the day.'

'So how did Cameron find out?'

'His lad must have told him. You can take all this openness and honesty shite too far. The sanctimonious old bastard has had it in for me ever since.'

All the time they were talking, Danny was scanning the helideck for threats, but Gemma seemed unworried.

'Dinna fesh yersel. I picked this spot for a good reason. You can see trouble coming. I came all tooled up.'

'With what?'

Gemma pulled a travel-size can of hairspray out of her pocket.

'It's not Mace, but it doesn't half make their eyes water.'

'You use hairspray?'

'You mean you canna tell?' she said, flicking her hair and striking a pose. 'Nah, I nicked this off Ailsa. The dozy cow has a drawer full of them. She'll never miss one.'

'So why the disappearing act?'

'Your Pied Piper drugged me, remember? I don't fancy being under his control again. He could have done anything to me.'

146

'But he didn't.'

'No, he didn't. That's creeping me out too.'

She didn't look her usual confident self. Danny was worried about her.

'So where have you been hiding?'

'The TLQ.'

'The what?'

'Temporary living quarters. It's near the mud lockers. The drillers used to stay there, but the HSE said it wasn't healthy or safe, so we had to let the dirty bastards sleep in the main accommodation. It's been locked up for years. I've got the only key.'

'Can we go there for a chat? If this wind gets any stronger, I'll be para-gliding without a parachute.'

'Nah chance, Danny. I don't want you going in and out. People will talk. I've got my reputation to consider. Besides, it's my private place. I go there when Ailsa is doing my head in. Or if I need somewhere for a quick ménage a mois.'

'Oh, Jesus, Gemma. Could you not wait till you get to shore?'

'Not for a full two-week rotation. If you lads go all that time hands-free, you must end up with balls like balloons.'

He could have given her the medical explanation for why that didn't happen. But he wanted to get off the helideck while he could still stand.

'So what do we do now?'

'I told you. You go away and you keep shtum. You don't tell anyone you've seen me, not even Cal.'

'That's a tall order, Gem. The platform's not that big. There are only two women on board and you don't look much alike. Someone's going to spot you, eventually.'

'I dare say, but not just yet. You're not the only one who knows where I am. There are a few people I trust. Even if they are mostly gormless eejits.'

'So what do you want me to do?'

'Tell you what. You grab the bastard who's doing this. I'll punt him over the side. You're going to find him, Danny. I got faith in you. So go investigate. I'll keep the radio charged. You can call nursey again when you find out something worth knowing. And if I see anything, I'll leave you a note.'

There was a clattering behind him. He twisted round just in time to see Snakey's head appearing above the green-painted deck. He spun back to warn Gemma, but she was gone. Snakey was waving him over with a face like thunder.

'What do you think you're doing up here?'

'I thought I'd throw out some bread for the helicopters.'

'I don't appreciate sarcasm, Mr Verity. You think you're a private eye, don't you? Think a lot of yourself but you're on thin ice as it is. The helideck is off-limits. It's not safe in these conditions.'

'Well, thanks for looking out for my welfare. I was just heading down. What brings you out of the warm and dry? And how did you know I was here?'

'Never you mind. Let's say I've got eyes everywhere. I'm more interested in who you were talking to. Secret assignation with our Pied Piper maybe?'

'I thought I was the saboteur.'

'Maybe you are. Or maybe you're in cahoots with them. You know more than you're saying, of that much I'm sure. I'm still the OIM. I'm judge, jury and executioner out here. It's my job to keep this platform safe and you're withholding information. That's a sacking offence.'

'So are you going to arrest and lock me up again?'

'I wouldn't give that idiot, Blair Scrogie, the pleasure. He'll only try to let you out again. Then I might have to arrest the both of you, not to mention those arse-licking pals of his.'

'If I'm free to go, I'd better get back to sickbay. I have a patient waiting.'

'Oh yeah? Who is it this time?'

'Callum Jarvie.'

'There is a God after all. I hope it's nothing trivial.'

'Another bang to the head. But it looks like he's okay.'

'Pity. Might knock some sense into the lazy bastard, if we're lucky. I imagine that takes him off your suspect list, does it?'

'Well, I suppose he could have head-butted the nearest scaffolding pole and then thrown it overboard... I'd say that puts him a couple of places below you on the list.'

'Do you really think I would sabotage my platform?'

'I don't know who or what to believe anymore.'

'And you've honestly no idea who is doing this?'

'I have a few leads, but no solid evidence. Not yet. If you want to keep us safe, you had better use your divine powers to drive this storm away. Otherwise, I don't suppose Callum Jarvie will be the last casualty.'

Chapter
Twenty-Seven

SNAKEY HAD NOT COME alone, but his minders stepped aside and let Danny back down the stairs into the comparative warmth of the accommodation. The heating system had given up as soon as the main generators failed. A frost was forming on the outside of the module. Inside, the body heat emitted by a hundred or more crew, all confined to their increasingly fetid quarters, was enough to raise the temperature to a bearable level.

There was no hot water and a reluctance to take cold showers. Fortunately, the ventilation system was powered from the emergency generator. Otherwise, the accompanying stink of body odour would have been overpowering.

Even in the sickbay, it was getting a bit ripe, and Danny decided it was probably in everyone's best interests if he let his patient go back to his cabin. Not that Callum seemed keen to leave. When Danny complained about the smell, he nodded.

'The fans aren't here as air fresheners, mind. We need them on to keep the gas out. If they pack in, we're supposed to abandon the platform. God knows what we'd do in this weather. Camp out on the helideck?'

Danny looked at him sharply, but there was no guile in the man's expression. He didn't see how Callum could have known where he'd just been. It *had* to be a coincidence.

His patient seemed to have recovered fully. Besides wanting to free up the only sickbed he had, Danny figured he needed to mull things over. He was keeping too many secrets now, and they were gnawing away at his conscience. He didn't know how long he could restrain himself from telling Callum that Gemma was still alive.

Gradually, the anger and sense of injustice that had been keeping him going for the last days ebbed away, leaving him with nothing but the dregs of regret and self-recrimination.

After all, it was his choice to take this job; he had no one else to blame for his latest disastrous career move. Necessity played a part, sure, but it had been his decision. Of course, he would never have been in this situation if he hadn't joined the army. For about the hundredth time, Danny wondered why on earth he'd signed up. He'd enjoyed the training. Afterwards, he was posted to RHQ in Hampshire, got promoted to corporal and everything seemed to go well. Then he made the mistake of blowing the whistle on his commanding officer. The army "suggested" a change of career and a change of location.

After retraining as a medic, they sent him out to Cyprus for a spell, where he met Kelly. They fell in love. Got married. Could have lived happily ever after there. But army life isn't like that. They posted him back to the UK. Kelly was livid. In the end, she agreed to go, but things were never the same.

Then came the two tours in Afghanistan. She said the experience changed him; she found it hard to cope. Even when he got a posting back home in Yorkshire, she always seemed on edge. Complaining about the hours, the amount he drank. She got friendly with some of the female officers on the base. They were a smart, single crowd and with them, she would go on nights out in York. Danny tried not to mind, but his jealousy and suspicion grew. He quit the army to save his marriage but failed. They still had an uncomfortable number of debts to pay off. According to Kelly, this was his decision. His problem. Working offshore seemed like a quick fix. Kelly decided otherwise. She waited until he was stuck out in the middle of the North Sea on his first offshore trip to announce that she was leaving. So here he was. Trying to put his life back together. Trying to be a medic and a copper all rolled into one. Jack of all trades and master of none.

He thought back to his conversation with Jack Blake. He'd told the chary old fool the truth. With any luck, Snakey would have assumed that Danny was lying. He was still on Danny's list of suspects, but he couldn't imagine why the OIM would want to wreck his beloved platform. Still, he'd long ago given up expecting people to behave rationally. If they did, half the policemen and most solicitors would be out of a job.

For want of a better plan, Danny wandered through the accommodation, taking stock of the crew, and the platform's failing utilities. The corridors and stairwells had an eerie abandoned appearance, only lit dimly by the glow of the emergency lights. Many of the crew appeared to be hiding out in their cabins, only emerging for meals. The few that he passed avoided eye contact as if they were not sure of his allegiance. Danny wasn't sure either.

Snakey was unlikely to invite him to join his gang, nor was he part of the operations posse or the maintenance mob. The drillers looked at him as if he might be edible, and the scaffolders seemed to consider him a dangerous intellectual. The stewards were perhaps his natural allies in the platform hierarchy, but even there the medic stood apart, as an unsightly gall hanging from the organisational tree.

Under better circumstances, this independence might have made him the ideal peacemaker. He was determined to continue his investigations to the bitter end, but felt alone and isolated; a private investigator on hostile territory.

In the absence of any better plan, he decided to find that other fish out of water, Blair Scorgie. Maybe he had something to offer.

There were two TV lounges on the platform. The smoking lounge, close to the management offices, had been taken over by those loyal to Snakey and the established authority. It made sense; they were mostly old hands, who had started in the Cuillin field back when smoking was the norm. This also seemed to have swayed the minds of Olly and the wavering drillers, most of whom liked a cigarette or two to steady their nerves.

Ironically, an oil platform was about the only place in the UK where you could legally smoke indoors. *Strange*, he pondered, until you realised that you really didn't want people wandering outside with a lit cigarette.

Blair Scorgie and his rebel alliance had holed up in the non-smoking lounge. It was close to the control room and Blair could scurry between the two without too much danger of confrontation. The few members of his unhappy band that felt the need for the occasional cigarette were banished to what was laughingly called the internet cafe. It was a tiny room at the back, containing two PCs with cracked monitors and a couple of wonky desks for laptop users.

It seemed that things had reached an impasse. Snakey had possession of the permit office. He still signed permits to work and gave out orders, but most were pointless edicts. If anything he commanded actually happened, it was by coincidence. On the other hand, Blair had a big whiteboard covered with his strategic plan, which he continually modified as the ever-changing reality of the situation spiralled out of his control. He was full of ideas but had no authority.

Danny guessed that Snakey had the reliable support of about a third of the platform, and Blair Scorgie had less, maybe a quarter. The rest were getting on with their jobs as best they could and trying to ignore both of them.

He was relieved to see Stevie, one of the few people he trusted, on the Alpha, climbing the stairs from the laundry. Two stewards were trying to wash clothes by hand, but it was a losing battle. Damp overalls hung in rows and mesh sacks full of oil-stained garments lay in heaps on the floor.

The laundry and the mess were clearly in the neutral zone, but even there, arguments would break out and occasionally fists would fly. Still, no one wanted to go hungry or walk around in dirty underwear, so a pragmatic truce was maintained most of the time.

Stevie seemed happy enough to see him, but refused to be drawn on platform politics.

'I'm not on anyone's side but my own,' he said. 'Those tossers are like two fleas sitting on a dog's back, trying to work out how to make its tail wag.'

He invited Danny down to the tech station where, despite Stevie's patronage, the inhabitants greeted him with suspicion.

'Hey, medic! I hear you are kissing Scorgie's ass now, yes?' Vlad said.

'Shut yer face,' Callum said. 'The medic's alright. He fixed me up pretty good. If you're going to piss him off, don't forget he's got a bottle of chloroform and a wicked collection of scalpels in his bag.'

Danny hung around with the techs for most of the morning drinking tea that looked like it came straight out of an oil well. They even gave him his own mug and, although it was cracked, chipped and missing a handle, he felt inexplicably grateful for the gesture. He soon realised that this tight-knit band was working with complete autonomy now. They were keeping the platform's vital functions going, patching up problems as they arose and making their own decisions.

Every so often, operators would come asking for help or equipment. They always seemed to travel in pairs, possibly under instructions from Blair. Relationships between them and the techs appeared cordial, but only on the surface. The techs spoke to the operators in tech speak. The operators slagged them off whenever they were out of earshot.

Vlad trudged off to check the fuel levels for the emergency generator. Danny offered to help.

'Maybe you used to work in a gas station? This is not the same. Very complicated. I cannot waste time explaining everything to amateurs.'

'Complicated, hey?' Callum said, once Vlad had left. 'There's two hand valves and a pump. And we've got a proper gauge rather than a dipstick. That's a bit high-tech for the North Sea, I guess.'

He too wandered off to fix the erratic HVAC controls, muttering a threat to reboot them with his size nines.

He left Danny instructions on how to hold the fort.

'If anyone phones up, just mumble some gibberish and they'll think you're a mechanic. You can take messages but don't promise anything. And you can look at the monitors, but don't press any buttons.'

Danny promised and scouted around for something to read. He found a couple of porn magazines and a dog-eared copy of *The Old Man and the Sea*. He started reading it, hidden inside a motorcycle mag, just in case someone came back and accused him of literacy.

He nearly got to the end of the first chapter before the lights went out again. The battery-powered emergency lights flickered into life, but all the power sockets were dead. Had Vlad opened the wrong valve? He slid back the door and stuck his nose out to see if anyone was around. He smelled burning, so he grabbed his hard hat and gloves and jogged towards its source.

Chapter Twenty-Eight

DENSE BLACK SMOKE SPIRALLED around the module deck, whipped up by the relentless wind. It was impossible to identify where it was coming from as it swirled through the passageways between the steel-clad packages. Danny charged up a flight of stairs to the first landing to get a better perspective. The smoke looked thicker on the far side of the deck, and it was a fair bet that the emergency generator was somewhere in there.

There was a yellow phone booth nearby, and he dialled 2222 for the emergency response team. To his surprise, someone picked up the phone immediately. It was Asim Holroyd; he wasn't impressed by Danny's knowledge of the Alpha's layout.

'Don't you even know where you are, man? What direction is this smoke coming from? Is it on the west side?'

It was so long since Danny had seen the sun that he wasn't sure which way was west. The gales had been pounding them from the south-west for days now and despite the eddies and gusts, he was pretty sure it was blowing the smoke towards him.

'Yeah, west-ish anyway. Near the red crane and the module that looks like a big egg box.'

Asim's sigh of exasperation was loud enough to be heard over the wind noise and static.

'I'm sending a fire team. You get back inside and let them deal with it. The OIM will call everyone else back into muster stations.'

That'll be fun.

He followed Asim's instructions and headed back inside, but only long enough to pick up his emergency triage kit, a smoke hood, and a torch. On the stairs, he passed Ailsa and told her where he was going. She promised to let the muster checker know, but she had that vacant thousand-mile look in her eyes again, and Danny wasn't convinced the message would get through.

He poked his head around the door of the tech station. It was deserted. Hopefully, they were all at muster, but Danny had a bad feeling. Where was Vlad? And why were the rest of them not in the tech station? There was no reason for them to be out and about during the blackout. This was their refuge and unquestionably they would have come here first.

The PA chimes sounded. Danny was expecting the OIM's muster call. Instead, he heard the Pied Piper's artificial voice again.

ATTENTION ALL PERSONNEL. A VIKING IS DEAD. HIS BODY BURNS. BURY HIM WITH HIS GRAVE GOODS AND MOURN NO MORE. VALHALLA AWAITS!

What was this crap about Valhalla? Was the fire raging on the platform a funeral pyre? For whom?

Danny caught up with the fire team as they approached the generator module. Magnus Tulloch, the only man on the platform who looked like a Viking, was leading them, his bushy blond beard just about visible through his smoke-stained mask. Magnus waved him back, and he was happy to comply. He could taste the smoke now; it was thick and acrid and burned his throat.

He found a smoke-free upwind perch from which to watch proceedings. Magnus and his team were wrestling a giant hose. They stood on either side with one hand on the shoulder of the man in front, like a parade of elephants., hitting the fire with a massive quantity of foam which bubbled and hissed as it stuck the hot metal walls of the module. Wisps of flame leaked out through cracks in the wall and the dull orange paintwork on the beams blistered.

For a long time, the deluge seemed to have no effect. Then, gradually, the flames retreated into the module and the smoke turned from black to smog-grey.

Eventually, the smoke died down sufficiently for the team to investigate inside. The main door was wide open, either left open deliberately or blown open by some initial blast.

Magnus clipped a line to his harness and edged forward with two of his team standing ready to haul him back out should the fire flare up again. He prodded various items of burned debris with his foot, then stopped and kneeled by a bundle of rags. He turned them over carefully with his insulated and fire retardant gloves. The molten remains of a plastic hard hat fell to the deck, and Danny could see an equally molten face beneath.

He turned about and threw up onto the open grate steps and offered a silent apology to anyone foolish enough to be standing below. He'd seen severe injuries and corpses in his time in A&E and he'd become hardened to most things, but burns bothered him. The idea of being trapped in a burning module, of dying in the flames, made his stomach churn again, but he forced himself to look at the body.

Perhaps what disturbed him most was how fire wiped away a victim's humanity and left them featureless. Looking at the corpse, it was hard to tell where the uniform finished and the man began. Even a skeleton seemed less dreadful. You could persuade yourself that its former owner had greeted death with a bony smile, though the evidence often told a different story.

Magnus motioned Danny forwards. 'It's still hot,' he said. 'Don't go in too far. We'll check for more bodies once things have cooled down.'

Yes, for all Danny knew, the entire tech crew could be lying in there. Everything was covered with black ash and charred insulation from the generator.

He checked over the body with gritted teeth, but the fire had certainly done its work. There was no way of identifying the victim. He couldn't even guess hair colour or skin colour. The overalls looked like they contained a medium-sized corpse of around average height. A description that applied to eighty per cent of the Cuillin Alpha's crew.

Danny felt an urgent need to get back to the accommodation and find out how many people were missing. Surely Snakey could tell him that much.

When he reached the mess room, everyone was still at muster, but there was no sign of Snakey. Ewan Haver was taking the roll call in the mess and he reluctantly confirmed that there was no one missing off his register other than Danny himself. Ewan seemed disappointed not to be putting him on the "missing, presumed dead" list.

He carried on to the control room, where he received a better welcome.

'Thank God you're alive,' Blair Scorgie said. 'We heard you were out with the techs when the fire started. No one seemed to know where you were.'

So the message hadn't got through. Ailsa Troup was really as dopey as she looked.

'We checked back at the tech station. When you weren't there, I didn't know what to think.'

Danny just patted him on the shoulder. He felt too full to speak. All the people he knew well, the ones he had come to think of as friends, were there. He was even happy to see Vlad, as grumpy as ever, covered head to foot in soot and looking like a portly chimney sweep.

'What happened to you?' Danny asked. 'There was a body in the generator room. I thought maybe. . .'

'I am outside, looking at fuel gauge when there is big bang. Much smoke. Much flames. I run like fuck.'

'Did you see anyone else while you were there?'

'No. No one there when I came. I know what you think, but is nothing to do with me. I do not touch valves or anything. I am not smoking. I will be blamed anyway. You people always blame the foreign guy.'

'My people?'

'Secret police, not-so-secret police, company boss, immigration man, all these people.'

'Hey! I'm not some undercover authority figure. I'm not your boss or anyone else's. I'm barely the boss of me most of the time.'

'Screw the bosses. I don't have to eat their shit. If I have to eat shit, I prefer my own. You understand, yes?'

'No. And whatever it is you're trying to say, it sounds completely gross.'

'I mean to say, maybe I don't know all these things. Maybe I do things the wrong way. But bosses say wrong things also. I prefer my kind of wrong to theirs.'

'Fair enough. That almost makes sense. I don't care, I just want to find out who did this. I want to stop any more people from dying.'

'We are all going to die someday. You cannot fix that, medic man. But if you can get me off this pile of shit without a body bag, then I will write to the Patriarch and make you some kind of saint, yes?'

Chapter Twenty-Nine

ALL THE CREW WORKING legitimately outside when the fire started were accounted for. That left the big question of the identity of the body in the generator module. It could be Mickey, but Danny was keen to know who else was missing. It soon became apparent that it would not be easy to account for everyone.

Blair had the master "Persons on Board" list, but after blustering about 'difficult circumstances', he had to admit that it was nowhere near complete.

'I tried to contact Jack Blake to get his help, but I couldn't find him and his associates didn't want to cooperate. I got the distinct impression they didn't know where he was.'

So there was missing person number two. As for the rest of Snakey's gang, it was anybody's guess. Danny took a deep breath and headed for the smoking lounge to see how many heads he could count before someone took a swing at his.

When he opened the lounge door, he was greeted by a fug of stale smoke. With no ventilation working, smoking was banned but a few hardened addicts were blatantly ignoring the rules.

The room fell silent. Every eye was on him. He felt like he'd just walked into a Glasgow bar wrapped in an England flag whistling "Jerusalem".

'Exactly *what* do you want?' Archie Grier asked, hauling his considerable bulk out of a tattered chair.

He was easily Snakey's oldest and scariest-looking minder.

'I've got some bad news, I'm afraid.'

'Have yer? Well, I've got some worse fer ye–'

'I've found a body,' he said, stopping Archie in his tracks. 'In the emergency generator module. Too badly burned to tell who it is, sorry to say. I'm hoping there's a muster list? I need to know who's missing.'

Archie glanced over at a hatchet-faced colleague, who nodded reluctantly.

'You'd best talk to Laws about that.'

'Thanks. By the way, where's Jack Blake hiding out these days?'

'Never you mind. You go see the preacher before you need a few prayers frae the man.'

Cameron Laws was sitting in his office with the door firmly shut. He didn't seem any better pleased to see him than the smoke-shack crew but when Danny explained what he needed, his expression softened.

'Of course. I took a roll call, but can't say it was complete. There are a few names missing. It should at least narrow down your search, I hope.'

Danny took Laws' list back to the control room and compared it with Blair's. Four crew members were missing from the Alpha: Scott (in cold storage), Mickey (God knows where), Gemma (Danny knew where) and Snakey. There might have been others missing or laying low. With no working generators and the platform lit only by battery-powered emergency lights, information was likely to become more unreliable and harder to come by.

Danny returned to the sickbay, opened the door, and froze. A corpse was on his sickbed. It was human-shaped and covered in a plain white sheet. Probably another dummy, he thought, maybe a sick practical joke set up by the Pied Piper. He went to pull back the sheet when the corpse sat bolt upright and gave him a toothy grin.

'Surprise!' Gemma said, jumping off the bed and punching him hard but friendly in the shoulder.

'Jesus Christ! You maniac! What in hell's name do you think you're doing?'

162

'Hold yer wheest, laddie. I'm only here to help. And I wanted to see if you'd shit yersel, of course. It gets pretty boring out in the TLQ by myself.'

'Well, thanks, but my sphincter control's better than that. What did you need to say to me that was so damned urgent?'

'I just wanted to see if you were doing your job properly. Your regular job, that is. Not this amateur detective crap.'

'What's that supposed to mean?'

'You are still the platform safety officer, right? Aren't you supposed to check those lifeboats once a week? Anyone would think you were neglecting your responsibilities.'

'You're mighty cryptic suddenly.'

'That comes of being presumed dead. I'm not so fussed about the concerns of mere mortals. I'm on a higher plane of existence and all that.'

'Don't even joke about it, Gemma. I've got at least one dead body on my hands. I don't need any more.'

'Aye, I heard about that. I'm afraid I cannae help you with that, 'cept to say I don't know who it is, and I had nothing to do with it.'

'That's pretty much what Vlad said. Why is everyone suddenly protesting their innocence? An investigator with a nose for trouble might get very suspicious right now.'

'Well, you keep that nose of yours pointing away from me, Danny. I dinna want to think where it's been. Just do your job, like I said. I'll be in touch.'

He almost expected her to clap her hands and vanish. Instead, she sent him out to check the coast was clear, then she pulled on a balaclava and hard hat to hide her face and unmistakable hairstyle and slunk out through the emergency exit.

He went looking for Callum, but the technician was nowhere to be seen. Stevie had gone too, so presumably, they had headed back to their hideout in the tech station. He didn't want to go wandering around the platform on Gemma's wild goose chase without some back-up, but there weren't many people around he could trust to come along. The ones he had crossed off his list of suspects were unlikely to want to leave the accommodation or they might ask too many questions about how he came by his information. That left Adam Chinaka.

'What is it you want?' Adam seemed confused.

'I have to check the lifeboats. I was supposed to do it before, but the wind was too strong. I am worried that maybe we will need them soon.'

'Yes, it is possible. Maybe there will be more fire. The helicopter cannot come and I am not a good swimmer. You are right. We must check lifeboats. But this is a job for cock swings.'

'For who? Oh, you mean coxswains. Though cock swings sounds better. I suppose you're right, but they are all in there.' Danny pointed towards the smoking lounge. It was true; all the lifeboat coxes were in Snakey's camp, except for Trev Sinnot who was still keeping a low profile.

'I see. Perhaps it is best not to disturb them. I will help.'

As suspected, Adam possessed little in the way of practical skills. He was a big muscular guy, though. Adam steadied the boats and watched Danny's back while he climbed aboard each one. It was no mean feat scrambling over the gantry and through the tiny hatch in a gale. At least the winds had gone from screaming to whistling in the last few hours. Otherwise, it might have been too dangerous to continue.

All the boats looked pretty much unchanged since his last inspection.

They started with the four active boats on the upper decks, their secondary means of escape if there were no choppers en route. Then they moved down to the cellar deck and the alternative abandonment station, which was only for use when none of the others were accessible.

They checked Lifeboat Six last; the one that Danny was really interested in. It was impossible to tell if anyone had been here since he discovered the hoarder's stash. Adam quickly noticed the lack of grime around the stern and the boot print on the decking.

'Someone has been on this one, I think,' he said. 'We must investigate.'

With Adam's help, Danny forced open the hatch and looked inside. It took some time for his eyes to adjust to the dim orange light, but he immediately sensed there was something wrong; a strange smell in addition to the usual aroma of diesel and grease. He scrambled down the steep steps. There, sitting bolt upright on the coxswain's chair, was Jack Blake. He had a fixed expression on his face. In the gloom, Danny could make out a trickle of drool down one side of his face. His glassy eyes were fixed on a spot somewhere over Danny's head and his mouth stretched into a rictus grin.

There was no doubt in Danny's mind. Snakey was dead.

Chapter Thirty

DANNY WAS RELIEVED THAT he had Adam Chinaka with him. He had a good idea where the finger of suspicion would point otherwise. After all, Snakey had locked him in the bond store and they'd had some very public arguments. Adam wasn't the most popular guy, but no one would suspect him of being part of a murder conspiracy.

'This is a woman's way,' Adam said, once Danny had persuaded him to climb into the lifeboat.

'A woman's way of what?'

'Dying. I did not expect Blake to be a coward and take poison, like Cleopatra.'

'Poison? You think Jack Blake poisoned himself?'

'What else? There are many things on this platform which are poison. I have read the labels. You can test for these things, yes? Cut out his liver and say what killed him?'

'Look, I'm just a medic, not a forensic pathologist. I can't test blood samples for toxins. I know where the liver is, but I'd rather leave it where it is, thank you very much.'

Adam had a point. Snakey looked like he'd been poisoned. Danny just wasn't convinced that it was self-administered. To keep Adam happy, he gathered up the bottle of water and the opened miniature of Glenfiddich. He was wrapping the half-eaten cheese sandwich in one of the lifeboat's sick bags when he found an almost empty bottle of chloral hydrate. Someone had lifted it from sickbay. In the prescribed dosage, it was an effective sedative. The amount missing would be almost certainly fatal. He slipped the bottle into his pocket. He didn't want anyone putting two and two together making five.

Adam was busy wrapping red and white tape around everything, including the lifeboat and its winch.

'What exactly are you doing?'

'This is scene of crime. I am securing.'

'That's great. You carry on and I'll go let Blair know what's happened. I guess he's in charge now. Unless you fancy the job.'

'International Oil send me from my home to train as operations manager. Maybe OIM one day. But here I am nobody, just another plant operator. Scorgie can be OIM if he wants.'

———

Danny decided to talk to Blair in private. Announcing the OIM's demise and the circumstances might just make a tense situation worse. Danny expected Blair to be secretly pleased that his rival was out of the way, but he was visibly shocked.

'That's terrible. Are you sure it was poison?'

'No, but that seems the most probable cause of death.'

'I didn't even realise he was depressed. I've been on a mental health awareness course but didn't notice any of the signs. I'd hate to think that my actions pushed him over the edge.'

'We can't be sure it was suicide.'

'Can't we?'

'We do have a killer in our midst.'

'Yes, I suppose so. But the other deaths could have been accidents, couldn't they? I mean, they were reckless acts, but I've never considered our saboteur to be a cold-blooded murderer.'

'Let's hope you're right. I don't like the idea of being picked off one by one, but you have to admit it's a possibility.'

The look on Blair's face was enough. Perhaps for the first time, he was feeling the weight of responsibility that was about to settle on his infamous coke-bottle shoulders.

Danny left him, and, when no one was looking, snuck into the radio room. Gemma's VHF radio was still in the drawer. Turned on, it indicated a fully charged battery. He squeezed the PTT button and prayed to all the deities he could think of that no one else was listening.

'Nurse. This is Danny Boy. Over.'

After a pause, a crackly voice replied.

'Danny Boy. This is Nurse. Please state the nature of your emergency. Over.'

'I've been reading *The Old Man and the Sea*.'

'So that's where it went. If you lose any pages, I'll make you eat the whole book. Anyway, what's your point, apart from showing off that you can read big words?'

'What happened to the old man? How did he die?'

'He's dead? That's news to me! When I left him, he was still alive and climbing into his wee boat. I thought he'd just chug off over the horizon.'

'Hard to launch a boat like that by yourself. Especially in bad weather.'

'Aye, well, there was a fella dropped by earlier. Some pal of his, come to give him a hand. Or so I thought. He left a wee while before you showed up.'

'Do you remember what this fella looked like?'

'Company overalls, white hard hat, medium height, medium build. Mr Average.'

'Thanks. That's a great help.'

'Don't mention it. Can I have my book back now?'

'It's in the tech station. Does Nurse ever do house visits?'

'Oh, aye. When the cats are away. They have a grand cheese stash in their wee fridge. Anything else I can help you with?'

'Have you seen an escaped lunatic?'

'Aye, he was on the loose last night, but I don't know where he's staying right now. Anyway, you're not supposed to call him a lunatic. It's not politically correct. I think the word you're looking for is fuckwit.'

'I'll remember that next time he locks me away. Danny Boy out.'

'Love you too.'

Gemma added some alarming lip-smacking noises, and then there was silence. So Mr Average had boarded the lifeboat ahead of Snakey? Most likely he'd slipped an overdose of sedative into the Scotch. Nothing like a peaty single malt to disguise the taste. Then he'd hidden somewhere on the boat. Perhaps he'd wanted to stay and watch his victim die. This Pied Piper was a genuine psychopath.

Still, at least someone other than him had caught a glimpse of their saboteur. Gemma's otherwise unhelpful description confirmed his observations. If Mr Average was their man, he could strike all the tall and short guys off his list. If you also took out those who were overweight or clinically obese, he could discount about half the crew. That left him with a lot of potential suspects, but it was a start.

It meant that the diminutive egomaniac, Derek Cochrane, was in the clear, but Danny was no nearer knowing what had become of him. The body in the generator also appeared to be of average build.

Danny had been half-convinced that Snakey had died in the fire, but now he was back to square one. If Gemma had really seen Mickey wandering about last night, then it couldn't be him. That meant there was someone else unaccounted for and, therefore, the muster list must be wrong. This was doing his head in. How was he supposed to work out what was going on? He didn't even know how many missing persons there were.

First, he went to talk to Magnus Tulloch and asked him if it was safe to examine the scene of the fire.

'Sure, it's cooled down enough to go in. The module is not about to collapse soon. Look out for falling objects, though. Insulation and the like. And you'll need a hood or a mask. The fumes might damage your lungs, right?'

Danny nodded and pulled out a respirator he'd found in sickbay.

'Any more bodies?' he asked. He thought Magnus would have mentioned it, but the thought had been preying on his mind.

'No, thank God. But there's a lot of loose debris so take care where you tread.'

Magnus wasn't wrong. The interior of the module had been destroyed. The floor was littered with twisted bits of panelling, mangled tubes and fused wire. His breath wheezed through the respirator. The acrid smell of the smoke reminded Danny of his survival training. Most of his fellow trainees were more fearful of the helicopter capsize drill, but it was escaping from the smoke-filled room that gave him the creeps.

At least the module wasn't as dark as the windowless maze of shipping crates they used for the training exercise. He shone his torch around the walls, looking for the source of the blaze. Judging by the intense scarring and thick soot marks, the fire must have started in the fuel tank, way up near the module roof. With trepidation, Danny climbed the vertical ladder and peered inside.

There wasn't much to see. The tank was nearly empty, but there was a hole near the bottom on the far side. Gingerly, Danny clambered around the tank. Next to the hole was a tangle of charred cable and what looked suspiciously like the remains of a cigarette lighter. So someone had drilled a hole in the tank, bunged it up with rags or whatever and then lit the blue touch paper remotely?

Danny followed the cable as best he could, but the arsonist had cut it off at head height right outside the module. The saboteur presumably wanted to use his remote control fire starter again. The thought sent a shiver down Danny's spine and he headed back to the relative security of the accommodation.

Chapter Thirty-One

'We need to call a muster.'

Danny was fed up of acting as a shuttle diplomat between the two camps. Without Jack Blake, he had hoped Blair could bring everyone together for a headcount. He thought the man would welcome the opportunity to assert his authority.

'Yes. That's a good idea.'

'So you'll do it then?'

'Certainly. It's just picking the right time.'

'How about right now?'

'Oh, I'm not sure that's such a good idea. What if–' His prevarications were interrupted by the ear-pounding pulse of the general alarm. Danny and Blair spun round to see Adam remove his finger from the GA button and pick up the microphone.

THE OIM HAS SOUNDED GENERAL ALARM. ALL CREW IMMEDIATELY REPORT TO MUSTER STATIONS AND AWAIT FURTHER INSTRUCTION.

'Nice one, Adam,' Danny said. 'Excellent projection. I'm not sure you needed the microphone. What happens when they realise there is no OIM?'

'There is always an OIM. I let you fight about who it is. When I am the only person left on this platform, I will be OIM.' Adam looked grim.

Blair nodded, but he looked like a rabbit in a railway tunnel. Unless he pulled himself together soon, the OIM would be whoever the mob decided it was. In the meantime, Danny had a chance to find out who was missing before all hell broke loose.

He started with the control room where the emergency team should be mustering. As expected, everyone was there, except for Jack Blake, of course. In the mess, Ewan Haver was taking the roll call while simultaneously keeping the crew's sticky fingers out of the biscuit jars. Danny did his own count and quickly confirmed that Ewan's list was accurate.

The rest of the crew were still clad in their overalls. They stood in the gym with blue plastic overshoes covering their work boots. It was a muster in name only. Olly was trying to keep them focused, but already a game of five-a-side pool and a killer darts match had broken out, each attracting groups of jeering spectators.

It made Danny wonder what other, more lethal, items were lying around the platform. Ewan's well-honed knives for one. And then there was the welding gear, not to mention those big copper hammers and the gigantic spanners the crew used to beat machinery into submission. Not that he could go around confiscating everything. He'd just have to hope that if a mass brawl broke out, none of the deadly items were ready to hand.

At least there were no firearms on board; this wasn't an Alaskan pipeline where they needed guns to keep the bears at bay or a West African platform where the seas were teeming with insurgents and pirates.

It took a while to quieten everyone down sufficiently to count heads. Danny perched on an exercise bench for a better view of proceedings. He checked his muster list twice. Gemma was officially missing, but otherwise, every living soul except for Mickey Walters was present. It seemed he might have precipitated a leadership crisis for no good reason.

It made no sense. Unless Gemma was wrong about having seen Mickey, he did not know who had perished in the fire. *Had Gemma been lying?* Danny refused to believe it. Could there have been a stowaway onboard? It hardly seemed likely, unless the Pied Piper belonged to some terrorist group and wasn't just a lone criminal. That seemed no more credible.

And then it struck him. Two names were missing from the muster lists.

———

The cordoned-off lifeboat was on the same level as the smokers' locker room. He grabbed a spare hard hat and strode out to take another look. Snakey was still in the same position. Someone had closed his eyes, but he looked as cantankerous in death as in life.

There was one other body to check. It should be in cold storage down on the cellar deck. What if the first victim of the Pied Piper's campaign was no longer resting in peace?

Only one way to find out. It wasn't a job he fancied on his own. He persuaded Tommy to come with him without explaining what he planned to do, then rounded up Adam and Cameron to give the party some semblance of authority.

'Did any of you know much about Scott? His surname was Viklund. Doesn't exactly sound Scottish.'

'It's Swedish,' Cameron said. 'His mother hailed from the Orkneys, but his father was from Malmö, I think.'

'So, if you were a complete psycho, you might call him a Viking. It seems our Pied Piper had some twisted respect for Scott, even though he killed him. That would make more sense if it were an accident.'

Danny led them down the north stairwell hoping to find some shelter. Although the wind was vicious as ever, the wave tips were no longer at eye level and they made their way to the makeshift morgue without getting soaked.

'We should say a prayer before we disturb Scott's rest,' Cameron suggested.

'If I'm right, that won't be necessary.'

Danny opened the compartment door and shone a torch onto the platform where they'd left Scott's body. His body bag was still there. It was empty.

'I don't understand,' Cameron said, wandering around the open tomb.

'He hasn't risen from the dead, I'm afraid. The charred body in the generator module must be Scott's.'

'But why would anyone desecrate his remains?' Cameron exclaimed.

'I'm not sure. Maybe the Pied Piper decided to give him a Viking funeral.'

'The sick bastard,' Tommy said. 'If I catch a hold of him, I'll put a fire up his arse, dead or alive.'

Tommy didn't look like he could run fast enough to catch a cold, let alone a murderer, but Danny said nothing. Somehow, it felt as if Scott had died twice. Was this part of the Piper's plan to throw him off the scent? If so, Danny was determined it wouldn't work.

'It is a long way to carry a body from here to the generator,' Adam said. 'He must be strong.'

Tommy leaned against the railings and stared up.

'It would be a struggle if you took the stairs. Suppose the bastard hauled it up? I can see the emergency generator exhaust duct from here. You'd need some kind of winch. No good just lowering a rope over the railings. Scott was a lightweight, but he'd still be too heavy for one man to lift.'

'Where is the man overboard winch?' Cameron asked.

'Just around the corner, next to the... oh.'

Tommy pointed at an empty stand. The winch, with its rope and rescue harness, was missing.

'I don't suppose there's any point searching for it?' Danny wasn't keen to look for another needle in the haystack, but he had to ask.

'Bastard probably threw it into the sea afterwards.'

'You're probably right. Look, can we keep this between ourselves?'

'Why would we do that?' Tommy asked.

'I'd rather let our Pied Piper think he's fooled us again. And I'm not sure it would be good for crew morale to know what's happened to Scott.'

'Suppose so.'

Danny wasn't sure he could rely on Tommy's discretion. Adam and Cameron agreed readily enough. Of course, he was keeping one big secret from them. Snakey's death.

The crew were going to find out eventually, and it might be better coming from these three than from him. Now was as good a time as any.

'I have something else to show you,' he said and led them round to Lifeboat Six. 'I've been trying to find Jack Blake. No one seemed to know where he was, but then an anonymous note told me to check the lifeboats. Adam and I came down earlier. I'm afraid this might be a shock.'

Danny helped Tommy and Cameron on board and waited. He didn't suspect either of them, but it would be interesting to see their reactions. Tommy came out and promptly threw up over the side. It was pretty spectacular; Danny was sure you couldn't fake that sort of response. He sat down on the deck and pulled his hard hat down over his face.

Laws was not far behind. He looked sorrowful but not surprised.

'I feared as much. Jack has been under a lot of pressure since this business started. I don't believe he was dealing with it well.'

'So you think he took his own life?'

'That's how it looks to me.'

Danny decided it was easier to stick with Laws' theory for now.

'I wonder how the crew will react. Are they going to pin the blame on someone? Blair, for example, or me?'

'Aye. Maybe. I had better address the crew. We've had more than our fair share of woes on the Alpha recently. I couldn't stomach more, especially if they resulted from a tragedy such as this. We need to concentrate on preserving the living, rather than avenging the dead.'

Danny sincerely hoped that a sermon from Cameron Laws might cool the hotheads among the crew. Sadly, that was even less likely than Snakey poisoning his own bottle of Scotch.

Chapter Thirty-Two

CAMERON'S ADDRESS WENT WELL. Even those who disliked Jack Blake seemed shocked and saddened by the news.

His plea to concentrate on the living rather than the dead rang particularly true for Danny. Without even the basic forensic capability, the dead were unlikely to yield any answers. However much red and white tape Adam wrapped around the place, Danny had neither the tools nor the skill to deal with any evidence. Even a simple survey of the crime scenes was unlikely to give him any significant clues.

He still thought that Gemma knew more than she was letting on, but if she wanted to play the mystic oracle and drip-feed him cryptic information, he supposed he'd just have to put up with it. She was his eyes and ears out and he didn't want to lose that by accusing her.

There was still one other living person who might help: Mickey Walters. Danny was sure he was still alive. *Where is he hiding?*

He couldn't imagine Mickey playing the Pied Piper. However, if the saboteur's moniker was a reference to the Piper Alpha disaster, it would put Mickey back in the frame. Mickey, Tommy, Snakey and Cameron were the only ones on the platform who had an obvious connection to Piper Alpha. But only Mickey had been on board during the fire that killed 167 workers thirty years ago.

And yet the North Sea oil industry was a pretty small world. Most of the guys working offshore at the time would have known some victims, even if they were just passing acquaintances. And then there were the relatives of the deceased. Some of their sons or daughters, nephews or nieces might well be working on the Cuillin Alpha. There was no way of knowing.

If the internet had still been available, Danny would have tried getting a list of the Piper Alpha crew and cross-checked their surnames against the crew here, but that horse had bolted long ago.

Whatever the truth, finding Mickey seemed to be the logical next move. Danny radioed Gemma but got no response. He tried not to assume the worst. There were plenty of good reasons for her not to pick up the radio, most of which he didn't care to dwell on. He slid open the fireproof door and poked his head into the main accommodation. There was no one about.

He could hear a rumble of voices and smelled the cigarette fumes seeping out from under the smoking-room door. Every so often, a stream of shouted profanities or manic laughter broke out. It was hard to pick out individual voices, and Danny had no intention of entering the lion's den again unless he had to. Instead, he headed to the fume-free eastern end of the accommodation.

The lounge was full, with the plant operators perching on the floor, playing cards under the dim glow of the emergency lights. Other members of the crew who had the luxury of a chair, strained their eyes reading the eclectic selection of books left behind by former colleagues, or engaged in stilted conversations while staring out of the tiny blast-proof window.

Ailsa was perched on a box next to the defunct coffee machine, looking decidedly uncomfortable.

'I didn't expect to see you here, Ailsa. I thought you'd be in your cabin.'

'It got super cold, there was no TV and I didn't feel safe by myself.'

'I thought you were a smoker?'

'Aye, but my mam's always on at me to give up. I thought maybe this would be a good time to try, what with the bond being closed and all. I prefer it in here. It smells a wee bit nicer and there's not as much swearing.'

In the background, Danny could hear Ewan Haver using the f-word as a noun, verb, and adjective all in the same sentence. You stopped noticing it after a while. He wondered how bad the smoko had to be for this end of the platform to seem like a pleasant place to hang out.

Danny attempted a cheerful 'hello' to the rest of the crew. Only Callum, sitting under the silent television, got up to greet him. Owen Shives immediately took his place, pursued by a chorus of complaints from his fellow operators.

'Oy! Give us back them cards,' Asim, who had a big pile of tokens in front of him, complained.

'Come get 'em yourself, if you want them.' Owen looked fed up.

'You've buggered up the game.'

'I don't give a toss about the game. I wanna go home. If there's no helicopter by tomorrow, I say we take to the lifeboats and head for the Trafalgar field or the Shetlands even. Maybe one of the support boats or the RNLI will pick us up on the way. Someone is bound to notice the transponder once we get out on the sea.'

A murmur of agreement rippled through the room.

'Better than stopping here and getting slaughtered one by one by some nutter,' Ewan Haver said.

'Or listening to Laws' bleeding sermons,' his baker-in-chief, Weevil, added. 'Maybe we should take him down the escape ladder and find out if he can walk on water.'

That raised a chuckle.

'Anything's better than listening to that arsehole Scorgie's inspirational speeches,' Asim said. 'I know Snakey could be a bit of a knob, but at least he had a plan. Scorgie's all talk and is full of shite. It's time we started looking out for ourselves.'

No one seemed interested in Danny's opinion. When someone finally spoke to him, it was only Callum asking him if he'd found any more dead bodies yet.

'Nope, thank God. However, Mickey and Gemma are still missing. I was hoping some of you might volunteer for a search party. If anyone knows who the Pied Piper is, surely it's Mickey.'

'What about our Gemma?' Ailsa asked.

'Our medic's got her hidden in his cabin, hasn't he?' Callum said, winking at Danny. 'She's been warming his bed all this time.'

'He has not. I looked,' Haver said. 'Not even any saucy photos of her on his phone.'

Danny bit back his anger. It was better to let Haver talk and maybe incriminate himself some more. So the chef had broken into his locked sickbay and searched his cabin? He could easily have raided the medicine cabinet. Danny tried to count his blessings. At least no one was accusing him of murder or sabotage. He let the conversation wander off into insults and speculation.

'Well, I've nothing better to do just the now. I'll help you look for your girlfriend and Crazy Walt, even if these lazy feckers can't be arsed,' Callum said.

His tech colleagues looked guiltily. They and a few others grudgingly agreed to join the search.

They split the volunteers into two parties: Callum took the techs, which left Danny with the odd squad: Magnus, Owen and Ailsa.

He went to the control room to see if he could round up Adam or one of the other operators. At the door, all he could hear was Blair bleating out his woes, and Cameron mouthing endless platitudes as he tried to paper over cavernous cracks dividing the crew. He decided against roping them in.

Danny collected a couple of handheld VHF sets from the radio room and set them to the channel that Gemma had been using. With any luck, she would be listening in and would know to stay out of their way.

There was a great deal of grumbling and a general reluctance to suit up, but eventually, the two search parties set out into the storm. Danny led his team to the exposed modules atop the main compressors and sent Callum down to the cellar deck to battle the spray and turbulence below.

As he stuck his head above the enclosure, the wind compression left him gasping for breath. He crawled on hands and knees to the sanctuary of an empty shipping container and then his team carefully worked their way through the half-dozen compartments on the compressor roof.

They retreated down the stairs and scoured the compressor module for any sign of life. Here was the heart of the gas process on the platform. It felt strange to pass through with nothing but the natural sounds of wind and rain disturbing their peace.

There was no sign of Mickey.

As he stepped through the door, Danny saw the scaffolding platform that caused so much angst and nearly led to Cocky being thrown overboard by the techs. There was about half a metre of scaffolding pole protruding next to the compressor enclosure door. Who in their right mind would leave a single pole protruding from the structure at the most hazardous point possible?

He decided to investigate, but as soon as he put his foot on the scaffold tower, the incongruous pole flipped up and the compressor door flew open, knocking him flying across the floor. He landed in a heap and clutched at his chest. Blood was seeping through his overalls. As the constellation of stars in front of his eyes coalesced into a swirling galaxy, he passed out.

Chapter Thirty-Three

THE WORLD GRADUALLY CAME back into focus. Danny found he was lying on his back on the cold module floor. The faces staring down at him didn't look overly concerned so he assumed he wasn't at death's door. Someone was pressing a paint-splattered rag against his ribs to stem the flow of blood. He felt like Gemma had kicked him with her steel-capped boots.

'You are lucky,' Magnus said. 'If the vent fans had been running, they would have blown the door open and you'd have been crushed flat. The fans can't run without the emergency generator, so the enclosure pressure must be way down.'

Magnus called the other team on the radio to let them know what had happened. Within a couple of minutes, they were all gathered round Danny like mourners at a funeral.

'Bugger off, you lot. I'm alright,' he gasped. 'Just give me some breathing space, for God's sake.'

Callum was temporarily speechless. For him, that was quite something. It didn't last long and soon he was talking nineteen to the dozen, organising his team and insisting on continuing the search for Mickey and Gemma. He agreed to keep in contact regularly. Once they'd swept their allotted area of the platform, they would meet up at the tech station.

Danny's team took some persuading to continue the search, but even in these icy conditions, it was at least more interesting than sitting inside, playing endless games of poker or staring at a blank TV screen.

Despite his sore ribs and the dizziness, he was keen to find Mickey. The trick was carrying out a thorough search for Mickey without exposing Gemma's hiding place. Despite Danny's best efforts, the team eventually stumbled upon her abandoned module, and Owen got excited.

'I bet the bastard is in here. I'd forgotten about the TLQ. Remember that twat Macgregor who was the heli admin back in the day? I was wearing my Hibs shirt when I rolled up on my first rotation and he was a mad keen Hearts fan. It's supposed to be temporary living quarters, but I ended up here for the whole of my first year offshore. What a shithole. Halfway between a caravan and a shipping crate.'

'Good place to hide, though,' Magnus stated.

The padlock was missing and the door to the TLQ was open. Hopefully, that meant Gemma had been listening in on the radio and had scarpered, but it could also mean that the Pied Piper had got here first. They entered cautiously and rooted around inside, but there was nothing to see. Gemma had done an excellent job of tidying her stuff away.

Where has she gone?

They continued with their sweep of the main deck, then trooped down to the tech station where Callum and his team were waiting for them.

'Did you find anything?'

'Not a sausage,' Danny said.

'Jesus! It's not that big a platform. There's nowhere left for those two to hide. They must have ended up in the drink. I can't see it any other way.'

'Mickey Walters is still our number one suspect. If he's drowned, I don't know where that leaves us.'

Owen was looking restless. 'Enough of this Miss Marple crap. I'm freezing my nuts off out here. Are we going in for a cuppa or what?'

The tech team looked at each other and finally turned to Stevie, their supervisor. He shrugged and, declaring the search party to be honorary techies for the day, opened the door to let them in. There were no spare chairs so Danny, Owen, Magnus and Ailsa had to perch on the swarf-strewn metal benches. They didn't mind. They'd all heard the rumour that the techs had rigged up some way of generating heat; it certainly seemed toastier in here than inside the accommodation module.

The smell emanating from the mechanical workshop next door reminded Danny of Bonfire Nights when he was a child. Plumes of smoke spiralling up from the stacks of damp wood, burning with the assistance of copious amounts of paraffin. He poked his head through the doorway and saw Vlad feeding fragments of broken palettes into a homemade brazier. There was a modified electric kettle perched on a metal grille with its remaining plastic fittings slowly melting into the fire, adding to the rich and toxic aroma wafting through the tech station. The spare mugs that Stevie pulled out of a filing cabinet looked equally hazardous to health.

No one seemed to care. The warmth it generated and the prospect of a hot drink were enough to banish any concerns about poisonous fumes and lung damage. Once everyone had a mug in their hands, Danny went over the incident in more detail. No one but him wanted to call it an attempted murder.

'Maybe it was another practical joke by this Pied Piper prick,' Stevie said.

'Very amusing, I'm sure,' Danny said.

He was reluctant to tell them about the drugs missing from the sickbay. It was a risk, but there was at least one person who could have stolen the drugs.

Ewan Haver said he'd snooped around his cabin and he had a long and bitter history of disputes with Snakey. In the short time that Danny had been on the Alpha, he'd heard him threaten to disembowel him with an apple corer, cut off his manhood with a meat cleaver and throw him out with the food waste. Danny had taken it all with a pinch of salt. They were two egotists with too much testosterone shut in a confined space together. He'd never seen either of them do more than bang tables and point fingers, but maybe something had tipped Haver over the edge. Haver was a popular suspect for many reasons.

'Wouldn't surprise me,' Callum said. 'We know he's a light-fingered fecker, and he's threatened Snakey with far worse than poison over the years.'

'But he's done none of those things,' Stevie countered.

'He's put a few fellas in hospital in his time.'

'He has?'

'It's common knowledge, I'm telling you. He did time for it. GBH, or so I heard. The fella has a fearsome temper.'

'If he spent time in prison, it'd be on his HR records,' Stevie said.

'Which are on a server somewhere, which we can't access because there's no power, and the network is down.'

'All the HR stuff goes to Blair Scorgie. And he doesn't trust computers. He keeps backups of all that stuff on memory sticks. Password protected, of course. I'll bet there are dozens in his desk.'

'That just leaves the minor problem of nicking the appropriate memory stick, powering up a PC, and deciphering Blair's password.'

'It's Cerberus. The dog with all the heads that guards Hades. Likes his mythology, does our Blair. Not great at spelling though, so he has it on a note stuck under his desk.'

'And the power supply?'

Stevie rummaged around in a cupboard and pulled out a portable inverter. 'There's enough juice left in the platform batteries to run a PC for hours. This device converts battery voltage to mains AC. Have to snip the plug off the cable to wire it in. I had better come with you. Don't want you electrocuting yourself. It's dangerous enough round here at the moment without letting amateurs loose on the wiring.'

Danny followed Stevie to the operations manager's office and sent Callum into the control room to make sure Blair didn't leave until they returned. Danny took a glance through the control room door. Blair looked like he'd put down roots and seemed in no hurry to go outside.

Chapter
Thirty-Four

Before they entered the office, Stevie made Danny swear not to divulge any personal information he'd come across.

'I don't mind you looking at Ewan's records, Danny. You've got a legitimate reason. But I'm not letting that nosy parker Callum rummage around in other people's affairs. He's an emotional magpie; he loves uncovering a juicy secret. I don't suppose he means harm, but I'd rather keep private files private.'

Stevie had an alarmingly large selection of keys, one of which fitted the small wall safe containing the laptop and half a dozen memory sticks. It only took him a few minutes to wire in the inverter and power up the PC. Danny logged on and began searching for the stick containing the HR files. At the second attempt, he was successful, and it didn't take him long to pull up Haver's records.

The rumours were true. He did have a criminal record, several for that matter. He'd done time for assault, robbery and handling stolen goods, plus a conviction for selling illegally imported methadone on the black market. But somewhere along the way, he'd gone straight, got a steady job, a wife and kids. His last run-in with the law was back in the late eighties.

Danny jotted down the salient details and prepared to shut down the PC. Stevie wandered off to use the toilet. Taking advantage of his absence, Danny speed-read his way through a few more records. It was very frustrating. He didn't want to leave without checking if there were any other crew members with convictions, but he was sure Stevie would make a fuss if he accessed any more files. Keeping one eye on the door, he fumbled for his memory stick and slipped it into a spare slot. According to Windows, it was going to take somewhere between 40 seconds and eternity to clone the entirety of Blair's records.

He thought he heard Stevie coming back and quickly lowered the screen. A head poked round the doorway. It was Callum.

'Sorry, mate. Don't mean to pry. Scorgie was looking for you. I told him you were down in the tech station. He's still there drinking coffee and blathering on. Jesus, that guy can spin out a story. I don't think they're going to get rid of him in a hurry.'

'Thanks, but I'm just about finished.'

'Find anything on Haver?'

'Yeah, lots. Any idea why he gave up a life of crime? Did he find God or something?'

'Not him. You should hear him and Lawsy going at it. Haver blames religion for just about everything.'

'Well, something made him change his ways.'

'Might be closer to home. His wife's a stunner. Or was anyway. Bit past her prime now, but I've seen photos of her from back in the day. She was Miss Aberdeen 1973 or something like that. If she told me to go straight and learn how to cook, I'd have done it too, no questions asked.'

'You might be right.'

'So what did you find out?' Stevie had crept up on them with surprising stealth.

Danny just had time to palm his memory stick, but he'd no idea how much data he'd extracted. Neither Stevie nor Callum seemed to have noticed his sleight of hand, so he blustered on regardless.

'There's nothing here that would give the police grounds to search his cabin, but I never was a regular policeman. I say let's do it anyway.'

'Agreed,' Stevie said. 'We should wait till lunchtime, though. When he's busy in the galley. Otherwise, you never know where the bugger's going to crop up.'

'Good thinking,' Callum said, casually inviting himself to the search party. 'He thinks the whole of the accommodation is his fiefdom. He's got more keys than Stevie. I reckon he has one for every lock on the platform.'

'He'd better not have a key for the gun safe,' Stevie said.

'The what?'

'The safe where they keep the shotgun.'

'Seriously? Why do you need a shotgun on an oil platform? Is it seal hunting season?'

'Don't be daft. It's a backup method of lighting the flare stack. You fire a special cartridge through the gas cloud and it catches fire. It's pretty neat to watch.'

'And nobody thought to mention that we had a gun on board? We have a murderer wandering around, you know.'

'Well, the Pied Piper has shot nobody, Doesn't even play the flute. Seems to prefer bashing folk in the head.'

'You'd better show me this gun safe. I've got another of those bad feelings coming on.'

The gun safe was in the control room, mounted on the wall next to the defibrillator and the first aid kit. It was a sturdy wooden cabinet covered with hazard stickers and padlocked shut.

With a great deal of reluctance, Stevie handed Danny the key. Inside was a long metal fire retardant box labelled: "Live Firearms. Handle with Care". It had its own in-built combination catch, but it was unlocked and ajar. He eased it open and stepped back. The box was empty.

Danny swore, long and loud, and punched the box, leaving a knuckle-shaped dent in the metalwork.

'So now we have an armed murderer on the loose.'

'It's only a double-barrelled shotgun,' Stevie said, looking like a man expecting to be blamed for the gun's absence. 'Not even a proper one; it only fires those special cartridges. You'd have to get right up close to someone to actually kill them.'

'Well, that's a relief. Anyone else got a nice surprise for me? Any weapons of mass destruction on board? Sarin gas? Nuclear warheads?'

'There are the radioactive sources,' Stevie said.

'The drillers use them for well logging. But they're very low level. I wouldn't like to find one in my soup, but they're pretty harmless.'

Ignoring the regulations, they all trooped out onto the main deck in their indoor clothes and marched across to the drill derrick. The radiation locker was a small lead-lined cabinet in the tool pusher's office. Olly Felmer assured them he had the only key and a detailed list of the radioactive sources on board.

'I've been doing this job for twenty years and I've never lost one yet. They go down the well, they come back up again, and they go back in the locker. What do you think yon nutter's going to do with it? You can't make a bomb with a few milligrams of caesium, pal,' he spluttered.

Danny apologised and headed back to the control room. Black anvil-shaped clouds had moved in to surround the platform. Horizontal rain whipped across the main deck, soaking the men in seconds. It was undoubtedly a change in weather, but not the one Danny had been hoping for. He cursed himself for not grabbing one of the operator's fluorescent weatherproof jackets on the way out.

Back in the control room, a disapproving Blair Scorgie who had finally emerged from his office to survey his tiny empire, greeted them.

'I appreciate we are in a state of emergency but that's even more reason to adhere to procedure. Leaving the accommodation without permission or proper PPE is a serious matter. Unless you can give me a reason for your flagrant flouting of regulations, I will have to take disciplinary action.'

Danny bit back the urge to tell him to shove his regulations where the sun didn't shine and broke the bad news instead. 'The shotgun is missing.'

'What do you mean, *missing*?' Blair asked. He rushed over to the safe and began examining it.

'Somebody got hold of the key and took it. As far as we know, the only people who have keys for the safe are you, Stevie, and maybe Ewan Haver.'

'Why on earth would Ewan have a key for the gun safe?'

'That's what I'd like to know. With your permission, I'd like to search his cabin.'

Danny didn't think Haver would have the shotgun stashed under his bed, but he had to start somewhere. He didn't rate his chances of finding it out on the platform either. It could be in some random corner of a forgotten module or at the bottom of a crate on the pipe deck. In any case, he had a feeling that a search of Haver's cabin might turn up something interesting.

Let's see if the keeper of keys likes people rifling through his things.

Chapter Thirty-Five

EXPECTING TROUBLE, DANNY ROUNDED up a posse, starting with the two biggest guys on the platform: Magnus Tulloch and Jed Santo. Blair declined to join them but offered Owen Shives, probably the smallest crew member, as his representative.

'Owen has... special skills. He'll be very helpful in your search.'

Danny raised an eyebrow but offered no objections. Maybe Owen was a martial arts expert like Asim. Or perhaps a champion sprinter.

They extracted the master key for the cabins from a reluctant Cameron Laws and made their way down to the auxiliary living quarters. Danny hammered on Haver's door. No response.

He was disappointed; he wanted to observe the man's reaction when they barged in. Perhaps it was for the best, though; Haver was unlikely to take it lying down, and it was easier to search the place without him.

The cabin was unusually tidy for an offshore installation. No used earplugs or out-of-date permits or damp towels were strewn on the floor. No personal items of any sort were visible.

Danny tried a few drawers, but they were all fitted with a variety of padlocks, some labelled with the names of absent crew members. It made sense for the platform regulars to have a permanently allocated cabin and locker to save them having to lug all their kit offshore each time, but it was frustrating the search.

'Shit! How are we going to open this lot?'

Jed offered to fetch some bolt croppers, but Owen raised a hand in which he held what looked like a set of hair grips.

'This is why I'm here. I'm good at opening things.'

'So you were a locksmith back in the day?'

'Something like that. I used to be a dab hand with car doors and all that, but I... err... had to give it up. I kept the tools of the trade, though. They come in handy. The lads are always forgetting their keys, or losing them down the bilge.'

Owen got to work with his lock-picking tools. It was alarming how quickly he was able to break through some secure-looking padlocks. There were nine lockers in the room all together, mostly containing piles of clothing, some of it not very clean, including a pair of trainers that smelled like they could have jogged away by themselves. Danny searched them all but found nothing.

He turned his attention to the locked drawer under a narrow, gun-metal grey desk, secured with combination padlocks. Owen made short work of those, too. He seemed to decipher the combinations by touch alone.

With skills like those, you don't need a key to open a gun safe. Danny made a mental note to check the locks in the control room for scratches.

The drawer contained a collection of keepsakes: jewellery, watches, photos, and even a lock of hair. Danny felt uncomfortable rummaging through Haver's family mementoes until he turned over a familiar-looking Royal Military Police badge. Danny didn't know what possessed him to bring it offshore with him, but it was undoubtedly his badge. What on earth was it doing in Haver's drawer?

He dug deeper and picked up a bracelet inscribed: "To Ruth. Love you always, Jack." He put it back and inspected the pile of photos. They included one of a smiling black family posing in a colourful African market, and one of blond children cross-country skiing. It was unlikely that any of them were from Haver's family photo album.

'Anyone know Mrs Snakey's name, by any chance?'

'Ruth,' Owen said. 'He used to say he was always ruthless out here. It was a crap joke, and I don't suppose she would have found it funny. She's dead now. Last Christmas it was. Cancer. He's never been the same since. Why do you ask?'

Danny showed him the bracelet.

'Jesus! Everyone knows Ewan's a nosy sod, but that's just plain creepy. Who'd steal a dead woman's bracelet?'

Magnus came inside to see what the fuss was about and made straight for the skiing photo.

'I took that in Norway last year,' he said. 'I wondered where it had gone. The dirty little bastard. What does he want with pictures of my children?'

Danny picked up the lock of hair. Thick mouse-brown curls. He would put money on it belonging to Gemma. *What is Haver doing with this stuff?*

Danny felt the change in pressure as the door to the stairwell opened and heard feet pounding along the passageway towards them.

'What the fuck do you think you're–?'

Haver's protestations were cut off as Magnus Tulloch's fist struck his jaw. He went down in a heap and landed on his backside in the passageway. Magnus yelled a stream of obscenities at him and swung a boot at his head. Danny moved quickly to block the kick and tried to calm the big driller, who was rapidly transforming into a blond berserker.

Heads poked out of cabin doors all along the passageway. Danny tried to explain without generating more conflict, but he was failing badly. It didn't help that Magnus was still bellowing at the top of his voice, calling Haver a pervert and a voyeur.

Soon there was a press of angry crewmen outside demanding to see if Haver had stolen anything from them. Danny had no choice but to take the drawer upstairs to the mess and lay the contents out on a table. Owen fetched Asim and between them they tried to keep the angry crew in order so Danny could make a list of what had been taken and from whom, before returning the item to its rightful owner.

They were doing well for a while until someone spotted a genuine Breitling watch among the treasure trove and suddenly half a dozen people remembered having lost one. Why anyone would bring a thirty thousand pound watch onto an oil rig was beyond Danny's comprehension. Some people would do anything to show off.

Fortunately, there was an inscription on the back. Archie Grier came forward. Danny was surprised that the grizzled, pot-bellied and pock-marked deckhand was the owner of the watch. Alarmingly, he was also intimate with someone who called him "squidgy bear".

'That's Solada. Ma girlfriend. She's frae Thailand, doesna spake much English. She wanted to buy this for ma birthday, so I gave her the money, like. They done this inscription for free. She's a dafty, calling me that, but she's young still. What can ya do, eh?' he grinned.

Danny wanted to ask him how young Solada exactly was, but he didn't think he would like the answer. Archie was pushing sixty and would be nobody's idea of a perfect partner. Archie's face hardened.

'Ma wife died. I was on ma ain for years. And now I'm nay. If you or the fucking Pied Piper or any other fucker tries to stop me getting back to Solada, I'll rip their fucking heid aff.'

Archie's little speech made Danny realise that however much he disliked the old deckhand and his unpleasant pals, in the end, they all wanted the same: to get home safely.

Danny got most of the purloined items back to their owners with no fights. Even Magnus seemed to have calmed down, though his colleague, Jed, was still keeping a weather eye on him. They had to lock Ewan Haver in the bond store for his own protection as much as anything. Some of the aggrieved crew had been threatening to cut various bits off Haver as keepsakes in return, and no one was eager to come to his defence.

———

When things had quietened down, Danny and Owen let themselves into the bond to conduct an informal interview. They perched on boxes of duty-free cigarettes, while Haver sat on the only chair, staring into his hands. Owen took the lead.

'So why did you take all that stuff, you twat? What was it for?'

'Ah, yer can go fuck yersel. I'm no saying nothing. I dunna talk to the filth.'

'What about the shotgun? The one we use for the flare. Do you know anything about that?'

'Yer what? Yer canna pin that on me. It was there last time I checked.'

'So you opened the gun safe?'

'Aye well, just for a look. I like to know that everything's put away in the right place. There's no law against that.'

'But only the OIM and the operation's manager are supposed to have keys to that safe.'

'And I wouldna trust either of them with a water pistol, let alone a proper gun.'

'What about the telecoms room? You been in there at all this trip?'

'And why should I?'

'Well, someone went in there and stole some network switches. Cut off our last link with the outside world.'

'You mean back when the Wi-Fi went down? Why would I do that? Wi-Fi and TV are the only things that keep a man sane out here.'

Danny felt he was wasting his time. Haver could stay in the bond indefinitely as far as he was concerned. Now the power was off, it wasn't like they needed his magic in the galley. Outside his domain, he was nothing but a kleptomaniac trouble maker with anger issues.

Chapter Thirty-Six

WITH NO HEATING AND only battery power, the whole accommodation module was cooling down. One by one, crewmen from both sides of the great divide shuffled into the mess, sniffing for food, and trying to avoid each other's gaze.

The biscuits were long gone and some hardy souls had started troughing their way through the wilting remains of the salad counter. Below, in the silent chiller cabinet, was nothing but some grated carrot, a few cubes of beetroot and a jar of pickled eggs.

Every so often, someone would peek through the serving hatch. There was talk of storming the galley and demanding food. Others suggested raiding the stores. There was little appetite for either plan. What were they going to make with slow-thawed chicken and raw cabbage? The time to start on cold baked beans and custard might be rapidly approaching, but for now, the crew were prepared to mutter and moan and wait to see what the galley staff could rustle up.

In Ewan Haver's enforced absence, Weevil elected himself head chef. He came out and climbed up on the counter in his work boots.

'Sorry lads. And lass,' he shouted, nodding to Alisa, who was putting on her serving pinny in readiness. 'Menu's a bit limited today. I mean, you'd think that on an oil and gas platform you'd have a gas cooker somewhere. Apparently, that's not allowed cos it might blow the place sky-high. Health and safety gone mad, eh?'

That raised a much-needed laugh among his audience, shortly followed by cries of 'get on with it', 'where's me grub, you tosser' and 'throw a shrimp on the barbie' in a fake Australian accent.

'Funny you should say that. That's pretty much what I had planned. Anyone mind if I completely flout regulations so that we can get some hot food?'

There was a big cheer. Even Cameron Law, hovering in the background, gave him a cautious thumbs up.

Weevil made a big show of bringing out trays of sausages. Ailsa rushed over to wipe his bootprints off the serving counter before she would let him put them down. Then he sent the two tallest stewards out into the mess and surrounding access ways, disabling smoke detectors, while another wedged open the emergency exit to generate much-needed airflow.

When Weevil returned to the mess, Danny walked over to see what sort of feast the chef was preparing. He immediately regretted it as a scuffle broke out behind him for possession of his hard-won dining chair.

A whiff of kerosene and smoke drifted out of the galley and Danny watched as Weevil leaned over a battered oil drum and stoked the contents with a length of angle iron. Flames licked around the rim of the drum and Danny could feel the heat. A stack of newspapers lay on the stainless steel work surface. Another steward stood by with a couple of extinguishers and a fire blanket.

There was a hiss and a loud crack as some damp kindling caught light and spat sparks up to the ceiling. Another cheer broke out.

Add some treacle toffee and parkin and it would be just like bonfire night. It was amazing how a little warmth and the prospect of charred food could lift the spirits.

Weevil lowered a canister of what looked like cold vomit, but was probably vegetable soup, into the fire, then placed a grill on the top ready to receive the sausages.

'Got to eat it all up,' Weevil said. 'Freezers are off. Even in a Scottish winter, everything will be thawed out and spoiled within a few days.'

'I was thinking of moving into your freezer,' Tommy said, pushing his way to the front of the sausage queue. 'Got to be warmer than my bleeding cabin.'

The rest of the crew lined up in a remarkably orderly fashion. Danny picked up his allotted rations: a cup of soup, two charred sausages and a stale bap, and perched on his first-aid box. It was the best meal he'd had in ages. He hadn't realised quite how hungry he was.

He felt briefly sorry for the techs who were presumably still huddling around their inferior brazier and missing out on this feast, though he wouldn't have put it past Callum to catch a couple of guillemots and barbeque them. Danny even considered saving a sausage for Gemma, but he thought the gesture was too open to misinterpretation. It was better to eat it while it was hot, anyway. He might try to sneak her some soup later.

Danny did not want the aroma of the barbeque and the memory of soup cloud his judgement, but he was inclined to cross James "Weevil" Weaver off his list of suspects. The Pied Piper had spent the last few days trying to make the crew's life a misery. Why would he suddenly turn around and give them sausages and heart-warming soup?

As their stomachs filled with warm food, even the most belligerent crew members found their mood lifting.

'Well done, lad,' Cocky said, unexpectedly patting Danny on the back.

'What did I do?'

'Locked up that pervert Haver. He's the Pied Piper right?'

'Yes, well maybe, I hope so.'

'Course he is. Stands to reason.'

'What makes you so sure?'

'He's a fucking weirdo, for one thing. I heard he was keeping a lock of everybody's hair, them as has any anyway. Probably planning some crazy voodoo shit.'

'I'm not sure that's quite true.'

'And he's a miserable fucker. Hates everyone. Nothing he'd like better than to toss the lot of us overboard into the North Sea.'

Just because Haver hated everyone, didn't mean he'd planned to murder them all.

There was still something bothering Danny.

He smiled nicely at Ailsa, but she wouldn't give him another cup of soup.

'Jamie says it's one each and no exceptions.'

'But it's for a patient.'

'And who's that then?'

Danny lowered his voice. 'It's Gemma.'

Ailsa's dull eyes lit up and she glanced around before hurriedly pouring him a big mugful of hot soup.

'So she's alright, is she? In yon sickbay, is she?'

'She's fine. I can't tell you where she is though. I promised.'

'Aye well, that's probably best. Tell her to look after hersel', eh?'

Danny promised and strode out of the accommodation, mug in hand, before anyone could ask awkward questions.

Fortunately, Gemma was waiting for him in the TLQ, but she wasn't at all pleased to see him. 'I told you not to come here. Use the radio, I said.'

'I brought soup.'

'Aye, I suppose that's okay then. You made sure no one was following you?'

'There was no one around. They're all huddled in the mess or the tech station. It's like the Marie Celeste.'

As soon as he mentioned the mysterious, abandoned ship, he regretted it. He pictured the derelict vessel out at sea, with all hands lost. It was too close to their current predicament for comfort.

Chapter
Thirty-Seven

'SO HOW'RE YOUR ENQUIRIES coming along, Officer Dribble?' Gemma's voice exuded sarcasm. 'Arrests imminent? Or is our resident sleuth still baffled?'

'Mostly baffled. I don't have enough to go on. If this were a proper investigation, we'd have interviewed everyone on the platform, plus their families and everyone who knew them. We'd have post-mortems on the victims and forensics would have been all over the place. And what have I got? A pile of handwritten notes, a few photos and Ewan Haver's keepsake collection.'

'I'd love to help, but I'm not cutting up dead bodies even for you.'

'Not sure I'd know what to look for if you did. I've watched a few post-mortems, but I spent most of the time trying not to throw up.'

'Soft as shite. I knew it.'

'Let's face it. I suck at being a detective. Even with my resources back then, I'd struggle to figure this out. Without it, I'm next to useless. I've got electronic copies of the HR records, but I didn't even think to print them out before the power went down. At least that might have given me some information. Now there's probably just enough battery power in Blair's laptop to find out if anyone else apart from Haver had a criminal record.'

'Don't bother yourself about the HR files. If you're wanting to dig the dirt on the crew, I know a better place to start.'

'Oh yeah? You got a little black book?'

'No. But Snakey did. More than just a book. He had files and files of information on every guy who'd ever worked for or with him. He said you couldn't get a machine to run smoothly if you didn't know what levers to pull.'

'That sounds as creepy as Haver's little collection. Did the rest of the crew know he was keeping files on them?'

'Some of them. Those he trusted. He used to brag about it. "Keep the troublemakers on their toes," he'd say. I don't know how much he really knew, but nor did they.'

'So could he have been blackmailing someone?'

'I doubt it. Unless you call spooking people into doing what you want blackmail.'

'Strictly speaking, yes. However, it would be hard to prove if he made no money from it. At the very least, it's bullying.'

'Oh, he was a bully, alright. I guarantee he was the school bully before he graduated to work bully. I never said he was a nice guy, but he got away with it because he was a good OIM. He kept the oil flowing and nobody complained about him, as far as I know.'

'But if they did...'

'Then he'd find something to use against them.'

'I think I'd better look at his files.'

'They're in his office. In a filing cabinet, just like the old days. You'll know which one when you see it.'

'How come?'

'It's barred and bolted and it has a padlock on it that must have come off the gates of Hell.'

'I'd better borrow some tools; don't want to involve light-fingered Owen.'

'Aye, don't go telling anyone what you're up to. There's plenty of folk would like to know what's in those files. I don't think you'll get to keep hold of them for long if they find out.'

Danny took heed of Gemma's warning. The only way to get the job done safely was to steal what he needed. Easier said than done. The tech station and the workshop were now fortresses, occupied twenty-four hours a day. But they weren't the only ones who had heavy-duty cutting implements.

The drillers were a bit more lackadaisical with their tools. There were bags and boxes full of all sorts of gear scattered around the derrick and the mud lockers. It looked like the entire drill team had downed tools and planned never to return. Danny took no chances and darted from pipe to post, glancing about him as he went. Apart from a distant deckhand standing with his back to him, he saw no one.

The third toolbox had what he needed: a pair of industrial-strength bolt-croppers and a hacksaw. He found an oily old hessian sack to stash them in and made his way back to the accommodation. There was a gents' toilet two doors down from the OIM's office and he hid a while in there, waiting for the coast to clear.

Eventually, the sound of clomping feet died away, and he felt brave enough to poke his nose out of the toilet door. The only people in sight were a couple of stewards, and they were preoccupied with preparing a cold meal for the crew from the remains of the barbeque.

Danny scurried along the corridor and opened the office door. Since Snakey's death, it seemed no one was brave enough to take over his desk, not even his successor, Blair Scorgie. Maybe they thought Snakey's ghost might return to his old seat of power. In the half-light, it wasn't hard to imagine that he was still haunting the place.

Gemma was right. The filing cabinet was unmistakable, and Danny's heart sank. The padlock looked way too thick for the bolt-croppers. He could probably get through the locking bar with the big hacksaw, but that would make a lot of noise. Surely, that would attract attention.

There was nothing for it. He *had* to try. By pulling a chair over to the cabinet and lying on his back across the seat, Danny found he could attack the metal bar from underneath at its narrowest point. Cutting into the metal made an unpleasant screech, but it wasn't as loud as he feared. Though the bar was pretty thick, it was soft aluminium rather than steel.

It took him about five minutes of intensive sawing. The section of bar he'd cut loose was still jammed through the handles of all three cabinet drawers, so he tipped tip the cabinet over and pull the bar out from underneath.

Danny hadn't reckoned on how heavy three drawers' worth of paper might be. When the cabinet was about halfway over, the weight became too much. He leaped out of the way just as the whole thing came crashing down onto the rubberised floor.

So much for his new career as a cat burglar.

He waited for the inevitable hue and cry, but none came. The cabinet had fallen drawers-side up and with the judicious use of his boot and a large screwdriver, he prised them open. He considered smuggling the contents away to examine them later, but this was as good a place to study Snakey's hoard as anywhere.

The first records were disappointing. They included the shocking revelation that one scaffolder had lost a testicle when his Rottweiler had turned on him, and that a former chef had been caught adding bodily fluids to the chicken soup. Hardly blackmail material.

According to Snarkey, four members of the current crew had criminal records: Mickey Walters, Ewan Haver, Owen Shives, and Trevor Sinnott. He knew about Mickey sabotaging TV satellite dishes and Haver's GBH charges. Given his lock-picking skills, it was no surprise that Owen had been arrested for stealing cars in his youth. Trev, it seemed, once got into a shoving match with the police on a picket line in the early eighties and spent a night in the cells. Only Haver had done time in prison. Nothing suggested any of them were still engaged in criminal activity.

Chapter
Thirty-Eight

THERE WAS A SHARP tap on the door. Danny nearly spun right out of Snakey's fake leather swivel chair. He glanced around, expecting Blair or Cameron, or maybe even the ghost of Snakey. It was only Stevie. He relaxed.

'What on earth are you up to, Danny?' Stevie asked.

'If you're on a secret mission, I think you failed. I heard that crash back in the TV lounge.'

'Anyone else notice?'

'A few, but I told them Vlad was working on the heating system. He never does anything quietly.'

'So you knew it was me?'

'Lucky guess. I brought this in case it was our Pied Piper,' Stevie said, waving a two foot long adjustable wrench in Danny's direction. 'If you don't tell me what you're up to, I might be tempted to use it.'

'Steady on, mate. That was Snakey's locked filing cabinet going for a burton. It was the only way I could get it open. I know he kept files on everyone. Maybe they hold a clue who the Pied Piper might be.'

'I'm not sure I like that idea. I mean, Snakey had a nasty little mind. He probably wrote all sorts of stuff about people that wasn't true. I'd throw the lot in the sea if I were you.'

'Sorry, but I've got to go through it all first. If I find information that's not relevant to the investigation, I promise I'll keep it to myself.'

Stevie didn't look convinced.

'I've got your file here if you're interested,' Danny said, and slid it across the desk towards him.

Reluctantly, Stevie picked up the slim folder and flicked through it. When he reached the last page, his shoulders visibly relaxed.

'He was like an elephant, was Snakey. Always poking his big nose into everything. And he never forgot an insult or someone who disagreed with him. All I did was suggest he came down to the tech station once in a while to see the guys who knew what was going on. He'd rather stay in his office and listen to his arse-kissing cronies. See here, it says I was "insubordinate" and "undermining his authority".'

He showed Danny the page.

'I'm not surprised if you called his mates "arse kissers",' Danny chuckled.

'Well, they are. Maybe I should have been more diplomatic, but at least this shows that he was listening for once.'

Danny worked his way through the last files, but there was nothing remotely helpful in any of them. Of course, he'd only gone through the first drawer, which seemed to hold information on the A shift crew. The second drawer had the files on the B shift who were all currently ashore, the lucky beggars. The third was dedicated to occasional crew, contractors like him, and a dusty pile of old folders marked "archive".

If he was pretending to be a private investigator, he ought to do this properly and go through the lot with a fine tooth comb. He sighed and grabbed a handful of files on crewmembers who were probably sitting in some pub enjoying their two weeks off.

'Don't suppose you fancy reading some of these, Stevie?'

'I suppose I could take a gander at these archived ones. No harm in that, eh? Poor sods are probably all dead by now. Not that dying would stop Snakey holding a grudge against them, believe me.'

The files for the off-duty crew seemed to be no more interesting than the previous bunch until Danny came across a printout of an email dated a day before he came on the platform. It was from the International Oil offices on the beach. The message itself was only a few bland platitudes from Jack

Blake's boss, but the interesting bit was the extract he'd forwarded from Aberdeen Police:

> THE CASUALTY WAS LATER IDENTIFIED AS KEN MUNDIE, AN EMPLOYEE OF INTERNATIONAL OIL, STAYING AT THE CLAYMORE HOTEL IN ABERDEEN PRIOR TO MOBILISING FOR THE CUILLIN ALPHA PLATFORM. A PASSERBY SAW ANOTHER MAN PUSH HIM INTO THE HARBOUR FROM ALBERT QUAY AT AROUND 01:30. THE MAN, DESCRIBED AS MEDIUM BUILD AND WEARING A DARK, HOODED JACKET, HAS YET TO BE IDENTIFIED. POLICE WERE CALLED AND, WITH THE ASSISTANCE OF PERSONNEL FROM THE HARBOUR AUTHORITY, RETRIEVED THE CASUALTY FROM THE WATER. HE WAS UNCONSCIOUS AND HAD SUFFERED A BROKEN JAW. HE WAS TAKEN TO A&E AT THE ABERDEEN ROYAL INFIRMARY WHERE HE IS IN A CRITICAL BUT STABLE CONDITION. OFFICERS FROM ABERDEEN POLICE ARE WAITING TO INTERVIEW HIM, IF HE RECOVERS SUFFICIENTLY TO GIVE A STATEMENT.

Danny's heart sank. All his assumptions were based on the idea that Scott was the first victim. This story meant it hadn't started with Scott but with a mugging or a fight down in Aberdeen docks several days earlier.

There were only a couple of dodgy pubs and a kebab shop at the docks; not much to tempt anyone. The report didn't hint at what Ken was doing when he was attacked. According to Callum, Ken was a heavy drinker, but alcohol was strictly prohibited on the night before a mobilisation. Maybe he was looking for a place to drown his sorrows. And then what? Had some fisherman beaten him up? Wouldn't it have been far more likely that Ken had met a colleague from the Alpha? Had an argument, probably fuelled by drink, and blows had been exchanged? Ken was near to retirement and he had come off worse. Perhaps his attacker hadn't meant to hurt him; maybe he lost his temper and struck out harder than intended.

Whatever the cause, the result was the same. One man escaped drowning, and the other was facing a GBH charge at the very least.

Stevie returned and leaned over Danny's shoulder.

'What are you looking at? I don't see why you're bothering about the guys who aren't even on board.'

Danny showed him the police report.

'Oh. I see. Poor old Ken. He's bloody useless, to be honest, but that's no reason to throw him in the sea. He's got kids and grandkids by the dozen. His family must be worried sick. Do you think our Pied Piper attacked him?'

'I do. Though maybe he wasn't the Pied Piper then. Maybe this is what started him on that road.'

'That's a lot of maybes. But it doesn't get you any closer to finding out who he is.'

'Oh, I think it does. This happened the night before Ken was due to mobilise last Tuesday. Our Pied Piper would have to be someone who lived in Aberdeen or someone who was also mobilising on Tuesday or Wednesday. Most likely he was on the flight that Ken missed.'

'You realise that includes me?' Stevie said. 'I saw Ken that night. We were stopping in the same hotel. The Claymore, round the back of the airport. I didn't kill him, in case you're wondering.'

'I didn't think you did. But you can help me make a list of who was on that flight. They were all new faces to me and I might have forgotten a few names.'

'Of course. Tuesday is the regular crew-change day. I could tell you who sat where and what newspaper they were reading. Always the same. They're institutionalised, the lot of them. If you're sure the Pied Piper was on that flight, your list of suspects just got a whole lot shorter.'

Chapter Thirty-Nine

STEVIE WAS AS GOOD as his word and produced a list with nineteen names, including his own. Danny was grateful, but didn't reveal they weren't his only suspects. As well as the passengers, there were still a fair number who might have had reason to be in Aberdeen that night.

He found a clipboard and attached a copy of the muster lists. He added a couple of extra hand-drawn columns so he could tick off who was on board when Ken Mundie was assaulted, and who was ashore.

Now he had the thankless task of asking each of the crew where they were on the fateful day. He tried to catch them in crowded areas, because they would be less likely to lie in front of colleagues. And less likely to punch him, for that matter. The first person he approached was Archie Grier.

'Go fuck yersel,' was his response.

Danny added another column to his spreadsheet. By the end of his survey, he had another nine ticks under the "go fuck yersel" heading. He assigned four to their proper column by cross-referencing information from their colleagues. The rest he added to his shit list of suspects.

Then he added the nineteen on the chopper and another eight who were onshore and could easily have been in Aberdeen. A long list, but most of them would have had little or no contact with Ken on or off the platform, and even less motive.

He needed someone to check his findings, so he got on the radio and called Gemma. It took a few attempts, but he made contact and agreed to meet her on the helideck. He had a fistful of paperwork and would have preferred somewhere less windy, but nursey refused to let him come down to the TLQ.

Standing bare-headed on the deck, she looked even more like one of those deities on a ship's figurehead. Danny made the mistake of mentioning this to her.

'I havna washed my hair for a week. Thank you very much. I reckon I look more like Medusa. Good thing there are no mirrors in the TLQ,'

'Why? Did they only put vampires in here?'

'Nightshift. Same thing really.'

He handed over his lists, and she sat down cross-legged on the netting to read.

'I see you put me down for "go fuck yersel". Inspired guesswork there, pal. Well, I've got no alibi, but it wasn't me and that's the truth.'

'I never suspected you. Didn't even need to ask.'

'More fool you. No wonder you were a complete failure in the police. But thanks for the vote of confidence.'

She tutted her way through the other crew members he'd crossed off the list. There were a few she queried, but in the end, she agreed with his deductions.

'I'd still have Snakey on my shit list.'

'He's dead, Gem.'

'Aye but I doubt that'd stop him if the bastard wanted to kill us all.'

Gemma wanted to lock up all their remaining suspects, the "dirty thirty" as she called them. Considering the list included several guys who were likely to put up a significant struggle, that was not feasible.

'If any of them bawbags complain, they must be guilty, eh?'

'I got locked up and I wasn't.'

'So you say, Danny. So you say.'

In the end, he shoved a piece of paper and a pen in Gemma's hand and told her to write a list of her prime suspects. He grabbed another sheet and did the same. Gemma was still sucking on her pen by the time he'd finished.

'Come on, Gem. I'm freezing my nuts off up here. What's your problem?'

She glanced up, then with the expression of a woman sucking on a lemon, with no gin or tonic in sight, she scribbled down two more names and handed her list over to Danny.

'It's no good. There are friends on that list. Or people I don't hate after being stuck with in the middle of the North Sea for weeks on end, which is kind of the same thing. But you never know, do you?'

Danny plucked the lists from under the netting and stuffed them in his bag. When he looked up, she'd gone. He staggered to his feet and braced himself against the storm. The wind was still strong enough to make walking difficult, but no longer sufficient to knock him from his feet. He turned round and made his way back to heli admin to check the weather and thaw out.

There was no one around. The spirit of Gemma Gauld haunted heli admin, even though she was still very much alive. The superstitious crew stayed away, just in case. Besides, the one tiny window was so encrusted with salt, all you could see was your haggard reflection. All the instruments on the wall behind Gemma's desk were dead, as was her multi-screened workstation. The only thing that was working was the weather station, hidden from view behind the remains of the radio console.

Danny clambered through the glass hatch. The display only showed the current conditions. He tried to find a trend of the wind over the last few days, but despite pushing all the buttons in various orders, all he achieved was to change the temperature reading from Celsius to Fahrenheit. It didn't matter. The significant figures had become engrained in Danny's mind. During the height of the storm, the wind speed never fell below sixty knots and some gusts were nearer eighty. The readout still showed sixty-eight, and the gusts were lessening. Gemma told him the maximum speed had to drop below seventy knots for a helicopter to come out.

That was under normal circumstances. Danny had a feeling the search and rescue chopper might brave stronger winds to get some help on board, or to airlift casualties. He wondered if there was some way to tell them to leave the medics behind and bring a tactical firearms squad, or the SBS instead.

He checked the sea state. That was more of a problem. The waves were peaking close to seven metres. No boat would set out in those conditions. Would anyone risk flying a chopper when there was no means of rescue? Supposing it ditched in the North Sea?

Maybe he needs to paint a big red X across the helideck to tell them not to bother landing. Until he recovered the shotgun, at least. He wanted no lives on his conscience, didn't know what damage it might do to a helicopter.

He looked back at the wind reading. Seventy-one. Perhaps help would be on the way soon. If he stared harder, maybe it would stay below the magic figure. Seventy-three. The gravity of his situation reasserted itself. He sighed and rubbed his face with his hands.

Whatever the Pied Piper had in mind for the endgame, they were not there yet. Things had been quiet for a while. He could have fallen victim to his last act of sabotage, or taken his own life, but Danny doubted that. This was not the end, but as the storm died, perhaps they were approaching the final act.

Danny felt overwhelmingly tired. His head was heavy, and it was hard to think straight anymore. There was an unpleasant stench filling the room; it smelled like rotten eggs.

Then the siren sounded. A continuous insistent tone that drilled into Danny's ears and jolted him out of his daze. Rotten eggs and alarms. That could mean only one thing: H2S. Deadly hydrogen-sulphide gas. A fatal dose would burn away your sense of smell. If he could still smell it, he had a chance.

The siren was screaming at him to get out. Danny staggered to his feet, his eyes filled with swirling black specks. He teetered for a few seconds before his legs gave way and he toppled backwards. He lay crumpled on the floor, gasping for air.

Chapter Forty

DANNY FELT NAUSEOUS AND his head was throbbing. Strong hands hauled him up and threw him on the deck. He imagined he must be riding out the storm in a lifeboat, but why he was at sea was a mystery. Maybe the crew had decided to give him a Viking funeral? There was no smell of burning wood and tar, just those rotten eggs.

Now he was being dragged, feet first, across an uneven deck. He kept his eyes tight shut for fear of what he might see, but when his head bounced over a sharp metal lintel, the shock forced his eyelids open.

His abductor was wearing a black latex mask, with a pig-like snout and eyes made huge by the sepia-tinted lens. The fiend was shouting, but the words sounded distant and distorted. Something about him being too heavy. He felt heavy. Couldn't even lift his head to see what new torment was in store, or reach out an arm to prevent himself from being dragged over yet another obstacle.

The masked figure grabbed him under his arms and lifted his shoulders off the deck. The devil dragged him out into grey North Sea daylight and laid him down on the cold deck. It wheezed loudly through its black snout, and, with a struggle, removed its hood. It was Mickey. He took a few deep breaths, replaced the hood and set off.

Cold drizzle settled on Danny's face. His head was sore and his back felt bruised and battered. He wondered why no one had thought to fetch the medic. Then reality dawned.

The next best thing, Gemma, arrived carrying a first aid kit and a bottle of water. Danny took a swig and was promptly sick over her boots.

'Thanks, pal. That's what you get for caring. I should know better.'

He tried to apologise, but she clamped an oxygen mask over his mouth before he could speak.

'Hydrogen sulphide poisoning. There'll probably be irreparable brain damage, but I doubt anyone will notice.'

'Was anyone else hurt?' he tried to shout through the mask. Gemma cocked her head and seemed to get the gist.

'Aye. Bastard flooded most of the accommodation with the stuff. At least the alarm worked. Most of us made it out in time. Stevie and the lads pulled out them that didn't make it under their own steam. You got lucky. Your guardian angel found you in the nick of time.'

'Mickey?'

'Aye, he was outside when the gas alarms went off. He grabbed the breathing gear and started pulling the guys out to safety.'

'I guess that puts him in the clear. Not that we ever thought he was the Pied Piper, did we?'

'I didna, but then I'm no detective. I hope you've got at least one suspect left.'

'Yeah. Just the one.'

'Well, you'd better hurry if you're going to arrest him. Your ride home is on its way.'

The confusion on Danny's face must have been evident, even through the mask.

'Didn't you hear it? There's a helicopter around somewhere. It flew past twice and then disappeared. It's bound to try to land here soon enough. And then the fun starts.'

'What do you mean?' Danny asked, plucking off his oxygen mask in frustration.

'The ship showed up just before the H2S did. I doubt that was a coincidence. The Pied Piper's not stupid. He won't wait around to see us rescued. He's got more mischief planned for the Alpha. You can be sure of that.'

Danny broke into a fit of coughing, so nurse Gemma patted him on the back. To be honest, it was more a thump than a pat and the heel of her hand landed smack on one of his most livid bruises. She clamped the mask back over his mouth and helped him to his feet.

'Have to get you to the new sickbay. Your one is out of bounds, and it probably smells like a driller's cludgie. I got Tommy to fetch some of your supplies, but the laddie doesn't know his arse from an aspirin, so I wouldn't hold out much hope.'

The new sickbay turned out to be Gemma's private retreat, the TLQ. Now help was on the way, it seemed she was out of hiding for good. The TLQ was about the only place outside of the accommodation suitable for a sickbay. The thought of trying to treat the injured crew in the squalid environment of the tech station filled Danny with horror. He wasn't even keen on sitting in there. You tended to stick to the seats if you weren't careful.

By contrast, the TLQ was about as spotless as you could get offshore. He still wouldn't have fancied having an operation out here, but it was ideal for triage and first aid. Looking at Gemma's current crop of patients, he hoped assistance would be on its way very soon.

Even the slow walk leaning on Gemma's shoulder hurt his lungs. He had to take a couple of gulps of oxygen before he could talk without a rattling cough drowning his words. 'How many?'

'Dead?'

He nodded.

'Only one. Thank God. Ewan Havers. I guess we all had a hand in that. No way he could get out of the bond and no one went back to let him out. Mind, without the Pied Piper, he would have been safe enough in there.'

Danny felt sick to his stomach. It was worse than H2S nausea. That would wear off eventually, the guilt would not. He looked around the TLQ at the other victims. Some were sitting up, white-faced, gasping for breath.

If they could breathe on their own, they should be okay.

It was the guy lying down with an oxygen mask on that concerned him. Ailsa sat by his bedside. Danny recognised him as one of the deck crew, but he didn't know his name. She was holding his hand and whispering a prayer. Never a good sign.

First-aiders were tending to a couple more. Danny wanted to help, but Gemma pushed him back into the chair. 'I'll tell you when you're fit to work. I'll not have you puking over my patients, you hear me?'

Danny heard her loud and clear. But he *knew* the identity of the Pied Piper. He *had* to stop him before he killed anyone else.

Chapter Forty-One

AT FIRST, DANNY THOUGHT the ventilation fans had started again. But that would have required electrical power and everyone who could have made that happen was either standing on deck or lying in Gemma's sickbay. The low thrumming sound continued to increase in volume and he realised it was coming from further away.

With some difficulty and even more reluctance, he sat up on the bedside and eased himself up to standing. He had a colourful collection of bruises, strained some muscles he didn't even know existed, and a persistent cough from the hydrogen sulphide inhalation. By all rights, he should leave the others to sort out this mess, but he couldn't.

The endgame was approaching. Brushing away Gemma's protestations, he pulled off the mask and staggered outside to stare up at the grey threatening sky. In a gap between the swirling clouds he could just make out a distant speck, growing ever larger. It was a helicopter.

More members of the crew joined him. There was a weary but sincere outbreak of cheering and some even waved at the distant chopper. Danny didn't join in. This wasn't a time for celebration. There was no sign of his prime suspect. First, he needed to find the culprit and lock him up.

Gemma appeared at his shoulder. 'Tossers, the whole lot of them. They'd cheer anything, even an incoming cruise missile.'

'Keep your eyes peeled. I can't see the Pied Piper allowing the chopper to land without causing some kind of trouble. Could he have booby-trapped the helideck? Rigged up explosives or a tripwire?'

'I walked the deck just a few hours before the bastard pumped gas into the accommodation. But you might be on to something. Maybe the gas attack was a diversion.'

Danny was already staggering towards the nearest access stairwell before she'd finished speaking.

'Come back here. I've not discharged you yet. You can't go killing yourself. Just think of the paperwork.'

He didn't get far. A small group detached themselves from the crowd of helicopter-spotters and surrounded him. They included Stevie, Adam, Owen and Mickey.

'Now everyone knows I'm not the Pied Piper I want to help,' Mickey explained. 'Those oil tycoons would happily let us all die, you know. It would save them all that redundancy money.'

Danny had wondered if being persecuted might have cured Mickey's paranoia. Apparently not. Still, he'd be useful in a search.

Mickey was explaining his wacky theories to a more than usually attentive audience.

'...and the name Pied Piper must be because of Piper Alpha disaster. You know what I think about the people responsible. Some of those directors are still around, pulling the oil company strings. Not much has changed. I understand his frustration, but I wouldn't blow up a platform just to make the point.'

'Who said anything about blowing the platform up?' Danny asked. 'Surely he was just trying to disable it, to stop the oil flowing and lining the oil execs pockets.'

'Maybe, but the bastard doesn't care who he hurts in the process,' Gemma said, elbowing Mickey out of the way and claiming centre stage for herself. 'I don't think he wants to see any of us getting off here alive. Danny was just away to check the helideck before he stopped for a wee chat with you slackers.'

'There is no need,' Adam said. 'I have told the fire crew to sweep the area and prepare for our evacuation. There is no booby trap. The problem is elsewhere. Mickey has seen it.'

'There was a device. Like a cylinder with a lot of straps and wires. I thought it was a new sensor, but now I think maybe it was a bomb.'

'And how long ago was this, Mickey?' Gemma asked.

'A few hours ago. Then there was the gas leak. Everyone was too busy to listen to me. It was only a small bomb.'

'Jesus fuckin' Christ. And exactly where was this little bundle of death?'

'In the compressor void. It's gone now. But I know all the best hiding places. I can help you find it again.'

'It cannot be big enough to cause structural damage,' Adam said. 'Not by itself. I am thinking he tries to make a big fire. Maybe ignite some gas.'

'I thought the gas was all going up the flare,' Danny said. 'The process is shut down, right? Surely it's safe enough when it's burning away up at the top of the stack?'

'There is still much gas left in the storage vessels. We do not vent them unless it is absolutely necessary. It is safer to keep the gas sealed away. It would take a massive explosion to break open a pressure vessel.'

'You don't need a big bomb,' Stevie said. 'You only need three things for an explosion: gas, air, and a spark. We have plenty of each on the platform. If I were a terrorist, I could make a few explosions, no problem.'

Adam was frowning.

'You are correct. We must look for the weak places, not the strong ones.'

'Show me,' Danny said. 'Where would you go if you were a terrorist?'

Gemma handed him one of the last two surviving handheld radios and clipped the other to her already over-stressed belt.

'I'd go myself, but I've some poor wee sick folk to look after. The ones you've abandoned. Try not to get blown up, Danny boy. Call me if you find anything. I might not send help, but at least I'll know where to look for the bits.'

Adam marched across the sickbay, cracking his hard hat on the low door on the way out. Danny scurried after him, clutching the radio to his chest like a lucky charm. Mickey followed him, darting from place to place like a sniffer dog at a festival campsite.

They walked through steel caverns filled with the giant pipes bringing oil up from the seabed. Beyond them were rows of mud-splattered valves, the size of small houses. Eventually, they reached a series of cylindrical vessels with domed ends and a bewildering array of smaller pipes and gauges.

'Maybe here,' Adam said.

They searched among the vessels, the valves, and the rest of the natural gas-processing system. Adam had a piping diagram, but it meant nothing to Danny. It might as well have been an underground map for a city he'd never seen, written in a language he didn't understand.

They clambered over scaffolding and crawled under equipment. Everything was covered with crud and rust and looked dangerous. Most of it had been here a long time. Unless the Pied Piper had an invisibility cloak, there was nowhere he could have hidden his last bombshell. Eventually, they gave up and crouched on the floor, staring blankly at Adam's diagrams.

'We cannot walk all the lines. The beginning is on the cellar deck and the end is at the flare stack. That would take many days.'

'What about those weak points you said we should look for?'

'Instrument piping. Sensors. Gauges, maybe.' Adam pointed at a row of dials which were covered with oily fingerprints. Danny wiped one with the sleeve of his overall.

'It says 600 bar. That's seriously high pressure, isn't it?'

'It is normal for this kind of vessel.'

'And this tubing's pretty thin.'

'There is no flow, so you do not need big pipes.'

'But it would be easy to break.' Danny waggled it to check exactly how easy and then thought better of it.

'Yes, but we have not seen any damage.'

'I did see some shiny new tubing up the gantry there.'

Adam marched over to the access ladder and hauled his considerable weight up to where Danny was pointing.

'Nothing stays clean on Cuillin Alpha for long. I think this T-piece was installed in the last few days.'

Danny watched as he attempted to follow the route of the new tubing along the walkway and over older flanges and valves until it disappeared through the bulkhead into the adjacent module. He waited for Adam to lower himself back down to deck level. They worked their way round to a door sealed in place with a series of levers and a large handwheel. Danny was about to spin the wheel when Adam grabbed his hand.

'This room should be pressurised. We do not know what is inside. Let us look first and leap later.'

Mickey pulled out a long metal torch which he placed up against the reinforced glass porthole. Through a thin layer of grime, Danny could make out a few pieces of derelict equipment. They included the bottom half of a turbine casing, looking like in inverted metallic sea urchin. Fastened to the side was a new piece of equipment that made Danny's stomach clench.

Straps and wires. A small bomb.

Danny called Gemma on the radio to tell her the bad news. All he got in return was a stream of compound swearing and then the radio crackled into silence. The battery symbol on the display went blank. The radio had waited for the most inappropriate moment to squawk its last.

Judging by Gemma's reaction, she must have got the message. He was sure she'd understand the implications. He was less sure what she was going to do about it. Then he heard the eerie howling of the PAPA siren.

'Prepare to Abandon Platform Alarm,' Adam said, in case Danny hadn't been paying attention during the mind-numbing online safety course. 'We must go.'

'We've got sick and injured crew. It won't be easy to get them into the lifeboats. Couldn't we let the gas out, or maybe disarm the bomb?'

'That is a dangerous idea. Either way, you must open the door and there will be much methane. We need gas masks and bomb experts.'

'How about these guys?'

The crew walking towards them didn't exactly look like a bomb disposal team, but they were wearing fireproof suits, helmets, breathing apparatus, and a variety of cutting implements.

'Fire team reporting for duty,' Stevie said, raising his mask to peer through the door. 'Gem said you'd ignore the alarm. She's given us ten minutes to see what we can do before everyone takes to the boats.'

The siren fell silent. Only for a short while, but it was still a relief to Danny's jangled nerves.

'I don't suppose you can tell if the device is on a timer or it's remotely operated?' he asked.

'Only by going in,' Stevie said.

'Might the door be booby-trapped?'

'Unlikely. I can't see any wires. It sounds like too much trouble for our Pied Piper. Most likely it's a spark plug rigged up to a simple timer. Only one way to find out.'

He handed out oxygen masks to Danny and Adam. He and another masked man started releasing the airlock door catches. There was an audible hiss and beads of condensation formed on the window. As the last catch was released, the door swung open and Stevie headed in. Danny resisted the urge to follow. There was only one guy here who knew what he was doing and it wasn't him.

Stevie carefully cut his way through the thick tie-wraps holding the device to the turbine and waved for his colleague to support the device. The last tie-wrap pinged loose. He lifted the bomb and carried it out into the fresh air. It was a real Heath Robinson affair, lashed together from spare parts and salvaged wiring. Danny could see why Stevie had been so confident it wasn't fitted with sophisticated booby traps.

'Now, let's see about disarming this nasty little piece of shit.'

Stevie waved his gas detector around to check there was no risk of explosion. Then he picked up a fire axe and began swearing and smashing the bomb into a thousand tiny pieces.

Chapter Forty-Two

THERE WERE A COUPLE of worn but comfortable chairs in the TLQ. All Danny wanted was to sit down, close his eyes, and take a long nap. Instead, he stumbled out onto the walkway in search of a vantage point. The helideck seemed the best place to start.

He tried to ignore that fact that Gemma's voice wasn't getting any fainter as he climbed the stairs. Either she'd got hold of a megaphone, or she was following him. At the top, he rested his arm on the cold, abrasive surface of the deck. He breathed in great lungfuls of damp air, coughing it back out again like a chain-smoker.

There was no one visible from deck level, so he dragged himself up the last few steps, into the teeth of the dying storm, eyes peeled for the Pied Piper. He staggered out onto the helideck, keeping to the holes in the safety netting, feeling drunk and disorientated. He stopped in the centre of the octagonal deck and surveyed the scene below. There were no signs of life, but out of the corner of his eye, he saw something move. He lifted his head and looked back at the rusting towers of the Cuillin Alpha. High on the flare stack, a figure was climbing the precarious, near-vertical ladder with what looked like a length of tubing held in one hand.

'At least we know what happened to the shotgun,' Gemma yelled, hanging onto a fire hose reel by the edge of the deck.

Danny hauled himself to his feet and stumbled towards her. 'He's going to bring down the chopper as it lands.'

'I should have brought the binoculars. I can't tell who it is from here.'

'I know,' Danny said. 'I think I have for a while. Just didn't want to believe it.'

'Aye, I see what you mean. He's got the build for climbing, sure enough. Unlike me. You'll have to get up there and try to slow him down. Send a monkey to catch a monkey, that's what I say.'

Danny nodded and bounded back down the steps, two at a time until he reached the main deck. A maze of shipping crates and abandoned equipment lay between him and the flare stack. He ran as best he could, swerving between containers and hurdling the obstacles in his path.

The bottom of the ladder had been made inaccessible. The first few rungs were hidden behind a padlocked barrier, with a sign stating: "No Unauthorised Personnel". Danny knew his quarry had got up there, so he fumbled around the steelwork until he found a handhold and hauled himself up and over the barrier. After a lot of flailing about, he got one foot on a wet and greasy rung of the ladder and started to climb.

He looked up and could see the ladder was split into three sections and enclosed with metal hoops. That might stop him from falling more than twenty metres at a time. *Not much comfort*, he thought grimly. As he reached the top of the first section, he was forced to stop and catch his rattling breath.

There was a walkway across to the next ladder about the width of his boot. He tight-roped his way along, clinging to the stack for dear life. The wind tugged insistently at his overalls, encouraging him to give up the struggle and let gravity do its job. Eventually, he reached the foot of the ladder and began the next stage of his ascent.

The stack was inclined at a gentle angle to direct the flame away from the rest of the superstructure. The further he climbed, the more he was suspended over the open sea. Should he fall now, it made little difference if he struck the water or the steel deck. Something about the movement of the waves made his vertigo all the more debilitating.

The figure above had stopped climbing and was staring down at him. The shotgun was hanging loosely by his side, with the barrel pointing down. It wasn't aimed at his head. Not yet anyway. There was nothing to do but keep climbing. A shotgun blast at this distance might not be fatal, but it would make clinging onto the ladder nearly impossible.

He reached the top of the second ladder without incident and started edging along the interconnecting walkway towards the final ascent. He was looking straight into the barrel of the gun now. Maybe it would be tricky to aim with one hand on the ladder, but Danny didn't want to find out. The man leaned forward and called down to him.

'Stay down there,' Callum said. 'Be sensible, fella. I don't want to use this on you.'

Chapter
Forty-Three

'ARE YOU GOING TO shoot me?'

'Not if I can help it, Danny. Sorry it had to come to this. I thought I could keep you and Gem out of it, but you *will* keep getting yourselves in the crossfire. How about you step aside this once and give me a clear shot?'

'And who are you going to shoot instead of me?'

'You know what I'm about. Sure you do. There'll be no rescue today. They didn't ask the Pied Piper's permission, did they? It's trespassing. I'm just protecting my property.'

'Your property. I think International Oil might have something to say about that.'

'They're not here. And all their useless fecking managers have abandoned their posts. I'm declaring myself King of the Cuillin Alpha. What I say goes.'

'Righto,' Danny said, stalling for time. 'But no one else has to die, right?'

'Hey! I never meant for anyone to die. You can blame those greedy oilmen for that. They were going to lay me off. They don't realise how much I do to keep this rust heap running. Without me to grease the wheels, the entire platform would grind to a halt. I just wanted to show them what they'd be missing. But some people just have to get in the way. Unintended consequences, that's all it was.'

'I believe you, Cal. I figured murder wasn't in the plan. I suppose it started going wrong back in Aberdeen. When you met Ken Mundie. That right?'

'The old fool should have retired years ago. Onshore, he was a drunk, and offshore, he was a liability. I went looking for him in those dives, down by the docks. There he was outside the Steam Packet, having a crafty smoke, so I gave it to him straight. "Pension yourself off," I says, "or I'll get the heliport lads to breathalyse you." The fecker tried to land one on me, so I had to fight back. I caught him smack on the chin. Over he went and into the water. I never meant for him to drown. It was just an accident.'

'But he didn't drown. Someone fished him out. He's in the hospital. Last I heard, the police were waiting to interview him.'

Callum looked stunned.

'Well, how was I supposed to know? The old soak fell right off the harbour wall into ice-cold water. His heart should have stopped there and then. Fecking unbelieveable. I suppose the whisky deadened the shock. Doesn't change anything.'

He was gesturing with his gun hand, and Danny took the opportunity to climb a few more rungs. Callum stopped speaking, and the barrel snapped back towards Danny's head. There was nothing to be gained by staring down the barrel, so he glanced back over his shoulder. The chopper should have landed by now. He could hear the rotor, but it was nowhere to be seen. Two more rungs and he might grab the gun. He just had to keep Callum distracted as long as he could.

'I imagine that if you'd known Ken was alive, you'd have stuck to your plan, and then maybe Scott would still be alive.'

'Maybe. But I didn't kill Scotty. The storm did that.'

'It was all about the sabotage. That was the plan, wasn't it? Stop the oil flowing, hit them where it hurts. Stop Snakey and his bosses getting their bonus. It would certainly have got him the sack if he hadn't died.'

'Yeah, well, let's just say I helped put him out of everyone's misery. Now there's one fella I won't be shedding any tears for. Nor that creep, Havers. Good riddance to both.'

One more rung. It might just be enough. The chopper was on the move again. Getting closer. Coming in for a landing.

'If you give yourself up, I'll explain it to them. Tell them it was all bad luck and accidents. It doesn't have to end badly for you.'

'We're way past the point of no return, Danny. I'm afraid it'll be a bad end for us all. You know they won't see reason. It's all about oil. Money comes first. People don't matter. They won't be getting any oil from here for a long while if I have anything to do with.'

Another rung.

Danny considered telling Callum they'd disarmed his bomb. Maybe it would weaken his resolve. Then they both spotted the chopper swooping towards the helideck.

Callum lifted the shotgun and aimed it at the goldfish-bowl cockpit.

Danny crouched and leaped for the gun. He had his hands around the barrel, only one foot on the ladder. If Callum let go of the weapon, both it and Danny would go tumbling down the stack. He didn't fancy his chances of surviving the fall.

At least the gun barrel was no longer pointing towards the helideck, but the business end was alarmingly close to his left ear. Danny shifted his weight, took one hand off the gun, and grabbed Callum by the throat. He hadn't ruled out the possibility of him letting go of the ladder, but he hoped his instinct for self-preservation would hold. Surely the King of the Cuillin Alpha wasn't about to abdicate yet.

As Danny pressed his thumb into his Adam's apple, Callum winced and kicked out. His boot connected with Danny's solar plexus, but there was little force behind it, and he held on. With a hop, skip and jump, Danny had two feet on the ladder and he was nearly level with his adversary.

Neither man could strike out hard without losing their grip on the ladder. What followed was more like a school playground wrestling match, taking place on a flaming tower suspended over an angry sea.

Danny's military training hadn't included this scenario, but he knew a few techniques for hurting people at close range. He tried kneeing Callum in the groin but ended up catching the butt of the shotgun instead and bit back a yelp of pain. Incensed, he let go of Callum's throat and, stiffening his fingers, jabbed away at his face until he connected with somewhere soft and painful.

Callum howled, let go of the shotgun and clutched at his left eye.

Danny, who was using his climbing hand as an offensive weapon, toppled backwards, still holding the gun. His shoulder crashed into the safety cage and his left foot slipped off the rung. He was left in a precarious position, wedged with one leg sticking through the ladder and the other folded into his chest. He tried to throw the gun away, but it, too, was wedged between the ironwork.

Callum took the opportunity to slip through the safety cage and clamber down the outside. He grabbed the shotgun and pulled it away from Danny. For a moment, the gun was right in Danny's face, but Callum steadied the butt against his shoulder and swayed it around until he was aiming it once again towards the helideck.

It was a one-handed, one-eyed shot. The helicopter was coming in fast, but he didn't need pinpoint accuracy. There was a loud retort and then another. The chopper kept coming. At first, Danny thought he had missed, but something was wrong. The flight path was no longer straight and the pilot was fighting for control.

As they reached the helideck, the nose came up a few degrees, and the fuselage rotated. With one last throw of the dice, the pilot slammed the chopper down onto the deck with enough force to buckle the landing gear. That slowed the rotation, but the helicopter was now sliding towards the edge of the helideck. Danny heard the engine tone change from a high-pitched whine to a low moan. The rotors slowed and finally stopped with the chopper less than a metre from a long drop to oblivion.

He realised he had been holding his breath and let out an audible sigh. He looked around for Callum and saw him climb back up the outside of the ladder's safety cage with the shotgun still in his hand. *With luck, the shotgun was the type that only held two cartridges*, he thought.

The pilots and a couple of crew were climbing out of the far side of the helicopter. They seemed understandably reluctant to leave the shelter of the fuselage. There was little chance that the chopper could take off. That meant that the helideck was out of action and they were stuck until a boat arrived.

There was no sign of cavalry coming. Gemma, despite her infamous powers of persuasion, had yet to find anyone crazy enough to climb up and help Danny tackle an armed and psychotic saboteur.

He was on his own. First, he had to untangle himself from the ladder without plunging to a watery death. His right foot had gone to sleep, and he was finding it increasingly hard to get a firm grip on the oily, wet rungs. Eventually, he twisted himself into a stable position with all four limbs on the ladder and his buttocks resting on the cold iron safety cage.

After a deep breath, he hauled himself up and started to climb. Until Callum gave up the gun, he wanted to keep him in his line of sight.

Things were warming up as they approached the billowing flare. He hoped Callum planned to stop before it got dangerously hot and his fireproof overalls smouldered. There was nothing below them but the open sea. The swell had lessened noticeably, but the thought of diving into the ocean from this height made Danny's head spin.

Finally, he emerged on a tiny ledge and realised there was one more ladder. It was so narrow that he hadn't noticed it until now. It led up to the flare itself, and he couldn't imagine why anyone would ever use it. He stared upwards and could make out a figure silhouetted against the blinding flames. He heard Callum calling his name, but the rest of the words disappeared in the thunder of the gas-fuelled inferno.

There was a blast of gunfire and he flinched, expecting a hail of lead to rain down on his head. Shot pellets ricocheted off the stack, and the gun came clattering down the ladder and tumbled into the sea below. Something else followed it.

A body, tombstoning, feet first, towards a watery grave. Danny watched Callum fall and disappear beneath the waves with barely a splash.

He watched for a long while, expecting the man to surface and make some gesture of defiance. But the sea had swallowed Callum and was not inclined to spit him back.

Danny banged his hand on the ladder until it hurt too much to continue.

'You stupid idiot! Why did you do that?'

He had thought of Callum as a friend and didn't want him to die, despite the betrayal.

He lowered himself, slowly, back down onto the ladder and began the long, wretched descent to the safety of the platform below.

Chapter Forty-Four

'THAT'S NOT THE END,' Gemma said.

'I saw him fall into the sea. Unless you think he's coming back to haunt you, it's over.' Danny wasn't sure what was on Gemma's mind. If it involved moving, forget it. He was perfectly content to keep lying here in the temporary sickbay forever.

'I've known Cal for years. I'm telling you he's not the suicidal type. He probably had a parachute or a zip-wire or some shite like that. I wouldn't put it past him.'

'You're being ridiculous. I'm not setting out on another wild goose chase. Dead or alive, he has to be out in the ocean somewhere. Have you any idea how difficult it is to spot a body or even a small boat in this kind of swell? He's gone.'

'That's your final word?' Danny nodded.

'Well, I think he must have surfaced by now. Just like a big ginger jobby. But I canna be bothered arguing about it.'

Gemma used the radio in the stricken helicopter to contact the coastguard and apprise them of the situation. It didn't take them long to come back with a plan.

She marched back into the mess and gave the crew the bad news. 'Right then, you boys had better get back out there and shift that heap of scrap off my helideck. As soon as it's clear, they'll send another chopper for the injured. The rest of you are going by boat.'

'Jesus, how long's that going to take?' Tommy asked, clutching at his distended stomach. 'We can't survive on biscuits and cold porridge.'

'A fast would do you good, you big porky roaster. I expect you'd like those fly boys to bring a takeout from the chippy, would you now?'

———

Moving the crashed helicopter was no mean feat. With everything else turned off, there was just enough power to operate the smaller of the two cranes. A team of guys with scaffolding poles levered the wheels off the deck far enough to lash it up with a few strops. Once the crane was able to take the strain, they manoeuvred it towards the edge. There was a collective intake of breath as it dropped a half metre or so and spun until the tail rotor struck one of the helideck supports.

'Oh well,' Trev, who was leading the salvage team, said. 'It was already bolloxed. A few more dents won't make much difference.'

The crane operator lowered the chopper faster than he intended. It struck the main deck with sufficient force to make the whole platform shake but remained intact. The team covered it with a tarpaulin and tied it down with rope.

'Well done lads,' Gemma said. 'Is there enough juice in the batteries to boil a kettle? I'm dying for a brew.'

According to the meter in the control room, the platform batteries had a few amps left. Despite Gemma's urging, Stevie refused to divert the remaining power from the emergency lighting to make her long-awaited cuppa.

Instead, Weevil lit his brazier and boiled a giant stock pot full of water. He even found a box of his homemade biscuits which were gratefully received, despite the ever-present danger of dislodging a filling or two.

The first chopper arrived two hours later, along with a few paramedics. It stayed just long enough to offload supplies and get the passengers on board before disappearing into the mist as quickly as it came. The remaining crew were left with a long wait for the rescue vessel to arrive from Aberdeen. Sadly, the supplies didn't include a few dozen portions of fried fish and chips. However, it was sufficient for the catering crew to knock up a decent hot meal for the first time in days.

When the vessel finally hoved into view, there was a lot of cheering and back-slapping and most of the crew lined the railings to watch it approach. As it came closer, Danny could tell that it was much bigger than the usual support vessels and that there was a helideck at the rear. It came to a halt in the deep water a few hundred metres away, pitching and rolling in the heavy seas.

'There's something I might have forgotten to mention,' Gemma said. 'We'll be taking a wee helicopter ride out there. The captain's too feart to come any closer in this swell. I don't like the idea, but the coastguard says it's the only way to get us all off, so I don't want to hear any moaning from you bunch of jessies.'

Danny would rather have climbed down a knotted rope and swung aboard like Tarzan.

They didn't have long to wait before they heard the familiar thrumming sound.

The helicopter burst through a bank of clouds on the horizon and swooped towards the platform. It was a search and rescue Super Puma and it made their usual Sikorsky S-92 seem luxurious and spacious by comparison.

Danny was past caring, as were the rest of the crew. They'd have done anything to get off the Cuillin Alpha. In any case, this would be the shortest flight they'd ever make.

Although the storm had abated, the wind was still strong enough to make it hard for a lightweight like Danny to stay on his feet. The downdraft from the rotor only added to his difficulties, and it was a relief to grab hold of the handrail and haul himself on board the waiting chopper.

The pilot seemed unconcerned. 'Standard procedure. We've done this plenty of times. It's just a matter of timing.'

The ship crested the latest wave. The pilot waited for a split second and then descended steadily, timing the touchdown to meet the ship as it climbed the next wave. It was a hard landing, but a long way short of the crash Danny was expecting. Once the pilot was happy that he was safely down and in no danger of slipping sidewards into the sea, his co-pilot opened the main hatch.

Many hands reached up to help the passengers down onto the rolling deck. The uninjured crew were taken off first. Though in dire need of a rest, Danny stayed back to help with the walking wounded.

It was an unpleasant gut-churning voyage to the Shetlands. Danny was no great sailor, so he avoided the ship's greasy cuisine and stayed outside as much as he could bear. The fresh air and a steady stream of sea-sickness pills kept him from throwing up and he reached Lerwick in surprisingly good spirits.

International Oil appeared to have booked out every hotel and B&B on the Shetland Isles to accommodate the crew of the Cuillin Alpha.

They allocated Danny a small room in a low-rent hotel on the edge of town. He wasn't complaining. It was warm and dry, and the bed had fewer lumps in it than his one offshore. He dumped his bag in his room, had a quick wash, and headed for the nearest pub.

It was already full of his colleagues from the Alpha. People that he had previously avoided like the plague now felt like extended family. Not having to live cheek by jowl with each other made all the difference. The tensions of the last few days evaporated and hatchets were buried.

Despite the jokes and banter, many of the faces wore a haunted look. He recognised it from his army days. They'd been through trauma and at times, hadn't been sure they'd make it back home in one piece. It would take a long time to recover; some might never be the same.

Danny soon regressed to his normal default state of assuming beer could cure all the world's ills. He propped up the bar and listened attentively to Gemma. She was explaining how all their troubles could have been averted if only the eejits had listened to her in the first place.

After that, it all became somewhat hazy. There were maybe a dozen pubs and bars in Lerwick and the crew seemed determined to visit them all. It was going to be a long and drunken night.

———

Danny woke hungover and disorientated. His dreams had been full of drills and helicopter engines, and his head felt like it was locked in a vice. The headache wasn't helped by the persistent reverberations emanating from somewhere by his left ear. It sounded like he was sharing the bed with an asthmatic pig. There was something wrong with the hotel room, too. He was sure the one he checked into had been much smaller than this one.

He rolled over, and all became clear. On the other side of the bed was Gemma, snoring contentedly. He should have known that she would have the best room in this tin-pot hotel. That only left the question of what he was doing in it, and more importantly, what he had done last night.

He recalled some drunken groping. He may also have fallen over while being helped out of his trousers. *Did we have sex?* It wasn't something you could ask a woman like Gemma without risking a punch in the face, so he would have to wait until his hangover, and hopefully his memory, cleared.

To say that Gemma wasn't his type would have been a significant understatement. He imagined she would say the same about him. He tended to go for willowy, athletic-looking women who eventually ran away from him. Gemma was more oak than willow. If she was an athlete, then she was definitely in a sport that favoured strength over speed. And yet she looked quite cute lying there. He had grown fond of her, in awe of her sometimes, and alarmed by her regularly. Their shared ordeal gave them something in common. Not enough to make a go of it romantically, though.

She woke up yawning, rubbing her eyes. Staring at Danny, she exclaimed, 'Jesus Christ! I thought that was just a bad dream. Tell me there's not a giant squid hiding in the bathroom.'

'No squid, just me.'

'Well, count your blessings, I suppose. I need a shower, I stink like a skunk on heat. Do us both a favour and don't be here when I get out.' She stomped off to the bathroom, peering inside first to check he wasn't lying about the squid and then slammed the door behind her.

He sighed relieved. Romance was dead and buried, with a stake through the heart, as far as Gemma was concerned. He scoured the room for his clothes, got dressed, and let himself out.

'See you at breakfast,' he shouted over the hiss of the shower.

'Aye. Maybe.'

Reality check complete, he made his way down to his box-sized room and sat on the bed, wondering what to do. His career as an offshore medic might be over. He could look for another posting, but would his prospective employers see him as a hero or a Jonah? He wasn't even sure he could bear to fly offshore again, but he needed the money, now more than ever.

Maybe the papers or the TV would pay for an interview. Or he could write a book. There had to be plenty of ways he could turn this to his advantage. If he could survive a near-disaster while solving a crime, surely he could deal with a few unpaid bills. Come to think of it, why not become a detective? Not with the police, that ship had sailed, but being his own boss? No one to tell him what to do?

It would be good to get Gemma's advice. She was the most pragmatic and practical-minded person he'd ever met. Ask her what she'd think of him as a private investigator. *Danny Verity, PI. I like it.*

Feeling fuzzy-headed, but more optimistic than he had been in a long time, Danny headed downstairs in search of the strongest coffee available. He ordered a full Scottish breakfast and devoured the lot. In the distance, he heard the familiar sound of the approaching helicopter coming to take him home. Not even that prospect could spoil his mood.

Acknowledgements

Emergency Drill began life on a crime writing workshop run by Will Sutton and Diana Bretherick. Without them, this book might have remained just an idea scribbled in an old notebook.

I'd like to thank all the Havant Writers for their many years of support and encouragement. And especially my star beta readers, Carol Westron and Lesley Talbot.

The Dunford Novelists helped hone the first chapters and gave me the confidence to enter *Emergency Drill* for the Debut Dagger award. Thanks to Leigh Russell and Dea Parkin of the Crime Writers' Association, for their continued encouragement. The Debut Daggers were a wonderfully uplifting experience, at a time when optimism and positivity was in short supply.

Thanks to Caroline and Jon at City Stone Publishing for all their expertise and hard work.

I'd like to thank my wife, Chris, the Blackwater girl, for all her support, her medical knowledge, and for lending me her name.

Finally, I'd like to thank you, the reader of this book. Especially if you've left a nice review on Amazon, Waterstones, Goodreads, etc. It makes a huge difference. And if you haven't done it yet ─ go on. You know you want to...

About the Author

Chris Blackwater is a writer and chartered engineer from Leeds, England. His first novel *Emergency Drill*, set on a North Sea oil platform, was shortlisted for the 2020 CWA Debut Dagger Award when it first came out.

His short stories have appeared in a variety of magazines and anthologies, including contributions to the much-missed *Mad Scientist Journal*.

Chris began writing to entertain himself whilst working on offshore oil platforms and remote power stations. His career has taken him all over the world to unusual locations and introduced him to some remarkable characters.

In recent years, Chris has gradually drifted down to the south coast of England, where he spends his spare time learning to sail and play the flute, though not at the same time.

Connect with Chris Blackwater on social media:
Website: chrisblackwater.co.uk
Facebook: @ChrisBlackwaterAuthor
Twitter: @BlackwaterChris
Instagram: @BlackwaterAuthor

About City Stone Publishing

Publisher with a passion for the written word and a heart that beats for our authors

We are an imaginative and enthusiastic indie publisher.

Our ambition is twofold:
To develop outstanding books and work alongside our authors.
To be a beacon of advice and a provider of services for indie authors.

We are not just about the books; we build relationships with our authors. Because we both write, we know what (indie) authors want. That is how we work: in cooperation and partnership with our authors.

From dark and gritty crime thrillers, adventurous fantasy, entertaining women's fiction, and intriguing contemporary novels to interesting and insightful non-fiction and visionary poetry, we publish it all.

Visit our website: citystonepublishing.com

EMERGENCY DRILL

239

Milton Keynes UK
Ingram Content Group UK Ltd.
UKHW011932230823
427374UK00001B/42